"Papa wrote me about the beginnings of the Spinsters' Club while I was away at seminary," Gil said.

"Did you think we sounded like a band of brazen hussies, advertising for marriage-minded bachelors?" Faith asked, almost afraid of the answer. But she saw a twinkle in his eye that reassured her.

"Not at all," he said. "You sounded like a plucky lot. I was only worried all the young ladies of the hill country would get the same idea and there'd be no one left for me when I finished seminary."

"Ah, now, where was your faith, Reverend Gil?" she teased. "Didn't you believe that the Lord would provide?"

"I'm only surprised you haven't made one of those matches, Miss Faith," he said. "I'd have thought those bachelors would have snatched you up when the group first started," he said.

He smiled at her, and she felt the jolt of it all the way through her heart.

Books by Laurie Kingery

Love Inspired Historical

Hill Country Christmas
The Outlaw's Lady
.*Mail Order Cowboy*
The Doctor Takes a Wife
The Sheriff's Sweetheart
.*The Rancher's Courtship*
The Preacher's Bride

*Brides of Simpson Creek

LAURIE KINGERY

makes her home in central Ohio, where she is a "Texan-in-exile." Formerly writing as Laurie Grant for the Harlequin Historical line and other publishers, she is the author of eighteen previous books and the 1994 winner of a Readers' Choice Award in the Short Historical category. She has also been nominated for Best First Medieval and Career Achievement in Western Historical Romance by *RT Book Reviews*. When not writing her historicals, she loves to travel, read, participate on Facebook and Shoutlife and write her blog on www.lauriekingery.com.

The Preacher's Bride

LAURIE KINGERY

Love Inspired

Recycling programs for this product may not exist in your area.

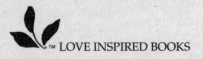 ™ LOVE INSPIRED BOOKS

ISBN-13: 978-0-373-82937-8

THE PREACHER'S BRIDE

www.LoveInspiredBooks.com

Printed in U.S.A.

Jesus said unto him, If thou canst believe, all things are possible to him that believeth. And straightway the father of the child cried out, and said with tears, Lord, I believe, help thou mine unbelief.

—*Mark* 9:23, 24

In memory of Tango, the dog of my heart

And as always, to Tom

Chapter One

⟞⟍⟋⟞

Simpson Creek, Texas, April 1868

I must be the most misnamed person in this whole town, maybe in the whole state of Texas, Faith Bennett thought, staring into the cool green water of Simpson Creek. Her parents had confidently given her that name, never guessing that by the time their daughter grew up, she would not believe in God.

It was a secret Faith shared with no one, not her parents, her neighbors and certainly not her friends in the Simpson Creek Spinsters' Club, of which she was a loyal member. She couldn't imagine what any of them would say if they knew. Her parents wouldn't know what to do about such a declaration if Faith ever made it. Her mother would worry and fret about her, and she didn't want that. Her friends in the Spinsters' Club wouldn't shun her, she thought. But they might not be so comfortable around her anymore, and they might wonder why she attended church every Sunday morning, just as they did.

A logical person would question why she enjoyed

being in church. Attending church on Sunday mornings was just what one did in this small hill-country town, she mused, and everywhere else in Texas. Faith found tradition comforting—singing the familiar hymns and listening to Reverend Chadwick preach. Even though she'd long since stopped believing in the God the preacher spoke about, she always found something uplifting in the sermons, which reinforced her belief in goodness and treating her fellow man with fairness and love.

So she continued to come here each Sunday morning, yet kept her secret—her name was Faith, but she didn't have any.

She only hoped that if and when she made a match—through the Spinsters' Club or however else it came about—the man she came to love would not mind that she was not a woman of faith. Somewhere there had to be a man who felt like she did, or if he was religious, wouldn't mind that she wasn't. The fact that she was a good, honest person was the most important thing, wasn't it?

It was probably time she joined her parents inside the sanctuary a few yards away.

"Miss Faith?" someone said behind her, and she whirled around, shading her eyes against the sunlight that filtered through the trees.

It was Gil Chadwick, the son of the preacher, and a fresh-from-seminary minister himself. Gil was staying with his father and sharing in his pastoral duties in preparation for being called to a church of his own soon.

"Good morning, Reverend Gil," she said, smiling up at him. He had a scholarly looking face, and wore spectacles when he read, but was saved from being too austere by a mischievous cowlick that often popped up at the back of his head despite his attempts to tame it. Any young lady, herself included, would be proud to be seen with the handsome unmarried preacher. But she was not a suitable match for a man of the cloth.

He pushed back a stray lock of chestnut-brown hair that had fallen low over his brow. "I'm glad I saw you coming down to the creek. I hope I'm not intruding on your prayers," he said.

Faith squelched the urge to laugh at the irony. "N-no, you weren't." She'd been thinking, certainly, but not praying. Instead of greeting her fellow worshipers before the worship service started, she'd felt the need for some quiet reflection. "It's just…so hot inside this morning, even with this," she said, lifting the ivory-handled fan she had brought with her, "I thought I'd spend a few moments in the shade first. Just looking at the water makes me feel cooler."

"It *is* very warm for late April," he agreed, running a finger beneath his stiff shirt collar. "Why, it's so hot a farmer told me this morning his hens are laying hard-boiled eggs." Humor twinkled in his hazel eyes.

She chuckled politely at the old joke, realizing he must feel the heat in his black frock coat and long-sleeved shirt almost as much as ladies did in their heavy layers of petticoats.

A silence broken only by the splash of some fish in the creek below stretched between them. She waited, but he seemed content just to gaze at her.

She heard the first few notes of "Stand Up, Stand Up for Jesus" waft toward them from an open window in the church. "Was there…was there something you wanted to say to me?" she prompted.

He blinked. "Oh, yes, of course, Miss Faith. I was merely wondering if—" He took a deep breath, as if gathering himself for a great leap, and went on, "If you might like to join me after church for dinner at the hotel."

She stared at him. She could not say his asking her out was a total surprise. She'd thought he had his eye on her for a while now. His invitation was both the fulfillment of a dream and the one thing she must not agree to, and she wanted to accept almost more than she wanted her next breath. But having dinner with him today would be the first step in a courtship, and for Gil's sake, she must not begin something she could not rightly continue.

The congregation began to sing, and she glanced once more toward the church. There wasn't time to think of a way to decline his offer in a way that wouldn't hurt his feelings.

"Perhaps we could discuss it more after church, Reverend Gil?" she asked. "We really should join the others inside." It would be harder after the service to get a private moment with him—in the short time he'd been in town, he was already very popular with the congregation. Hopefully during the sermon, she could think of an acceptable excuse to decline Gil's wonderful invitation.

Or find a way to justify accepting it, a rebellious voice within her insisted.

He sighed, darting a glance back over his shoulder at the church. "You're right, of course, Miss Faith," he said in that pleasant deep voice of his that curled so appealingly around her heart. "All right, then, we'll talk after church. I'll meet you under that old gnarly live oak in the back of the churchyard."

Faith nodded as she took his proffered arm, savoring his nearness. They really should go in separately, so no one got any mistaken ideas that the two of them were courting. But Gil's invitation suggested he wouldn't mind at all if it looked that way, and somehow she couldn't bear to let go of his arm.

Faith felt every eye on them as she let him escort her down the aisle between the rows of pews. She could almost hear the speculative hum rising in the brains of those who liked to be in the know.

Her father and mother looked up from their hymnbook and beamed delightedly at Gil as he stopped with Faith by the pew they were occupying. He acknowledged them with a smile as Faith settled herself next to her mother, then he strode on toward the front of the church.

Her mother cast a sidelong glance at her. Faith knew she was full of questions, but fortunately, she could not ask them now. Safe from parental curiosity for the present, Faith opened her mouth to sing the next hymn along with the rest of the congregation.

After they finished singing, Gil rose and strode toward the pulpit. "Good morning, congregation," he said, taking hold of the pulpit with both hands and grinning as they returned his greeting. "In just a moment Papa will bring us the message, but I wanted to remind you of next Saturday's wedding—our first in our new church building. Isn't that exciting?"

A chorus of murmured agreement arose from the congregation, and Faith knew everyone was remembering the smoldering ruin of the old church, burned to the ground by a band of evil men last summer. The town had worked diligently to rebuild it, and it had been completed just before Thanksgiving.

"Miss Caroline Wallace and her fiancé, Jack Collier, have asked me to remind everyone the whole town is invited," Gil went on. "The ceremony begins at one o'clock, and the reception afterward will take place in the church social hall. It sounds like a wonderful, blessed time will be had by all, so let's all plan to attend and support the new couple as they begin a life together."

Caroline and Jack, sitting on the opposite side of the aisle from Faith with Jack's twin daughters, waved at the folks around them, radiating happiness.

What a good, generous man Gil Chadwick is, Faith thought, as he returned to the front pew and his father took his place at the pulpit. Gil seemed genuinely happy for the engaged couple, yet a good many people in Simpson Creek knew that not too long ago, Gil would have preferred to announce his own upcoming wedding with Caroline. It was apparent he'd been taken with Caroline when he'd first arrived in Simpson Creek, but had unselfishly kept her company only as a friend until Jack realized he'd better get off the fence and propose to Caroline or risk losing her.

Faith knew some of the other members of the Spinsters' Club were interested in capturing the interest of the bachelor preacher before he was called to another town and left Simpson Creek. Gil wouldn't be single for any longer than he wanted to be.

"Our text comes from 'So then faith cometh by hearing, and hearing by the Word of God,'" Reverend Chadwick said.

He looked a little pale, Faith thought, and thinner than he had been. As he'd moved to the pulpit, his steps had been halting. Perhaps, like some elderly folks, he didn't sleep well, or suffered from some ailment.

His son had taken over the pastoral calls to outlying ranches that Reverend Chadwick had once made, but once Gil was pastoring his own church, the old preacher's congregation would have to realize *they* would have to come visit *him,* rather than the other way around. No doubt some woman of mature years would have to be found to keep house for the old preacher, for his wife had been dead for a score of years or more.

Reverend Chadwick raked a hand absently through his thinning, snowy-white hair. "H-hearing…by the w-word of God," the preacher repeated. "What d-does that mean, cong-congregation?"

Was she imagining it or was Reverend Chadwick having trouble speaking? His words suddenly sounded slurred, thick. He'd always been the most eloquent of men, his delivery smooth and polished.

Faith saw she was not alone in noticing something was wrong. Dr. Walker, sitting at the other end of the same pew, leaned forward, an expression of concern furrowing his features. Beside him, his wife, Sarah, bit her lip worriedly.

"Obviously…it means spending time…r-reading the Bi—Bi—" He stopped, and looked around in bewilderment, as if he could not find the familiar word. He looked to Gil as if entreating his help. His mouth seemed to droop on one side.

"Papa?" Faith heard Gil ask. Tentatively, he rose and started forward.

Reverend Chadwick put out a hand as if assuring his son that he was all right. And then he collapsed.

Behind Faith, someone shrieked in alarm.

She watched, horror-struck, as Gil reached his father first, followed close behind by Dr. Walker. With the assistance of the doctor, Gil gently turned his father onto his back and knelt so that Reverend Chadwick's head could be elevated in his lap. Dr. Walker loosened the preacher's shirt collar.

Faith could see that the preacher's face was ashen, his eyes closed. She could hear him breathing, but his respirations sounded rattley and snoring.

People began to leave their pews. An anxious murmuring arose. She heard her father praying aloud, asking the Lord to save the old preacher.

"I think he's had an apoplexy," Faith heard Dr. Walker say to Gil. "We'll need to carry him to my office."

Assisted by Sheriff Bishop, Gil lifted his father from where he'd been lying by the pulpit. The old man felt so light, as if a puff of wind could blow him away. *Lord, please save Papa. Please don't take him yet...*

It wasn't far to the doctor's office. Dr. Walker paced alongside Gil and Bishop, peppering Gil with questions—had his father complained of a headache? Dizziness? Unusual fatigue? Numbness or tingling of his limbs? Pain in his chest? To all of these, Gil shook his head. His father had been his usual cheerful self before church, and had eaten a good breakfast.

A number of people followed them, and some of these lingered in the waiting room with him. He was vaguely aware of Faith sitting in the midst of them, and he remembered with a pang the dinner he had hoped to have with her. But he couldn't think of her now, nor of the whispered prayers and conversations around him. Instead, he besieged Heaven with silent pleas of his own. And when he could think of no other way to ask that his father be spared, he added, *Lord, help me to be willing to accept Your will, if You decide to take him Home.*

* * *

"Is my father…still with us?" Gil asked, an endless time later, when Nolan Walker emerged from his examination room. Walker was followed by his wife, Sarah, who often helped him with his patients. Gil looked for clues to what Walker would say. Had his father gone to be with God, leaving only the shell of his body behind?

Nolan Walker nodded. "He's breathing, but as to whether he will live…" He shrugged. "I'm sorry, but I honestly don't know, Gil. It does seem to be an apoplectic attack, as I thought in church. It's in God's hands now, and the next few hours will be critical. If he lives, he may suffer paralysis and be unable to speak. I'll keep him here for now and watch him closely. His heartbeat is strong, and his breathing is regular at least. Perhaps by morning we'll know more."

"Is he…is he awake? May I see him?"

"He's still unconscious, but of course you may see him," Walker said. "Stay as long as you like."

Because it may be the last time you spend with him, Gil knew Walker was thinking.

Gil followed the doctor into his examination room on legs that felt wobbly as a newborn calf's.

Faith couldn't have said why she'd accompanied the pillars of the town, Mayor Gilmore; Mrs. Detwiler, the town matriarch; Mr. Avery, the bank president; and Mr. Wallace, the postmaster as they followed Gil and Sheriff Bishop carrying the old preacher to the doctor's office—she only knew she had to be there for Gil's sake, even though she could not bow her head and join the others in praying for the stricken preacher. She could not have gone home and merely hoped for the best.

And now she didn't know why she remained. It

wasn't likely Gil would be leaving his father's side soon. The others had departed, asking Faith to convey their best wishes to Gil.

A few moments later, Dr. Walker returned to the waiting room. "I'm glad you are still here, Miss Faith," he said in his down-east Maine accent. "I need to ask you a favor."

She blinked. "Whatever I can do, Doctor."

"I remember you were one of the nurses who helped us during the influenza epidemic, and I was hoping I could call on your nursing ability once again. Someone will need to watch over the reverend through the night. Ordinarily, my Sarah handles this, you know, but she's been so tired, since she's expecting…"

Sarah Matthews Walker, and her sister, Milly Matthews Brookfield, had been Faith's friends long before they'd met their husbands, but they experienced pregnancy very differently. Milly had never felt better in her life, and carried on her routine as a ranch wife just as energetically as before, but Sarah tired very easily these days and was looking a tad peaked, although her face remained as serene as ever.

"Of course, Doctor Walker, I'll be happy to help in any way I can," Faith said, pleased that there was actually something she *could* do for the preacher and his son, because she couldn't pray. "I'll return this evening after supper, all right?"

"God bless you, Miss Faith. You're a good woman. But as I told his son, Reverend Chadwick's condition is tenuous, to say the least. It's a distinct possibility he will pass away during the night or even before you return. That might be for the best, if he is not to regain consciousness. As a fellow Christian, I know he looks forward to Heaven, as we all do."

Nolan Walker assumed she shared his belief in the hereafter. This was not a time to disagree.

"Yes, Doctor. I hope he recovers, of course, especially for Gil's sake," Faith said. "I'll do everything I can to assist in that."

The doctor nodded. "I have every confidence in you, Miss Faith."

Would the physician still feel that way, and continue to look at her with such respect and gratitude, if he suspected her lack of faith?

"I wish we could talk you into eating something, Gil," Nolan Walker said as he walked Gil to the door of his office. "Sarah saved a plate for you."

Gil sighed. "I'm not hungry, Nolan, thanks. I'm not even sure if I'm doing right to let you talk me into going home for the night. What if…" He couldn't put his dread into words, but he knew the doctor understood.

Walker put a hand on his shoulder. "The parsonage is right across the street," he reminded Gil. "We could summon you in a minute if there's any change. You need to go home and get some rest. If your father survives the night—and so far he's holding on—you'll need your strength. Ah, there's Miss Faith now, come to sit up with him."

Just as the doctor had said, Faith Bennett had just opened the gate and was making her way up the walk. She wore a dark skirt and waist and her gleaming auburn hair lay neatly coiled at her nape. She looked all business, but her eyes softened as she caught sight of him standing in the doorway.

"Hello, Reverend Gil," she said, addressing him informally as he'd requested of all the townspeople when he'd come to town, to avoid the confusion caused by two Reverend Chadwicks. "How is your father doing?"

He shaded his eyes against the setting sun. "Just the same, I'm afraid," he said. His throat felt tight with emotion as he thought of his father lying crumpled and motionless at the base of the pulpit. He should be grateful that the old man still lived, he reminded himself. While there was life, there was hope, wasn't there? "He's no worse at least, thank God."

Her green eyes held endless depths of sympathy. "And how are *you* holding up, Gil? This must be so hard for you, seeing your father like this. It's good that you're going home to get some rest."

"I'm all right, Miss Faith," he said quickly, although nothing could be further from the truth. He felt so weary that he hardly knew how he would reach the other side of the street, and so shaky after watching the shallow rise and fall of his father's chest all afternoon that her sympathy caused his eyes to sting with unshed tears. "Look, I don't feel right about you having to sit up with my father all night," he said, making a vague gesture toward the doctor's office behind him. "Just let me go home for a couple of hours, and I'll be back. It's my place to do this—"

"Nonsense," Faith responded crisply. "You look done in, Gil. You need sleep. I've nursed before under Dr. Walker's direction, and he'll be right here if I need help."

"Yes, Miss Faith was one of our excellent volunteer nurses during the influenza epidemic," Nolan Walker said. "She's very competent. Your father couldn't be in better hands. Go on now—"

Sarah Walker appeared just then at the door, bearing a plate covered with a cloth. "Hello, Faith. Thanks for coming. Gil Chadwick, you're to take this home and eat it. I won't take no for an answer. Then go to bed."

Their gruff kindness warmed his heart. He would find a way to thank them one day. For now, though, he just silently accepted the plate and nodded to each of them in turn.

But Faith's heart-shaped face, her green eyes luminous with understanding, was the one that stuck in his mind later that night as he prayed and then struggled to sleep. Was she even now praying for his father and for him? *What a comforting thought that was—Faith on her knees in prayer for my father.*

Lord, show me if she is "the one" for me.

Chapter Two

"Summon me if there's any change, Miss Faith," Dr. Walker instructed her, his hand on the doorknob. "If the quality of his breathing changes, or he seems feverish, or becomes restless…"

"Or if he wakes?" Faith asked, determined to be hopeful.

"I admire your positive attitude, Miss Faith," Walker said. "Yes, call me if he wakes." It was clear he didn't expect that to happen, however. "Our bedroom is just beyond that wall," he said, pointing. "Just knock on it and I'll hear you. I'm a light sleeper, and I'm often wakeful anyway if I have a seriously ill patient here, so I'll probably come and check on him once or twice."

Faith nodded, and he closed the door behind him. For a while she busied herself with straightening the crisp sheets and light blanket over the preacher's slight form, checking the slow, steady pulse at his wrist and watching his chest rise, but at last she settled herself in the cane-bottom rocker. The wind sighed around the building, and the old house creaked back in reply.

She'd brought a book of Shakespeare's sonnets to

keep her company through the long hours of the night, for she'd known there would be little else to do to help her stay awake. Caroline Wallace had praised it and lent it to her, but she found the antique language of the poetry slow going and the flickering lamp light soporific. Her schoolteacher friend must certainly have an elevated intellect to penetrate the irregular spellings and obsolete words, Faith thought. If *she* persisted in trying to read it, though, she'd fall asleep, despite the still-warm cup of black coffee she sipped.

After a while she laid the slender leather-bound volume aside and walked quietly to the window that faced Fannin Street. A full moon hung low behind the church, bathing it and the parsonage in its ethereal glow.

The windows were dark at the parsonage. Was Gil sleeping or was he keeping a prayer vigil on his knees, beseeching his God to spare his father? She hoped the former—he would need his strength, regardless of the outcome of his father's illness. It would do little good to wear himself out pleading with a deity who either wasn't there, or if he was, had never given Faith much evidence that he cared.

She looked back at the unconscious man on the bed. What kind of reward was this for a lifetime of faithful service, being stricken at his pulpit, in front of his son and the entire congregation? Now, if nothing changed and his heart continued to beat, he would die a lingering death from dehydration and pneumonia, his body withering slowly. What had happened to the brilliant mind that had memorized practically the entire New Testament and psalms and could recite them, chapter and verse? Why hadn't he been granted the mercy of a peaceful passing in his sleep? If that was how God rewarded His faithful servants, she was wise to want no part of it!

She turned back to check on the preacher, and was astonished to see that his eyes were open and he was gazing at her.

She gasped, hardly able to believe what she saw. *"Reverend Chadwick?"*

He made no attempt to speak, but the faded old eyes were full of intelligence. *He knew her.*

"Can you...can you squeeze my hands?" she said, reaching under the covers and grasping his cool, gnarled hands. The right one lay limp and unresponsive in her grasp. She could not be sure she felt an answering pressure from the left, so slight was his effort. He continued to regard her, blinking occasionally, and she could *feel* appreciation radiating from his eyes.

"I'll get Dr. Walker," she said, feeling a rising excitement. "He'll be so encouraged!" She turned, about to rap on the wall behind her, but looked back one more time.

The old man's eyelids were once again closed.

"Reverend Chadwick?" she called softly, but there was no response. Gently, she shook the old man's shoulder. "Reverend Chadwick? Please open your eyes again. Squeeze my hand, sir, please?"

He lay immobile, as if he had never opened his eyes. She sagged back down on the chair, unsure now that she had really seen what she thought she had. Had she forgotten that she had sat down again and perhaps fallen asleep? Had the sight of his opening eyes been but a fleeting dream born of wishful thinking?

Faith was still thoroughly discouraged when Dr. Walker came in to check his patient near dawn. She told him what she thought she'd observed, then watched as he bent to listen with his stethoscope to the old preacher's heartbeat and his breathing, and check his reflexes.

"Come to the kitchen," he said, beckoning. "I'll make some fresh coffee."

"But…" She glanced back at Reverend Chadwick.

"It will be all right to leave him alone for a little while," he assured her.

Once they'd reached the kitchen, he spoke again. "It's best not to speak frankly in front of a patient, even when the patient seems completely comatose," he explained. "Hearing seems to be the last sense to go. A soldier in my care once came out of a coma and reported everything that was said in his presence while he was supposedly insensible—much to my embarrassment, for I had told another army doctor right at the bedside that I didn't think the fellow would make it." He gave a self-deprecating chuckle.

"Then you believe the reverend's brief waking was a good sign?" she asked, hopeful again. "You don't believe I fell asleep and dreamed the whole thing?"

He studied her. "You seem too responsible a lady to let yourself doze," he said. "It's quite possible he awoke and knew you. But does it mean that he will recover?" He shrugged. "I couldn't say as yet. It's not a bad sign, certainly, but I've seen unconscious men have moments of apparent lucidity, then die anyway. We'll have to see if he wakes again, and I'll be more hopeful if it lasts this time. We must continue to pray," he added.

Faith winced inside, but kept silent. *If only she believed prayer would do some good.*

"I'll heat water and help you give him a bath," Dr. Walker said. "Perhaps the stimulation of that will help bring him back to consciousness. And then you'll go home and get some well-earned rest yourself."

Faith glanced out the south-facing window, and saw the faint light of dawn.

"The sun's coming up," she murmured. "I expect Gil will arrive before long. I imagine it's been hard for him waiting through the night for news. It would be wonderful if he found his father awake, wouldn't it?" She wanted to give him that gift—the sight of his father conscious and in his right mind, no matter what other damage the apoplexy had left.

"It would," he agreed, as he pumped water from the kitchen pump into a deep iron pot. "And I'd have a better idea of his prognosis." The doctor's blue eyes held a Yankee shrewdness as he set the pot on the stovetop. "You're fond of Gil, aren't you?"

The question had come out of nowhere, and she could not stifle a gasp nor summon a quick denial.

"H-how did you know?" she asked, feeling a telltale flush spreading up her neck.

The corners of the doctor's mouth quirked upward. "We doctors are trained observers of signs and symptoms, and human behavior," he said gently. "This is probably not the appropriate time to tease you. But there's nothing wrong with being fond of a man of such sterling character, and I know my wife wouldn't mind if I pointed out you're a kind and generous young lady as well as a pretty one. You might make a very good wife for the young preacher."

He couldn't know how wrong he was about that. She bit her lip, not knowing what to say, wondering if Dr. Walker would hint of her feelings to Gil. She cleared her throat, trying to find the right words.

He'd seen her dismay, though, and waved a hand. "I'm sorry, Miss Faith, forgive my frankness. My wife is always telling me I'm so used to dealing in life and death matters that I think I can say anything that pops into my head. It's none of my business, and I won't mention it again."

"No apology is necessary, Doctor," she said.

Before either of them could say anything else, they heard footsteps, and Sarah appeared in the kitchen, dressed in her wrapper, yawning, her golden hair still confined in its nighttime braid.

"Good morning, dear," Dr. Walker said, kissing her before he updated her on the events of the night. Faith looked on, wistfully envying the obvious tenderness between husband and wife.

Gil had slept the sleep of exhaustion despite his anxiety over his father. Now he hesitated on the front step of the parsonage. He stared across at the doctor's office. What would he find when he crossed the street and entered the doctor's office? No one had come during the night to tell him matters had worsened, and yet he dreaded seeing his father in the same helpless, insentient condition he'd been in when Gil had reluctantly left him yesterday.

Lord, please give me strength to accept Your will.

"Good morning, Gil," Sarah said when she opened the door. "Go on in and see your father. My husband and Faith are in there with him."

Her smile gave Gil the courage to do as she suggested. A surge of hope lightened his steps as he walked forward. The doctor's wife wouldn't have smiled if things were still the same, would she?

Faith was just tucking in a fresh sheet at the foot of the bed. His father was propped up on pillows, but Gil couldn't see his face because Dr. Walker was bent over him, listening to his chest with his stethoscope.

Dr. Walker straightened and turned to greet him, as did Faith. Now Gil could see his father's face, and saw the gleam of recognition as he saw his son at the door.

"Papa!" Gil cried, and rushed to the bedside, trembling with joy. He sank down by the bed, taking his father's gnarled, blue-veined hand in one of his, while reaching up to touch his father's whiskery cheek.

"Good morning, Gil," Dr. Walker said. "Your father decided to wake up when we were giving him a bath a few minutes ago."

Tears stung Gil's eyes as he stared into his father's face. The hand he held gripped his weakly, and the old man's attempt at a smile was still droopy on one side, but his eyes radiated the same joyfulness that threatened to overwhelm Gil.

"Can he—" Gil began to ask, then turned back to the old man on the bed. "Can you…talk, Papa?"

"Mmmhh," his father said, then he shook his head in a clear expression of frustration.

"Give him time, Gil, he only just woke up," the doctor said with a gentle smile. "We should be very encouraged by that alone."

"I…I am," Gil said, smiling back at his father. "I love you, Papa," he said, his voice thick with emotion. "I'm just so glad I'm able to tell you that again."

His father stared back at him, his eyes also full of love.

"Here, sit down," Dr. Walker said, indicating the chair at the bedside. "Faith tells me your father woke up briefly during the night, then drifted off into sleep again."

Gil looked across the bed. There were violet shadows under Faith's eyes, and she looked weary, but her gaze reflected the same relief and joy he felt.

"Yes, it was so quick I thought I might have imagined it," she said. "But then when he felt the warm water on his face, his eyes popped open and he's been awake ever since."

The old man's eyes were drifting shut again. Walker beckoned Gil and Faith to the door.

"I'll see you later, Papa," Gil whispered, and kissed the top of the old man's head.

Once in the hallway, Gil asked, "What…what do we do now?"

"He's been able to drink sips of water," Dr. Walker said. "Later, I'll see if he can swallow a little chicken broth. Assuming he can, I'll want to keep him here another night, then you can take him home."

"I'll take good care of him, Doctor," Gil promised, still hardly believing he was going to get the chance to do so.

"I'm sure you will," Walker said. "And Faith will help you. She's agreed to organize the Spinsters' Club to nurse him. I told you what an excellent job they did during the influenza epidemic."

"Yes, but he's my responsibility," he said, reluctant to obligate Faith and the other young ladies to the care of a sick old man.

"You'll certainly get plenty of time to fulfill your responsibility to your father," Walker said. "But it's going to be too much for just one person. You'll need help. Until he regains full movement—and there's no guarantee he will—someone will have to feed him, do his laundry, exercise his limbs, help him learn to speak again—if he can, and that's by no means certain—help him get out of bed when he's stronger… And don't forget, the needs of the congregation will continue. I'm sure the church board will be asking you formally, of course, but unless you're unwilling, I expect you've just become the acting pastor of Simpson Creek Church."

Gil blinked, raking a hand through his hair distractedly. "I've been so worried Papa would die, I hadn't given it a thought. I suppose you're right." He hoped he was equal to the task.

"I'll get started arranging his nursing care right now, Doctor," Faith said, heading for the door that led out of the office.

"You'll do no such thing, Miss Faith," Walker ordered. "You've been up all night, and you're to go straight to bed, understood? Your organizing can wait till after you've slept at least."

"Yes, *sir,*" Faith shot back, her grin so sassy that it made both men grin, too. "I'll see you both later."

"I can't thank you enough, Miss Faith," Gil told her.

Her smile was all the reward he needed. It warmed his soul.

"That's a good woman," Dr. Walker said, after the door had closed behind Faith. His gaze locked meaningfully with Gil's.

The doctor's message was clear enough. "I believe you're right, Doctor," Gil said.

Before going to bed as Dr. Walker had directed, Faith took a few minutes to update her mother on the reverend's condition and the need to revive the Spinsters' Club Nursing Corps. Louisa, her cousin who lived with them now, was not present because she helped Caroline teach, and it was the last day of school.

"Is there anything I can do to help, dear?" Lydia Bennett asked. "Your father and I are so proud of you, the way you're taking the initiative to help the preacher. At least this time there's no risk of contagion."

Faith wished she had her mother's belief in her father's pride in her. Unfortunately, she knew differently. But she'd never distress her mother with that truth.

"Mama, you wouldn't mind if the Spinsters' Club met here after supper tonight to sign up for their nursing shifts, would you?" she asked, smothering a weary yawn. They would have to teach the new spinsters about their nursing duties, too, she supposed, by pairing those who had never nursed with the ones who'd been in Simpson Creek during the flu.

"Of course you may, Faith. It's the least we can do to help. I'll call on the ladies while you're sleeping and notify them of the meeting. Let's see, there's Louisa, Maude, Polly, Ella, Kate, Jane and Hannah. Have I forgotten anyone? There's fewer of them available than when the epidemic struck…"

"Yes, Sarah, Emily, Bess and Milly are all married now," Faith mused aloud. "But we should have enough willing helpers among the others, I think. Gil will be able to help his father at night, and if all goes well, Reverend Chadwick will need us less and less…"

If all goes well. There was so much that could happen, even now. In his weakened condition, the old preacher would still be easy prey to pneumonia and other infections. Not for the first time, she wished she believed in prayer. But she might as well aim her thoughts to the dirt, she thought, as believe there was Someone beyond the sky who would hear her.

No one in the Heavens had listened when she had pled for her brother Eddy's life when he was bitten by a snake. If there was a God, wouldn't He have listened and spared a small boy? And when she had begged to feel her father's love again?

She had always wished for the courage to ask the question of Reverend Chadwick. But now he, too, had been struck down, and only time would tell if he survived.

Chapter Three

"Thank you, ladies, for coming together on such short notice," Faith said, after all the members of the Spinsters' Club had helped themselves to lemonade and cookies and sat down in the Bennett parlor. "Especially you, Caroline—we didn't really expect you to have time, what with your wedding and all—goodness, I hadn't realized!" she said, as a thought struck her. "I suppose Reverend Gil will have to be the one to conduct your wedding this Saturday?"

"Yes, Jack and I spoke to him about it this afternoon. It'll be the very first wedding he's performed, imagine that," she said with a smile. "Of course, it will depend on the state of his father's health. Do you suppose we could all pray for our preacher right now?"

Everyone bowed their heads while Caroline led them in prayer. Faith lowered her head, too, out of respect, but she always felt like such an outsider when others prayed.

"All right," Faith said when the prayer was over. "We're here to organize shifts for nursing Reverend Chadwick. If all goes well, the plan is for him to go

home from the doctor's tomorrow morning. I'll take the
first shift, and see if the routine I have in mind works.
We will be at the bedside in the daytime, ladies, while
G—that is, Reverend Gil—" she corrected herself hastily as she felt the heat rise in her cheeks "—will see to
his father at night." She cleared her throat, hoping none
of the others had seen her blush. It would not do to let
them know how much she cared for the young preacher.
"This should involve less intense nursing than during
the epidemic because there shouldn't be feverish cri-
ses, but our diligent care will still be vital to whatever
recovery he makes."

Hannah raised her hand. "Your mother told me he
was awake but unable to speak."

Faith nodded. "So far, he can't speak," she confirmed, "though he has tried. I'm sure it must be frus-
trating. He is also paralyzed on his right side. So he'll
need much effort from us. From what Dr. Walker has
told me, he must be turned from side to side every few
hours, bathed, fed nourishing broth and have his limbs
exercised a few times a day. There'll be laundry to do.
We must work hard, ladies, or he'll get pneumonia."

"It sounds like a tall order," Maude said soberly.

Faith knew Maude was more aware of what such
nursing care involved than the others did, for her father had been a doctor. "Yes, and if any of you feel
you're not up to doing this, no one will blame you,"
Faith said. "The married ladies will provide food for
the preacher and his son, but those who can't nurse
could do this, too."

Polly closed her eyes and put up a hand as if volun-
teering for martyrdom. "*I* would do *anything* to help
our preacher," she declared in a tone more suited to the
stage. "I'd be willing to work every day, if you like."

Faith guessed Polly was thinking a good deal more about how the old preacher's illness would give her increased time around his son than she was of the reality of nursing a helpless, sick old man.

"We're *all* devoted to Reverend Chadwick, Polly," Maude sniffed, clearly annoyed at Polly's histrionics. "That's why we're here."

"I'll remind y'all that we're caring for our preacher so his son will be free to attend to pastoral duties as they arise, so he will not always be at the parsonage," Faith said, hoping Polly got the hint. "Now, unless there are any other questions, here is a schedule for those willing to sign up," she said, laying the sheet of paper she had prepared beforehand out on the table, along with a pencil. "Those of you who have never nursed before might like to pair up with someone who is more experienced the first time you go." She had already signed up for several shifts herself.

Faith watched as the members of the Spinsters' Club milled around, the newer ladies partnering with the experienced ones, then stepped over to inspect the list. She was proud to see that every lady had committed herself for at least one shift over the next two weeks. That was far enough ahead to plan, she thought. Even Caroline, who must have a couple of dozen things to do before her wedding, had put herself down for the day after tomorrow.

Her cousin Louisa's face was troubled as she looked over the schedule. "But, Faith, you've signed up for the day of the wedding."

"It's all right," Faith said quickly. "*Someone* will have to be at the parsonage with Reverend Chadwick during the wedding, Louisa. I don't mind." It was probably best that she avoid the event. She was sure she could remain businesslike around Gil at the parsonage, when she was there in an official capacity. But at the wedding, with everyone dressed in their best and romance in the air, it would be far too tempting to flirt with Gil. If she wasn't there, perhaps Gil would notice one of the other spinsters, and begin courting that lucky lady. The thought wrenched her heart, but it was for the best, she told herself, no matter what sort of spark she'd thought she'd seen in Gil's eyes.

It was only my imagination, she told herself firmly. *All the more reason to sit with the old preacher while the others attended the wedding.*

"Oh, but I'll switch with you," Louisa persisted. "It would be a shame for you to miss it. You've known Caroline for a long time, while I'm still rather new here."

"What a kind, generous offer, Louisa," Caroline said. "Faith, why don't you take her up on it? Didn't you tell me you'd already made a new dress for the wedding?"

Faith blinked, wishing she hadn't told the bride-to-be about the blue dress. She'd started making it right after Jack Collier had finally gotten serious about courting Caroline, when she realized she might have a chance with Gil after all. That was before she'd come to the realization she was the wrong woman for Gil.

She was neatly caught now on the horns of a dilemma, despite her best intentions. If she didn't agree to let Louisa switch with her, Caroline would wonder why. She might even think Faith didn't want to celebrate with the happy couple, and be hurt.

"That's very nice, Louisa," Faith said desperately. "But you haven't had any nursing experience. Why don't you sign up with any of the experienced ladies, or did you intend to work alongside one of them earlier in the week?"

Louisa appeared surprised. "Faith, have you forgotten I took care of Papa before he passed on?" Louisa asked. "He was bedridden for months, remember?"

Faith swallowed hard. She *had* forgotten about the lingering illness that had finally taken her uncle. Louisa was every bit as competent a nurse as she was, maybe more so.

"I had forgotten," she admitted. "All right, Louisa, thank you." Surely, at the wedding, she could manage to keep from noticing Gil too much. And she'd contrive to stay away from the bouquet toss. Perhaps if she struck up a conversation with Mrs. Detwiler, the talkative older woman would keep her so occupied that she would not be tempted.

The grandfather clock in the corner of the room struck nine.

"Oh, look at the time," Caroline said, rising. "I have to be getting home. Milly's coming over to do my final dress fitting in the morning."

One by one, the other ladies started gathering their things.

Except for Polly. "We haven't even spoken of any Spinsters' Club business yet," she complained. "Haven't there been any letters from bachelor candidates arrive at the post office lately, Caroline?"

Caroline shook her head. "I'm afraid not. Oh, by the way, Faith, I've told Papa you'll be stopping by to pick up any bachelor mail that might arrive."

Faith started to agree, but before she could open her mouth, she saw Polly's lower lip jutting out dangerously.

"*I* could do it," Polly declared in a voice that dared anyone to disagree. "Sounds like Faith's going to be pretty busy running the nursing corps when she's not at the parsonage herself. And I see you took the lion's share of the slots, Faith."

There was an unspoken accusation in the other woman's voice, and from the indrawn breaths and shocked expressions around the parlor, everyone else noticed, as well.

Faith forced herself to take a calming breath before speaking. "I'm not sure what you're trying to say, Polly, but I did so out of a desire not to burden anyone else unduly. I only help Papa at the newspaper office when he needs me, and I don't have younger brothers and sisters to mind, so I have more time to devote to the preacher's care. Would you like to do it with me tomorrow?" she asked Polly. "I'd be happy to have your help."

The other woman's eyes lost their pugnacious glint, and she looked away. "I can't. Tomorrow I promised my mother I'd watch the younger children while she goes to San Saba. It's just so boring keeping Teddy, Johnnie and Lottie out of trouble. I swan, Lottie is the worst of the three!" She tittered, but none of the other ladies joined in.

"It's fine with me if you want to pick up the bachelor letters, Polly," Faith said. "That would be a big help."

"Perhaps after the wedding's over and the preacher's condition stabilizes, y'all could plan some new sort of event, or write a new advertisement in the newspaper for eligible bachelors," Caroline suggested. "Good evening, ladies. Faith, I hope all goes well tomorrow," she said as she left.

One by one, all of the Spinsters' Club members departed, until only Faith, Louisa and Polly were left.

"I...I think I'll go read for a while," Louisa said, excusing herself with an uneasy glance toward Polly.

Polly waited until Faith's cousin went upstairs, then

grabbed her reticule and motioned for Faith to follow her out onto the front step. "I…I'm sorry," Polly murmured. "I don't know what makes me snippy like that," she said. "I admire you, Faith, I really do. You're such a confident, admirable woman and I'm just…me. I want to be looked up to and useful, too! I thought Bob Henshaw admired me—" she shrugged and heaved a great sigh "—but then he went back to Austin…"

Faith was touched by the sadness on the woman's face. She just wanted to be loved—and who didn't? The defection of her beau had been a blow to her confidence, especially when the other two men who had come to Simpson Creek at the same time had made commitments to their matches. Bess Lassiter had married her rancher from Mason and moved there a month ago, while Hannah and Mr. Von Hesse had just announced their engagement.

"You'll find the right man someday, Polly," Faith assured her, and put a bracing arm around the woman's trembling shoulders. "There'll be unattached fellows at the wedding reception, you know. Prissy mentioned her handsome cousin Anson is coming for a visit, and she'll probably bring him along. Matches have been made before at weddings."

"Pshaw, I've met that Anson Tyler before. He's far too impressed with himself to notice little old me. But there's another gent whose eye I'd love to catch…" Polly murmured.

Faith had a sinking feeling she knew who that was—Gil Chadwick. Well, Gil's choice of ladies was no business of hers. He was a grown man with sound judgment.

"And meanwhile, I know you will be a big help to Reverend Chadwick. He's going to need some nursing care for a long time, you know—far longer than the two weeks I've scheduled so far. Meanwhile, I'd be happy to let you take a couple of those slots I had put myself down for, Polly," she said.

"That's all right," Polly said quickly. "We'll see how it goes. As you said, he'll be needing help for a long time. Thanks for listening to me, Faith." She gave Faith an impulsive hug, then scampered down the steps into the night.

Faith watched until Polly disappeared around the corner. She needed to go in soon, for tomorrow would be busy and start early. But for now she just stood there, enjoying the peace and the sweet scent of the honeysuckle that wafted from the tall bushes surrounding both sides of the step. The night was clear, and she thought she heard the hoot of an owl from down by the creek...

"Is she gone?" asked a voice from behind the honeysuckle.

Faith was so startled that she nearly fell off the step. Her arms flailed as she strove for balance, but finally she righted herself. *"Who's there?"* she demanded, but the voice was familiar and she thought she recognized it.

Gil Chadwick came out from behind the bush, looking more than a little sheepish. "I'm sorry if I frightened you, Miss Faith," he said, chuckling. "I've been waiting for your meeting to be finished to speak with you about tomorrow, and I thought everyone had left, so I was just on the verge of knocking at the door when I heard you coming out with Miss Shackleford. If I'd tried to make it back to the parsonage, she'd have seen me..."

Perhaps she shouldn't have, but Faith couldn't help but giggle at the look of dread on his face.

"You laugh," Gil said ruefully, "but Mrs. Detwiler

warned me Miss Shackleford has 'set her cap for me,' whatever that means. And just in case she's right, I need to avoid that young lady for a while, especially while I'm so worried about Papa."

She wanted to ask what it was he didn't like about Polly, but that would be amusing herself at Polly's expense. "Yes, how is your father? I thought you'd be at the Walkers' with him."

"I was, until the good doctor sent me home. He said Pa was doing as well as could be expected and he'd watch over him tonight. Mrs. Walker told me to make sure the house was ready for Papa to come home tomorrow, but I've already cleaned the place and made his bed with fresh sheets..." He shrugged.

"Sounds like you're all ready for your father's homecoming," she said. "You must be so happy after all he's been through," she said, aware she was babbling. But she was just so pleased to be in his presence, to know that he had waited because he wanted to speak to her. *Alone.* "We spinsters are all set to pitch in, too, Gil. One of us is signed up to be with your father every day for the next two weeks. What time do you want me at the parsonage tomorrow? I want to be there when you bring him home, of course."

"Right after breakfast, about eight? Oh, and I wanted to show you what Mrs. Patterson loaned me from the mercantile."

Curious, Faith stepped down off the step into the sparse grass that was all that would grow so near the giant live oak that shaded their house.

"I was so concerned Polly'd spot it, if not me," he confessed over his shoulder, then pushed the object away from the side of the house toward her.

It was a chair, with a back and seat of leather and

wheels on the sides. "It's for Papa," he said with a smile. "Mrs. Patterson said I could use it as long as Papa needs it. Wasn't that kind? And Dr. Walker says if Papa continues to improve, he can soon get up in it and spend more time out of bed. He can sit outside, when the weather's good, and even go to church."

She smiled back at him, buoyed by Gil's hope.

Gil left the chair and came closer to her. "I can't thank you enough for what you're doing, Miss Faith," he said. "God bless you."

The intensity of his gaze spurred her heart into a gallop. "I… Thank you, Gil, but there will be several of us helping. We love your father, you know."

He nodded, then took her hand in his and gave it a squeeze. "I know," he said, "but you're the one who's put our Lord's teachings into action and mobilized the ladies. I'm very grateful." He let go of her hand and backed away. "I'll see you tomorrow, then. Good night."

"Good night…" *Oh, dear,* she thought as she went back inside the house, her pulse pounding, her hand tingling from his touch. Rationally, she knew she was not for Gil, but convincing her heart was another thing. And unless she had greatly misread the look in those hazel eyes, Gil Chadwick was attracted to her, too. But taking care of Gil's father was going to put her in Gil's company frequently, even with the other ladies helping her. How could she keep herself from encouraging him?

Sooner or later, she would have to have an honest talk with him, the one she had planned to have after the church service, but she dreaded it. Not only would it mean forgoing the courtship he seemed to want to begin, but Gil would never see her as admirable ever again. And what if her secret got out? She might well become an outcast in Simpson Creek.

Chapter Four

Word had spread that the preacher was going home this morning, and when Gil and Dr. Walker pushed the old preacher across the street on a wheeled litter, the townspeople formed a cheering gauntlet through which the litter passed.

Reverend Chadwick beamed crookedly at this evidence of the love his congregation bore for him, and raised a hand in a weak attempt at a wave—or maybe it was a blessing. Faith, watching from the front step of the parsonage, wasn't sure.

Once inside the parsonage, Gil and the doctor lifted him gently into his bed. Reverend Chadwick looked around him, obviously recognizing the familiar surroundings, and gave a happy sigh before closing his eyes. Even the brief excitement of being moved back to the parsonage had exhausted him.

Faith's and Gil's gazes met across the preacher's bed. Gil's hazel eyes gleamed with the same triumph that warmed her. No matter what else happened, they had accomplished this much. They had brought his father home.

"Dr. Walker said he would tire easily," Faith whispered. "I'll just go into the kitchen and start making dinner."

Gil took the worn Bible off the bedside table and lowered himself into a chair at the side of the bed. "I think I'll just sit with Papa and pray awhile," he said.

Faith hadn't been inside the parsonage for many years, but she found her way down the hallway into the kitchen at the back of the house. She had no idea what she was going to prepare for the noon meal, but Sarah had told her she was going to bring over a kettle of stewed chicken, so perhaps Gil could eat the chicken and the preacher could sip the nourishing broth.

When she reached the kitchen, Faith found she had not been the only one thinking of the Chadwicks' need for nourishment, for while they had been preparing the preacher for the move back to his house, the married ladies of the town had let themselves in and brought enough food for a regiment. In addition to the promised pot of chicken, the side table was filled with hams, fresh-baked loaves of bread, baskets of rolls, jars of jelly, preserves, green beans, applesauce, baskets of eggs and crocks of lemonade, cold tea and apple juice. On the floor sat bushel baskets of potatoes, apples, peaches, a sack of flour and one of cornmeal. Goodness, they'd thought of everything! She would have to move some of these things to the root cellar beneath the house or they would spoil before they could be eaten.

About noon, when Reverend Chadwick had awakened from his nap, she was ready with warmed broth which she spooned little by little into his mouth. Dr. Walker had warned her of the danger of the old preacher aspirating liquid into his lungs if she was not careful, but he did very well, as long as she went slowly and kept a napkin at the ready. She could tell from the way he blinked in exasperation when some leaked out of the right side of his mouth that the process frustrated him a little, for the old man was not used to being helpless. But after he'd taken his fill of broth and washed it down with apple juice, he gave her a crooked smile.

She helped ease him back onto his pillows. "Why don't you rest a little, Reverend Chadwick? I'm going to go make sure Gil has some dinner. When I come back, we'll exercise your limbs a little, all right? We've got to get you back into fighting trim—the town needs you." She could tell by the gleam in his eyes he appreciated her thinking such a goal was possible.

Faith found Gil in the parlor, sitting at a roll-top desk and writing something, his Bible open next to the paper.

"Gil, dinner's ready," she said. "Can you stop for a while?"

He turned in his chair and smiled at her. "Only if you'll eat with me," he said.

She nodded. She'd intended to do that, but his invitation pleased her more than it should.

"I've been struggling with my wedding sermon," he told her, once he'd said a blessing over the meal. "It'll be short, of course," he added with a chuckle. "No one wants to hear a preacher drone on for very long. They want to see the groom kiss his bride and begin the celebration."

She cut a piece of chicken and took a bite. "Didn't your father write down his sermons? Can't you use one of those?"

He swallowed some lemonade and shook his head. "Papa never writes anything down. It's all in his head, along with whole chapters of the Bible he's memorized."

"Your papa wa—*is*—" she corrected herself hastily "—an amazing man."

Gil nodded. "If I'm ever half the preacher my father has been, I'll be thankful. Besides, I'm trying to come up with something that hasn't been said thousands of times before."

She thought about that for a moment. "I think folks like the tried and true in a wedding. Tradition is comforting," she said.

"I suppose so," he said. "I hope I can find a way to make it traditional and fresh at the same time, however."

Just having a preacher other than his father conducting the service would make it fresh enough for the people of Simpson Creek, she thought.

"I think the world of Miss Caroline and Jack," he went on. "I want to do my part to make their wedding day special for them."

"I'm sure you will. But…it doesn't bother you?" she asked at last, giving way to curiosity.

He didn't pretend he didn't know what she meant. "Because I kept company with Miss Caroline for a little while, back during the winter? No, not really," he said. "I'm happy that she and Jack were able to resolve the things that were keeping them apart. God showed me Caroline was for Jack, not me. And the more I'm around the two of them, the more convinced I am of that."

"God…showed you," she said, hoping her doubt didn't show. "How does that…happen? To *you,* I mean," she added quickly, not wanting to reveal that she never prayed anymore, and had never experienced God showing her anything.

He speared a couple of green beans with his fork as he considered her question, and nothing on his face revealed that he found her question unusual. "I prayed about it, of course, but He doesn't always answer out loud. It was more of a feeling, *here,*" he said, flattening his hand over the center of his chest. "And sometimes He shows us by the way events work out. That's what happened in this case. Jack finally declared his true feelings, and now he and Miss Caroline are about to get married." He looked more carefully at her. "You didn't think I was hiding a broken heart, did you?"

His direct question gaze flustered her. "No…I—I'm… Perhaps I shouldn't have asked you that. It's none of my business after all." She pretended great interest in a mockingbird which had just landed on the lantana bush outside the kitchen window.

"I didn't mind, Miss Faith," he said. "Not at all. I think it's good for believers to talk about how they feel God's leading, because He has different ways of leading different people."

But I'm not a believer, she thought.

"Miss Caroline and I really hadn't progressed beyond friendship," he told her. "I would never let my feelings grow to the point where my heart would be wounded without seeking His guidance on the matter."

If that was true, she felt better. For if there was a God who cared about His faithful followers, He'd never let Gil fall in love with a woman like her—one who did not believe as he did.

"I wish I'd grown up in Simpson Creek," he said then. "It's a good place. Good land, good people."

Reverend Chadwick had become pastor here during the war years, while his son was in college. Gil had served in the army after graduating, then been wounded only a few months before the war's end. He'd gone straight into the seminary after he'd recovered.

"I'm glad you like our town," she said, wondering

where this was leading. "If you had been raised here, you might have been the only single man who returned to Simpson Creek after Appomattox."

"Or one of those who didn't live to come back," he said soberly, his eyes thoughtful. "Which is why you ladies started the Spinsters' Club, isn't it—the lack of unmarried men? Papa wrote me about the beginnings of the Spinsters' Club while I was away at seminary."

"Did you think we sounded like a band of brazen hussies, advertising for marriage-minded bachelors?" she asked, almost afraid of the answer. But she saw a twinkle in his eye that reassured her.

"Not at all," he said. "You sounded like a plucky lot. I was only worried all the young ladies of the hill country would get the same idea and there'd be no one left for me when I finished seminary."

"Ah, now, where was your faith, Reverend Gil?" she teased. "Didn't you believe that the Lord would provide?"

He smiled at her, and she felt the jolt of it all the way through her heart.

"I'm only surprised you haven't made one of those matches, Miss Faith," he said. "I'd have thought those bachelors would have snatched you up when the group first started," he said.

This bantering tone was new from him. She shrugged and looked away to hide her confusion. "So far it hasn't happened… I haven't felt 'led' to any of the gentlemen who've answered our advertisements so far, either."

"Maybe for a reason."

The sentence hung in the air, heavy with meaning. *Oh, dear, what did he mean by that? What was she to say?*

Just then a loud, urgent rapping at the front door startled both of them. Faith dropped her fork. Gil jumped up from the table, nearly oversetting his chair.

"Who can that be?" he wondered aloud. Faith followed him as he headed down the hall toward the sound.

Billy Henderson stood on the doorstep, his face tearstained, his eyes swollen. "Pastor Gil, you gotta come quick! My ma got a letter just now, and she's terrible upset. She won't tell me what it's about or let me see it. She just sits on the sofa and sobs."

"I'll come," he said quickly, remembering that Billy Henderson's father had been sent to prison after assaulting Caroline Wallace at her schoolhouse. He'd been in on the conspiracy to kidnap Jack Collier's twins which had taken place at the same time. His imprisonment had left his wife and son alone in Simpson Creek, fearful of the time Henderson would be released, for he'd also been a brutal husband and father. Daisy Henderson and her son had been planning to move away from Simpson Creek in hope that her husband wouldn't be able to find them, but they hadn't left yet.

He turned back to Faith. "Will you and Papa be all right?" he asked. He hated to have to leave on the very first day his father was home, and still in such frail condition, but one of the congregation needed him now, too.

"We'll be fine, Gil. Go ahead," she said. "Dr. Walker's right across the street if I need help."

"Bless you, Faith," he said, as he dashed down the steps after Billy Joe. "I'll be back as soon as I can."

He found Mrs. Henderson just as Billy Joe had described her, weeping on a horsehair sofa and clutching a damp handkerchief. A crumpled sheet of paper lay in her lap.

"Ma, I brung the rev'rend," Billy Joe said, speaking loudly over his mother's sobs.

She looked up and blinked at Gil as if she'd never seen him before.

"I'm Pastor Gil, Reverend Chadwick's son," he reminded her gently. He wasn't sure if he'd seen her at church since the day of the assault and kidnapping in March. Folks said she kept mostly to herself these days, shamed by her husband's despicable actions.

"Oh. Yes, of c-course," she said. "S-somehow I was expecting to see your father…forgot about what happened to him…"

He brought a chair close to the sofa and lowered himself into it. "That's all right," he said. "Your son said you were upset by the arrival of a letter. He's pretty worried about you, so he came and got me. Is there some way I can help?"

"I just couldn't tell him!" she wailed. "Here, read it!" She yanked the letter off her lap and extended it to him with a shaking hand.

Gil unfolded the rumpled paper, aware of Billy Joe watching him, his eyes troubled, his gaze darting between Gil and his mother. Gil bent his head and read the letter to himself:

Dear Mrs. Henderson,
I regret to inform you that your husband, William J. Henderson, was killed in an altercation between himself and another prisoner yesterday. He died instantly after being stabbed in the chest. We are shipping his body home to you for burial, and it should arrive at the same time as this letter.
Yours truly,
Emerson Fogle, Prison Administrator

* * *

Gil looked up at Daisy Henderson, who had covered her eyes with her sodden handkerchief. Muffled sobs still escaped from her shaking body.

Compassion welled up within Gil. The man had beaten her for years, and abused his son for as long as he had lived, yet she still sorrowed for her husband, Gil thought. She had been William Henderson's faithful wife, despite the way he had treated her.

"Mrs. Henderson," he said gently, "is it your wish that I tell your son what the letter says?"

She nodded, raising red-rimmed, tear-drenched eyes to him and then her son.

Billy Joe had drifted to a position in between Gil and his mother.

Gil took a deep breath. "Billy Joe, I need you to be brave," he said. "Your father is dead. He was killed in a fight between himself and another prisoner," he said.

Billy Joe had already been pale with worry, but now the color drained from his face. Gil rose and put a bracing hand on the boy's shoulder. He was only about twelve, Gil knew, but at this moment he looked much younger.

"I'm very sorry, Billy Joe," Gil said. "You'll need to be strong, for your mother will need you to be the man of the house now."

Billy broke away from Gil then, his face growing red as the tears flooded his cheeks. "I'm not sorry!" he cried. "My pa was mean to me an' Ma every day a' his life. We was gonna hafta leave town, and now we don't need to! We can stay here, Ma!" He knelt by the couch and buried his face in his mother's skirts, crying just as she had been.

Daisy Henderson stroked her son's rumpled hair

as she raised her tearstained face to Gil. "That's why I'm cryin', too, Reverend," she admitted. "I'm feelin' guilty 'cause I should be grievin', but what I mostly feel is relief."

"No one could blame you for feeling that way, Mrs. Henderson," he said. "In time, perhaps, you will be able to remember your husband's better qualities, the good times..." He wondered if the brutality the dead man had exhibited had erased all that from her memory. Surely there had been a time when Henderson had cherished his wife?

She shrugged. "Maybe someday," she said. "But right now his body's at the undertaker's, waitin' to be buried. Might you have some time to say some words over him tomorrow? I'll have to borrow some widow's weeds, too, I expect, just to be proper."

There was a defiant glint in her eyes that hinted she secretly wanted to put on her Sunday best and celebrate her unexpected freedom.

"I'll be happy to say some words at the graveside," he assured her. "And again, I expect folks will understand if you choose not to wear mourning very long. It's only natural that you're experiencing a lot of conflicting feelings, Mrs. Henderson, under the circumstances."

"I don't know how I'm going to pay for his buryin', Reverend," she said bitterly. "I've been taking in washing, but... He left me with next to nothing, you know."

Gil did know about her financial situation from conversations with his father. The church's Fund for the Deserving Poor had been helping the mother and son keep food on the table even before this. "Don't give it another thought, Mrs. Henderson. I'm sure the church can help you with that. Would you like me to have a word with the undertaker?"

She rose, gathering her dignity around her like a shawl with many rips and holes in it. "I'd be much obliged, Reverend. Thank you for coming—and not judging me."

"The Lord understands what you're feeling, too, Mrs. Henderson," he assured her.

He was conducting his first wedding on Saturday, and tomorrow he would conduct his first funeral, Gil mused as he walked back down High Street from the Hendersons' house. How he wished he could get advice from his father on what to say over a grave when the widow felt—understandably—more reprieved than bereaved. He could tell his father, but his father could only stare back at him, his eyes full of answers he couldn't express. He would have to pray for wisdom and trust that the right words would come to his mouth.

He wondered what Faith would say. Of course he couldn't divulge what Daisy Henderson had confided in him, but like most of the town, she'd known about Henderson's brutal character.

He wondered if his father had confided the things he knew about the townspeople to Gil's mother, secure in the knowledge that his wife wouldn't gossip. Had his mother had insights about people that she'd shared with his father? His mother had been gone for years, but he remembered her as a very wise lady. Surely his father had shared his concerns with her. Being a pastor would be a lonely business, indeed, without a helpmate.

Not for the first time, Gil thought about how much he needed a wife himself. Immediately Faith's face appeared in his mind. *Is she the one, Lord, or is it just my wishful thinking? I want to act according to Your will. I don't want to make a mistake again, like I did before, a mistake that could make me unfit to serve You.*

But the image of Faith continued to burn itself across his brain. He could imagine telling her all about what had happened today, and all his days. About his doubts and his fears. He would never need to fear that she would be indiscreet with what he confided to her. The words of the Book of Proverbs came to him: "The heart of her husband doth safely trust in her."

Faith Chadwick. It had a good ring to it.

Chapter Five

Faith was peeling potatoes at the kitchen sink when Gil returned to the parsonage from the undertaker's.

"Is everything all right?" Faith asked, after reporting that his father was dozing again. "I mean…if it's all right for me to ask, that is?" she added quickly.

There was certainly no reason not to tell her the news, even if he couldn't tell her all of it.

After he told her about the death of Mrs. Henderson's husband, Faith's lovely green eyes were troubled. "That poor woman, and poor Billy Joe," she murmured. "Perhaps in time she'll see it as a blessing in disguise…"

He didn't tell her that Mrs. Henderson already did. "The burial will be tomorrow morning," he said.

Faith looked thoughtful. "There probably won't be any other people there, will there? Caroline will be with your father tomorrow, but I could stay here during the funeral, so she could attend—she and Billy Joe were close, you know, because she was his teacher. It would be a comfort to him. And I'll tell the spinsters and others about it, so they'll come, too, and Mrs. Henderson won't feel alone…"

He was touched by the way her compassion immediately moved her to help in a practical way. "That would be very kind."

"And perhaps you could take her some of the food the townspeople have brought by for you and your father? They've brought more, even after I put away the bounty of this morning. I found this on the doorstep while you were gone," she said, pointing to another already-plucked chicken, a cake and a pie. "It's more than any two people could eat all week, especially when one of them isn't up to taking solid food yet. Which reminds me, Dr. Walker stopped by and said we could try giving him some soft food very slowly at supper tonight."

"Sure, I can take Mrs. Henderson some of the food," Gil said. "It's good that you thought of it. And you don't have to prepare supper—I can see to it," he said. "It's all right if you want to go home." He could remember his mother being just such an energetic individual, with the members of the congregation being as much her concern as his father's.

"It's already cooking," she said, lifting the lid of a pot on the stove and a savory aroma filled the air. Unless his nose misled him, beef stew simmered within. "Besides, I want to be here when the reverend first tries swallowing soft food. I think he should try applesauce to begin with—Dr. Walker said to make sure it was watered down at first, so it was more like a thick liquid than solid food—until we're sure he can swallow well."

So that his father wouldn't choke. Gil sighed. His father was going to have to learn to eat all over again, as if he were a baby. Gil said a quick prayer for patience, both for his father and himself—and one of thankfulness for Faith's nursing ability.

"I thought once you came home, we could get him up in the wheelchair for a little while," Faith went on. "The doctor says the more he's up, the better, but he won't be able to tolerate being out of bed very long at first."

"All right, let's try it now," he said, gesturing in the direction of his father's room. Minutes later, when they had lifted the frail old man into the wheelchair and wheeled him out into the sunshine-lit parlor, the look in his father's eyes was all the reward any son could have asked.

Later that evening, Gil told his father the whole story about Henderson's death, including the parts he couldn't tell Faith. His father listened attentively, and Gil found it helpful to speak his thoughts aloud, even though his father couldn't advise him.

"Mrs. Henderson and her son need our prayers as well as any help we can give them, Papa," he said. "But of course you knew that as soon as I told you what had happened."

His father nodded.

Gil sighed. "Papa, I can't help thinking how sad it must be to live one's life, and have the person who should be closest to you only feel relief that you're gone," he murmured. "I'd like to think someone would miss me when I die."

His father nodded again, and jerked a shaky finger at the daguerreotype portrait of him and his wife which sat on the top of a bookcase.

"I know you miss Mama," Gil said. "I miss her, too."

His father then pointed at the thin gold band he wore, the ring that had once been his wife's, but now fit his thin, gnarled finger. Then he pointed directly at Gil. He mumbled something unintelligible, then looked exasperated at himself.

Was he asking Gil what Gil thought he was asking?
"Are you saying I need a wife, Papa?"

The old man nodded emphatically and repeatedly, then turned his left palm upward while shrugging the same shoulder, as if he was asking what Gil thought.

Gil was pleased that he had judged correctly, and that his father had guessed what had been so much on his mind of late. "Yes, I've been doing some thinking about that very thing, Papa," he said, grinning. "Did you have anyone in mind?"

His father shrugged, but there was a distinct gleam in his eyes.

Gil knew his father probably wouldn't have told him, even before his stroke. He'd always encouraged Gil to make his own decisions—with the Lord's direction, of course. *If only he'd always included prayer in his decision making...*

"You're not being much help, Papa," he said, letting his father see that he was teasing. But then he gathered himself to ask a daring question. "What do you think of Faith Bennett?" He found himself holding his breath as he waited for the answer.

His father's gaze went to the ceiling, as if to indicate he was thinking about it. Then he looked back at Gil, held out the hand that hadn't been affected by the stroke and pointed his thumb up.

He approved! Gil felt a surge of encouragement. "So you think that's a good idea, Papa?" he asked in confirmation.

His father took hold of the hand he couldn't move with his good hand, and held up the hands, clasped together.

Gil didn't have to guess at the message—*Pray about it.*

* * *

"Cup," Faith repeated patiently, sitting by the preacher's bedside and pointing to the object he had been drinking tea from, with her help, a little while ago.

"K—kkkk—" he repeated, managing the hard consonant but not the rest of the word. "K-k-kkk," he said again, then fisted his left hand and pounded it in the mattress, his face furrowing in frustration.

"You're doing better, Reverend," Faith assured him. "Remember, only days ago you couldn't say even that much. If you keep working on it, I just know your speech will come back in time. Perhaps you'll even be preaching to us again one day."

He gave a skeptical snort, then a look which said, plain as day, *I don't believe it, but you're sweet to try to make me think so.*

Faith couldn't help chuckling aloud. "They say when you're feeling ornery it's a sign of recovery," she said, and he flashed his crooked smile.

She heard the door open, and a moment later Caroline appeared. "Your son conducted a very comforting graveside service, Reverend," she said as she entered the room. "The apple doesn't fall far from the tree, I suppose."

Pride twinkled from the old man's eyes, but he made a gesture that showed he wanted to hear more.

"Mrs. Henderson and Billy Joe are doing as well as could be expected," Caroline went on. "I think it helped her to have others there to support her, thanks to Faith getting the word out."

Reverend Chadwick reached a gnarled hand out and patted Faith's arm, clearly commending her.

"It was the least I could do," Faith assured him, warmed by his regard.

"Gil's escorting Mrs. Henderson and Billy Joe back home, but he said to tell you both he'd be back soon," Caroline said. "Thanks for making it possible for me to attend, Faith. I know Billy Joe appreciated it. You can go home, now that I'm back. You must have other things to do. Unless you wanted to see Reverend Gil?" she added, when Faith remained seated.

"Oh…oh, no, I didn't…guess I was woolgathering," she said, hoping Caroline hadn't noticed the heat she felt blooming in her cheeks. She didn't want the bride-to-be, or anyone else, to guess she had any special feeling for Gil Chadwick—a feeling she must continue to conceal.

"Yes, of course," she said, jumping to her feet. "I *have* neglected my chores at home lately… Now, be sure to go slow when you give the reverend his dinner—maybe some more applesauce and the mashed beans, with sips of water in between. And you'll need to exercise his limbs this afternoon, and have Gil get him up in his wheelchair—"

Caroline waved a hand. "You went over all that this morning," she reminded Faith, chuckling. "I can handle this. Now shoo!"

Faith hastened home, forcing herself not to look down the street when she left the parsonage to see if Gil was coming.

By the time Saturday arrived, Gil's father's condition had improved so much that he was spending much of the day out of bed and in his wheelchair. Even though he still couldn't speak intelligibly, and his right hand remained useless in his lap, he seemed in all other ways much improved, so much so that Dr. Walker agreed with Gil that his father could come to the wedding.

"Just for the ceremony and an hour or so at the reception afterward, but I'll be there, and I'll have his nurse for the day take him home sooner if I judge he's getting too tired," the doctor told Gil. "Even happy events can be fatiguing, of course."

"You hear that, Papa? You can go, but don't you dare try to get up and dance with the bride," Gil said, grinning at his father.

His father pointed at himself. "G-g-good," he said. The word was slurred and indistinct, but recognizable nonetheless.

Gil whooped with triumph and swooped his arms around his father in an exuberant hug. "You're saying you'll be good? Oh, Papa, God is good, too!"

Anyone passing through Simpson Creek Saturday afternoon must have thought it a ghost town, for everyone was at the church. George Detwiler had even closed the saloon for the day.

The wedding procession had to be delayed while the entire congregation, including the bride and groom, greeted Reverend Chadwick in his wheelchair, but no one seemed to mind. Now, as Sarah began playing the "Wedding March," Louisa Wheeler parked the old preacher next to her by the last pew and slid in next to Faith, who was sitting with her parents.

"Don't they look wonderful?" Louisa whispered, indicating the bride and groom standing in front of Gil at the front of the church, flanked by Jack Collier's twin daughters.

Faith nodded, watching with misty eyes. There was no doubt the rancher who had finally won the schoolmarm's heart was a very good-looking fellow. But a shaft of sunlight had found its way through a golden portion of the stained-glass cross window behind the preacher, and it illuminated Gil's light brown hair as if he wore a halo.

Gil Chadwick was not for her, she reminded herself once again, but there was no harm in looking, was there?

She hadn't realized she had sighed aloud until Louisa, misreading her reason for sighing, leaned over and whispered, "They must be so happy…the twins just adore Caroline, you know."

Faith just nodded again, not wanting to miss any more of Gil's resonant voice saying the old, traditional words of the marriage vows.

"I now pronounce you man and wife. You may kiss your bride."

Gil took the opportunity to take a deep breath while the bride and groom kissed and everyone applauded. It was done. He had married his first couple, and had not stammered as he led the couple in the recital of their vows. His hands hadn't shaken, despite his nervousness. He'd managed not to drop the ring, even though Jack Collier's hands trembled when he'd handed it to him. He'd spoken about the wedding feast at Cana at which Jesus performed his first miracle, and had kept his sermon eloquent but to the point.

He looked over the heads of the new couple and the congregation to where his father sat in his wheelchair, and was gratified to see the old man beaming proudly at him, as if to say, "Well done."

Then the attendees rose to their feet as the new husband and wife began their march back up the aisle as the music swelled again.

Next to his father, he spotted Louisa, his father's nurse for the day, and then his gaze landed on Faith, sitting on Louisa's other side, heart-stoppingly lovely in a dress the color of bluebonnets, and he looked no further.

He could have sworn she'd been looking at him until a second before his eyes had found her, but it was just as well that she no longer did. This way, he could feast on the sight of her as she watched the new husband and wife pass by.

Did she have any idea how pretty she was? His pulse quickened at the thought of spending time with her at the wedding reception. Now that it seemed clear his father was on the mend, Gil planned to make it clear to her and anyone who cared to notice that he was interested in her. Faith—what a perfect name for a future preacher's wife!

"Did you notice how Reverend Gil was looking at you just a moment ago?" Faith's mother remarked as they waited to congratulate the bridal couple. "I believe he's sweet on you, dear."

"Oh, I'm sure you're imagining things, Mama," Faith told her mother, hoping no one had heard her. Sometimes Lydia Bennett's voice carried more than she meant it to, for she was slightly hard of hearing and didn't realize how loudly she spoke.

"Time will tell," her father said. "About time our young preacher found a wife and settled down. I don't reckon he could do any better than our daughter."

It was rare to hear her father express approval of her, yet his words made Faith wince inwardly. *Just about anyone would be better for him than me.*

Once in the social hall where the wedding reception was to be held, her parents drifted toward other older couples they were friends with and Faith joined a cluster of Spinsters' Club ladies.

"How are you doing out on the ranch with your husband off on that cattle drive? I'm sure you must miss him dreadfully," Faith said to Milly Brookfield, whose baby son, Nicholas, was being handed from lady to lady, much to his delight and theirs. Clearly he'd inherited much of his British father's charm.

"I miss him every minute of the day," Milly admitted. "But I'm doing all right. Little Nick keeps me busy."

"I've begged her to come stay with us while Nick's gone, but she got all of our father's stubbornness," her sister, Sarah, said. "I even suggested renting the Spencers' house because it's still standing empty just down the street, if she thinks it'd be too crowded at our house."

"Nonsense," Milly retorted. "What kind of ranch wife would I be if I stayed in town the whole time my husband's away? Besides, I'll have Jack and Caroline as my neighbors, as soon as they get back from their wedding trip," she said, nodding toward the bridal couple, who were speaking to old Reverend Chadwick and Mrs. Detwiler nearby.

"Milly, I just can't rest easy about your being out there so far away with only the cowhands who stayed behind, as loyal as they are," Sarah said. "Why, anything could happen."

"By 'anything,' I know you mean Comanches, sister," Milly said, "but they're not likely to come raiding because there's only a handful of cows with young calves left on the ranch, and only half a dozen horses. And I don't think outlaws will be a problem, either—they've steered clear of Simpson Creek since Prissy's husband's shown himself to be such a no-nonsense sheriff."

Prissy, already glowing with the radiance of a woman expecting her first child, beamed at the compliment.

"We'll all have to make it a point to come out visiting often, both as a group and individually," Faith said. "Perhaps we can organize a party, like we did to celebrate young Nicholas's birth."

"I'm afraid I won't be up for any trips out that way until after our baby comes," Sarah Walker said, glancing down at her own rounded form.

Prissy clapped her hands together. "I have an idea— we'll have a party to celebrate Sarah's baby coming, here in town!" Prissy cried. "We should probably have it at Papa's house, rather than ours, because Sam's in the middle of adding on a room and it's all sawdust and confusion," she added. "You could come into town for that, couldn't you, Milly?"

"Sure," Milly agreed. "And yes, Nicholas and I will stay overnight with you then, Sarah."

"I'll look forward to it," Sarah said.

"Prissy, your papa and Mrs. Fairchild will be getting married soon, too, won't they?" Faith asked the sheriff's wife.

"Yes, though they're just planning a quiet ceremony with the family and a few friends," Prissy murmured. "My guess is they're talking to Gil about that right now," she said, nodding to where her father, the mayor, and the widow he'd been courting were now in earnest conversation with the young preacher. "Papa seems years younger since she's come into our lives," she added with a happy sigh.

Faith remembered it hadn't been so long ago that Prissy was very distressed about the fact that her widowed father was romantically interested in Mrs. Fairchild, a woman whom he had known from his school days. What a difference a few months—and Prissy's own contentment with Sam Bishop—had made.

"Goodness, we might as well rename ourselves The Brides' Club and a Few Others," Polly hissed in Faith's ear just then, yanking Faith abruptly out of her peaceful musing. "I can't believe we were ever once a band of enterprising misses looking for husbands. Land sakes, all we've talked about are babies and the husbands of the lucky few."

Faith fought to control her feeling of irritation at Polly's spiteful remark. "Well, Milly sure didn't wait on someone else to bring about her wedded bliss," she pointed out, keeping her voice low. "Why don't you suggest an event we could plan?"

"As a matter of fact, I've been thinking of that very thing," Polly said, her face smug as she turned to the rest of the spinsters. "Ladies, I think the Spinsters' Club should hold a box social, with the prize going to the most beautifully decorated supper box before the bidding. Only Spinsters' Club members' boxes will be eligible for the prize, though there'll be the usual bidding by husbands for their wives' boxes, of course. I've taken the liberty of drafting an advertisement to be posted in the neighboring towns—perhaps Caroline's young brother would take care of that for us?"

Faith's irritation faded. Polly had actually made a plan and wasn't just carping with no solution in mind. "Who'd be the judge?" she asked. "And what would be the prize?"

"Why, Reverend Gil would be the judge," Polly said. "And the lucky winner would get to sit with him at the picnic supper that would follow."

Too late, Faith saw where Polly's idea had been leading. It was only another thinly veiled plot to position herself next to Gil Chadwick. Faith smothered a sigh. There was no guarantee of victory, but Polly was willing to risk it.

"That's a good idea, Polly," Maude Harkey said, apparently unsuspecting of Polly's motives. "Have you asked him if he'd be willing to judge?"

"No, I wanted to pass the idea by you ladies first," Polly said, all innocence. "But now that you've approved the plan, I think I'll go speak to him this very minute. What man wouldn't want to be the prize of a contest?" She left the circle of spinsters and sashayed in Gil Chadwick's direction.

"I see what she's up to now," Prissy said, her eyes narrowed. "Cousin Anson!"

Startled, Faith stared at Prissy. *What was Prissy up to, calling her cousin like that? What was it she wanted him to do?*

Chapter Six

A broad-shouldered, dark-haired man with a faint resemblance to Prissy turned from where he had been conversing with young Dan Wallace. "Yes, Cousin?"

She nodded pointedly at Polly, who had been stopped by Mrs. Detwiler just before she had reached Gil. The old woman appeared to be complimenting her on her dress. Polly smiled and bent her head to listen, but her gaze kept darting over Mrs. Detwiler's head toward Gil.

"Remember what we talked about?" Prissy called, nodding meaningfully toward Polly.

"You want me do that right *now?* But Dan and I were just talkin' about my new sorrel stallion…"

Hands on her hips, Prissy stomped her foot with exasperated impatience. "I wanted you to do it several minutes ago. *Hurry!*"

Faith could see the conversation Gil, Mayor Gilmore and his lady was about to conclude, but she still didn't know what Prissy expected Anson to do.

"Prissy, what are you up to?" Faith asked.

"I told Anson to distract Polly, so she wouldn't plaster herself to Reverend Gil like I'm afraid she's about to do," Prissy said, not taking her worried eyes from her cousin, who was still ambling unhurriedly toward Polly.

What had Prissy told her cousin to do? Faith watched, fascinated, as Anson reached Polly and Mrs. Detwiler and favored both women equally with one of his dazzling smiles. If she hadn't seen it with her own eyes, she wouldn't have believed the way Mrs. Detwiler's eyelashes began to flutter and how Polly's whole face brightened.

Faith stared. "What can he be saying to them?"

Prissy giggled. "It's a pleasure to watch a charming man at work, isn't it?"

Faith saw Mayor Gilmore and Mrs. Fairchild leave Reverend Gil's side, hand-in-hand and beaming. Then Gil looked around as if searching for someone, appeared startled as he saw Polly near him, then visibly relaxed as he saw that her attention had been snagged by Anson. Gil resumed peering over the room, then his gaze stopped as it landed on her.

Milly chuckled. "Looks like the coast is clear for you, Faith, dear. Go to Gil now."

Faith's jaw dropped. "What do you mean? I can't—"

"Oh, yes, you *can,*" Prissy whispered, giving Faith a nudge.

Gil started toward them.

"Looks like you won't have to move an inch, Faith," Sarah murmured. "Ladies, I think the rest of us need to go get some punch."

Before Faith could something to keep them with her, the three ladies deserted her, chuckling all the way to the punch bowl. Some friends! Then she reminded herself they didn't know how strongly—or why—she was trying to resist flirting with the very man who now approached her with a smile that threatened to melt her steely resolve.

"Miss Faith, you're looking lovely today, if I may say so," Gil said as he reached her side.

Don't blush. Don't let him see how much the compliment affects you. But she might as well have spoken to the wall as to her body, for she felt the color flooding her cheeks and her pulse kick into a gallop.

"Why, thank you, Reverend Gil," she managed to say. *And you look like the handsomest man that ever walked the streets of Simpson Creek.* "Uh…th-that was a lovely wedding sermon you gave."

His smile broadened and his eyes sparkled with pleasure. "Thank you," he responded. "My very first, you know."

She nodded. "But not your last, I'm thinking," she said, nodding toward Mayor Gilmore and Mrs. Fairchild.

He glanced back at them. "Yes. It will feel a little odd, marrying a couple who are so much older than myself. I'm sure they wish my father could do it," he admitted.

His humility touched her. As beloved as Reverend Chadwick was, his son must feel he had very large shoes to fill. "But surely he could sit by you in his wheelchair, and perhaps lay his hand on them in blessing," she said. She had seen the old preacher do that, had even been the recipient of such a blessing. Yet she had lost her ability to believe.

He blinked. "What a good idea. What a wise woman you are to think of that."

Faith felt her heart warm at his appreciation, even if she felt she didn't fully deserve it. "At the rate he's going, he may even be able to *say* some words of blessing by then. His other nurses have told me he's been practicing saying the names of things all day long." She looked over to where Gil's father was sipping punch, his wheelchair next to the table where Louisa and the Wallaces were sitting.

Gil grinned proudly. "He's determined," he agreed. "I asked him if he was getting tired, but he shook his head. I think he takes strength from being around his congregation." He paused, his attention caught by something at the bridal table. "Oh, look, they're cutting the cake. Would you like a piece, Faith?"

Faith nodded. She would enjoy Gil's company for now, for a wedding reception was not the time or place to explain her difficult truth to him. As they walked side by side to the table where the pieces of cake were being laid out, she saw with some amusement that Anson Tyler was still in earnest conversation with Polly, and Polly appeared to be having the time of her life. She seemed to have forgotten all about speaking to Gil Chadwick.

Once they'd obtained their slices of cake, plus an additional one for his father, they sat down at the table with his father, and told Louisa they would stay with Reverend Chadwick so she could circulate for a while.

Sitting here with Gil and his father, conversing with some of the older married couples sitting nearby, Faith pretended she didn't see the group of younger women gathering near the bride in an open area of the hall.

Milly came over to their table. "Get up there, Faith. Caroline's about to throw the bouquet," she said.

"Oh, no thanks, I'm fine here," Faith demurred. "I'm helping the reverend with his cake." She had no wish to take part in the tradition ritual, especially in view of her resolve about Gil.

Sarah had come to join her sister. "Go on, Faith. Are you a true spinster or not?"

"I don't like making a spectacle of myself. Let Polly win," she muttered, feeling Gil's gaze on her. "You know how much she wants to."

Faith saw Reverend Chadwick frown crookedly, then, with his unaffected left hand, make a shooing motion. She could hardly refuse the old preacher's urging without looking like a spoilsport.

"I don't think you'll have to worry about Polly," Prissy said, joining the others. "I saw her and Anson strolling around out in the churchyard, arm in arm. My cousin's an excellent decoy!"

Faith looked at the group, and saw that Prissy was right. Polly wasn't among the young ladies lined up to catch the bouquet. Maude Harkey was there, and Jane Jeffries, Ella Justiss, Kate Patterson and her cousin Louisa—as well as a trio of younger girls barely old enough to put their hair up, but no Polly. *How surprising,* she thought. Anson Tyler was either taking Prissy's request very seriously or he'd found something unexpectedly appealing in their fellow spinster. Faith fervently hoped it was the latter, and that Anson wasn't just playing a game. Polly was searching for love, and Faith hoped she wouldn't get hurt in the process.

Faith decided to give in gracefully. But even after she had joined the others waiting for the bouquet to be tossed, she was so lost in thought that she missed Caroline tossing the bouquet, and flinched when it hit her in the head. Blushing with embarrassment as everyone in the hall began to laugh and clap, she smoothed some curls that had been knocked askew before she picked up the ribbon-bound cluster of wildflowers.

"Better wake up, Faith!" Caroline teased, merriment dancing in her eyes. "Looks like you'll be the next bride!"

Faith ducked her head to avoid the stares and amusement as she returned to her seat next to Gil. She should have stuck to her guns about staying put at the table.

"Well done, Miss Faith," Gil praised, grinning.

"Don't laugh, your turn is coming," she said darkly. "I see the groom getting up, so the garter toss will be next."

"Oh, I'm sure that members of the clergy are exempt," Gil protested, but without any real alarm.

Sure enough, just then Jack Collier invited the bachelors to gather up front.

"Go on up there, Reverend Gil," Milly urged Gil. "There's not all that many bachelors. That's why I started the Spinsters' Club after all."

"Yes, go on, Reverend Gil," the mayor urged.

"Why, Mayor Gilmore, you're unmarried also," Gil retorted. "Seems like you need to be right up there with me if I go."

"Ah, but my lady and I have already set a date, as we spoke about with you a little while ago," Gilmore countered, giving Maria Fairchild a fond look. "So I have nothing to prove."

Eventually, Gil let himself be persuaded and joined Caroline's younger brother, Dan, a couple of other youths and Anson Tyler, who had ambled back into the hall with Polly just in time to join the others.

"Oh, pooh, Cousin Anson can't bear to lose any contest, whether it's horse racing or a shooting match," Faith heard Prissy fuss. "Why did he have to come back right now? He'll grab that garter whether he has any intention of marrying or not."

And so he did, jumping for the backward-thrown

garter as if he were part bullfrog. Gil made a good effort, but he was a little too far to the right to reach it, and Anson plucked it neatly out of the air. Everyone clapped and the other men slapped Prissy's cousin on the back and congratulated him. Waving the little article triumphantly, he returned to where Polly jumped up and down, clapping her hands.

"I was counting on you, Reverend Gil!" Milly said in mock reproof as Gil came back to the table. "You let us down!"

"Don't listen to my sister," Sarah told Gil. "You gave it a good try—that's what counts."

Faith was secretly relieved. If Gil had won as she had, there would have been far too much attention paid to the two of them. Before she even had a chance to explain to Gil why they could not be a courting couple, the gossips would have it that she and Gil were as good as wed.

Perhaps she was getting ahead of herself, though. Gil had sought out her company today, but it would be presumptuous of her to assume he would ask to call on her until he actually did so. Looking across the hall, she saw that Prissy's cousin Anson was once more deep in conversation with Dan Wallace and a couple of other men, while Polly hovered uncertainly at his side, as if uncertain whether he expected her to linger.

Deep within her, however, Faith knew that she had not imagined the way Gil's eyes had lit up when he approached her, or the warmth in them when his gaze was focused on hers. He was attracted to her, she could feel it in her bones. It would just be a matter of time until he asked Faith to accompany him to dinner again, to some event or even just on a walk.

And until he *did* make the next move, she would

be in an agony of anticipation, wanting to accept, but knowing she must refuse.

"Miss Faith?" Gil murmured, and Faith realized with a start he had been trying to get her attention for a moment or two.

"Oh! I'm sorry," she said. "You were saying?"

He smiled. "I was saying, I think Papa's getting tired. If you'll excuse me, I'll help Miss Louisa get him home. But I'll be back," he added, and she did not miss the gleam of hope in those hazel eyes that she would still be at the party when he returned.

She gave him a bright smile, then turned to his father, who was indeed looking worn out. "Reverend Chadwick, I'm so glad you were able to come."

The old preacher said "Mmmm t-too."

If she stayed until Gil returned, he might ask to walk her home. That might be a good thing—during their walk, she would get the chance to explain her position when he asked if he could see her again.

But she couldn't face it just yet. Some of the wedding guests had started to depart, and once Gil had left with Louisa and his father, she made her farewells to the bridal couple and escaped to the sanctuary of home.

"You left the reception before all the excitement," Gil informed her the next morning when she arrived at the parsonage to care for his father. She had come earlier than usual, knowing Gil was getting ready to preach today. His father would remain at home, though, for Dr. Walker had already decreed that a day of rest was in order for Reverend Chadwick after the long time spent at the wedding the day before.

She felt guilty that she had not waited for him. "Oh?

I…I'm afraid I was tired…" she murmured. "What did I miss?"

He grinned. "Just as I returned, Dr. Walker and his wife were leaving. Apparently their baby had decided it was time to make an appearance."

"Sarah—she had the baby?" Faith cried. Sarah hadn't seemed the least bit like a woman about to give birth, although her form had certainly indicated the time was near.

Gil chuckled. "Not until the wee hours, but yes, the Walkers are the proud parents of a baby girl, and both mother and baby are doing fine. Dr. Walker stopped by to tell me just a few minutes ago. They've named her Elizabeth, which, as luck would have it, is both Sarah's and Nolan's mothers' names. And the proud papa tells me the wee one has bright red hair, just as he had as a baby."

"How wonderful!" she said, clasping her hands together. "I can't wait to see her!" She would wait a day or two, though, for Sarah would need time to rest before receiving visitors.

"Well, I'd best be going," he said, grabbing his well-worn black leather Bible. "I'll see you and Papa after church."

She found the old preacher sitting up in his wheelchair in the parlor, staring out at the church next door with an expression that could only be described as frustrated.

Her heart went out to him. She wanted to be at church, too, watching and listening to Gil's voice as he preached. "I know you want to be there, Reverend," she said. She knew it would not help to remind Gil's father that he had lain at death's door so recently and his condition was still frail. "And you will be, soon, especially if we do everything we can now to get you back into fighting trim. Let me help you exercise your hand and arm, and then we'll work on your words, all right?"

He nodded, his gaze still focused on the church where folks were starting to arrive.

She would have her work cut out for her to provide encouragement and therapy for the old preacher *and* prepare Sunday dinner by the time the worship service was finished—even considering that Gil would be among the last to leave the church. Perhaps she could combine tasks by coaching Reverend Chadwick on his speech while she prepared the meal.

She would stay until after dinner, when the old preacher would probably take a nap. If that happened, would Gil ask to escort her home? A polite gesture because she lived only a short distance from the church down Fannin Street. But would they keep walking past her house, past the school…

Would this be the day she would have to expose herself as a nonbeliever to Gil, and end the regard for her that she saw in his eyes?

Chapter Seven

Gil was guiltily aware that his mind was only half on his preaching that morning, too eager to finish the service so he could go home and see Faith. If the opportunity presented itself, he wanted to do what he'd been unable to do after the wedding yesterday, and begin their courtship.

After stumbling a second time over a passage of Scripture he'd been quoting, he mentally reined himself in. *I'm sorry, Lord. Help me to keep my mind on Your service and Your people, not just Faith, while I am in Your house.* Then he added to himself, *This must be why ministers should be married—so they won't be distracted all the time.*

Then he could concentrate more easily, even afterward when it seemed each and every one of his congregation felt the need to engage him in conversation. Of course he wanted to speak to Mrs. Henderson, even though the mourning-clad widow would have stolen meekly past him, and inquire about how she and her son were doing in the wake of Mr. Henderson's death. He was pleased to see a number of the Spinsters' Club ladies approached her after that and included her in their conversation.

Finally the last church members left the churchyard, and Gil was free at last to cross the lawn between the church and the parsonage.

A savory aroma greeted his nose as he opened the door. His father sat in his wheelchair at the table, and Faith was just carrying a pot of chicken and dumplings toward it from the stove.

"H-h'lo, s-son," his father said, and looked very pleased with himself.

"Hello, Papa, Miss Faith." His throat suddenly felt very thick with thankfulness.

"We practiced that for a long time this morning," Faith told him. "I think he's really making progress."

Gil had to agree.

She filled Gil's glass with lemonade. He took a grateful sip, parched after a morning of using his voice. It was soothingly cool. She must have stored the pitcher in the root cellar until just a few minutes ago.

The food was as delicious as it looked. Faith asked him all about the church service as she helped his father cut up his chicken. Gil guessed she was asking the questions she thought Reverend Chadwick would want the answers to—how many people had attended, if someone had expressed any special need for prayer, if anyone was reported ill and so forth. How perceptive she was!

As he answered Faith's questions, he saw his father listening attentively. From time to time the older man would make a halting attempt to make a comment of his own. His speech was still mostly garbled, but Faith seemed able to decipher what he was trying to say even better than Gil could.

The old man was drowsy after the big meal, so Gil helped him lie down in his room for a nap. He returned to the kitchen to find Faith already doing the dishes.

"You didn't have to do those," he said, picking up a towel to dry them.

She smiled at him. "Nonsense. It'll take only a few minutes. I wouldn't dream of making a mess in the kitchen, then leaving it for someone else to clean up."

He was glad she had lingered, for it gave him the perfect opportunity.

"Faith, may I call on you tonight?"

Gil saw a flash of something trouble the green in her eyes before she shuttered them with her lashes. Could it be she was concerned about his father being alone?

"Papa goes to bed even before the chickens these days," he told her. "I think it would be all right for me to leave him for a short time, with your home so close to the parsonage," he told her, but the shadow didn't leave her eyes.

Faith took a deep breath, scrubbing hard for a moment on the pot in which the dumplings had cooked. Then she laid it aside and dried her hands on her apron.

"Gil, there…there's something you need to know. About m-me," she began, turning away from him and gazing out the window that overlooked the church.

His heart skipped a beat and he felt a stirring of apprehension slither down his spine. What was she about to confess? An unsavory past? Surely not. Integrity radiated from her. No, a past mistake was something *he* would have to tell *her* about at some point, not the other way around.

She wasn't about to say she held some affection for someone else, was she?

"You can tell me anything, Faith, you know that." His voice sounded a lot more steady than he felt.

She looked over her shoulder for a long moment, studying him, then turned back to gaze out the window again.

"I…I do not think you should court me," she said. Then she added quickly, "Don't get me wrong, I am more than happy to help you care for your father."

"Have I—have I done something to offend you, F— Miss Faith?" he said, retreating into formality when he really wanted to rush to her and apologize for anything he had done wrong.

She whirled, looking as distressed as he felt. "No, of course not, Gil! To be honest, there's nothing I'd like more than your calling on me this evening—or any other time, for that matter," she assured him, wide-eyed, then looked away once again, as if fearing she'd said too much.

"Then what could it possibly be, Faith?" he asked. "Please don't be afraid to tell me."

"I think you should know that I…" Faith took another deep breath, as if the air had suddenly been sucked from the room. "I'm not a suitable lady for you, Gil."

He took an involuntary step toward her. "Why would you say such a thing? I think you're eminently…suitable." Such a cold, unfeeling word, *suitable*. It didn't come close to expressing how right he felt she was. She was perfect for him. *Wasn't she?*

"No, no, I'm not," she insisted. "I— This is hard for me to say, Gil, and I hope you will handle this information with discretion, for I've not told anyone else for good reason. It could…that is, I could well become an outcast, if it was known."

Gil felt a cold ball of dread in the pit of his stomach.

"You may rely on my discretion, of course," he said. "But if you've sinned in some way, you know as a Christian you need only to acknowledge your sin to God and pray for forgive—"

"I don't believe in God, Gil," she said, interrupting him in a rush of words like water pouring through a breaking dam. "I have no faith. Ironic, isn't it, considering my name?"

He stood stock-still, unable to believe what he had just heard. "Y-you don't…believe?" He had never heard such an admission. Even outlaws he had counseled in jail cells believed in the Almighty, even if they chose not to obey Him. "But why?" he asked at last.

Faith turned to face him now, her eyes blazing. "Why?" she repeated. "You think you can explain it away?" she demanded. "You think you can give me some kind of easy reason that a loving God could allow my brother to die of a rattlesnake bite despite the prayers of your father and the whole town? Your father is a good man, a man of prayer. So if he couldn't save my brother with his prayers, and the whole town's prayers didn't matter a hill of beans, it must be because there is no God. Or if there is," she said, her voice breaking at last, like a piece of thin window glass finally pushed with enough force to splinter, "He doesn't care about the people He supposedly created."

He'd imagined she been going to tell him she was a fallen woman. This was so much worse. *Faith didn't believe in the God he served.* She was right—as a preacher, he couldn't marry a woman who didn't share his faith. But his disappointment that she could not be his was the least of it. *Faith was wandering in darkness, lost!*

She had carried this grief, this secret, inside her for

years, he realized. "Did you never tell your parents about your doubts?" he wondered aloud. "Surely they could—"

She whirled on him. "Oh, they never stopped believing," she snapped. "I didn't want them to wash my mouth out with soap for admitting such a shameful thing, or put it down to a passing whim brought on by grief. And then," she said, her voice growing bitter, "I found my father alone on his knees, begging God out loud for another son to carry on his name, and his business—as if he had no child left who could help him, no daughter who needed to know she was loved, even if the Bennett name would die with her!" Angry tears slid down her cheeks now, tears she sought to dash away with her fingers. "But when no more children came, *they* didn't stop believing."

For a moment he could only stare at her, aching for the hurt she had felt as a girl. Hurt she was still feeling. He didn't know Robert Bennett, the editor of the Simpson Creek newspaper, very well, but how could he have failed his daughter so completely?

"What did he say to you when he discovered you had heard him, Faith?" Could any loving father have failed to comfort a child when he realized what she had overheard, and mistakenly believed she wasn't loved and valued?

"He never knew," Faith said, her tone wooden. "No mouse ever scurried away more quietly than I did that day."

"And your mother?"

"I never told her what I heard," she said.

She hadn't wanted to risk hearing that her mother felt the same way.

Help me help her, Lord. Give me the right words.
The words he chose next were of critical importance.

If her life depended on it, Faith could not have dis-
cerned what Gil was thinking. "I...I'll understand if
you'd prefer that I not care for your father anymore,"
she said at last, when the silence stretched on too long
for her to endure.

"Faith, I don't prefer any such thing," Gil said then.
There was sadness in his eyes, but his voice was as
warm as ever. "I would like you continue helping with
Papa—as your time permits, of course—for as long
as you're willing. I know he enjoys your company and
appreciates what you're doing for him. And so do I."

She let his words echo in her mind. She shouldn't
have been surprised that Gil would continue to be as
kind as a man of the cloth should be. Not all of his
congregation would be so understanding, though, nor
would they have continued to let her nurse a family
member once they knew she was a nonbeliever. Some
might even call her a heathen.

"Th-thank you," she breathed. "I'd be glad to continue."

"And I can understand why such a tragic loss might
undermine your belief in the Almighty," Gil went on.
"Many have found their faiths shaken, especially in recent times, after the war and the influenza epidemic."

Faith waited, sure she knew what was coming. Gil
would point out those who lost loved ones found comfort in their faith, even if they questioned the Lord's
caring for a while. And she would be expected to feel
shame.

But he didn't.

"You must have felt very alone since your brother's

death, Faith," he said instead, "because you didn't feel safe in telling anyone how you felt."

Faith's jaw dropped in surprise. *How could he know exactly how she felt?* Her heart gave a painful squeeze. She hadn't even realized herself how alone she'd felt until he had voiced it, or how much she had longed for someone with whom she could be genuine.

"Yes," she murmured, her throat choked with emotion. Now it would come—the question of why she attended church if she didn't believe in the God who was spoken of there. But he didn't ask, and when he didn't, it left her floundering for what to say.

"You see why you should choose someone else to court," she said. "A good Christian lady who shares your beliefs. Perhaps you should look at some of the other ladies in the Spinsters' Club."

His next remark neither agreed nor disagreed with what she had said.

"Faith, it sounds like you're in need of a friend," Gil said. "A real friend, someone who accepts you, the *real* you," he said. "I'd like to be that friend, if you're willing."

"Why?" Did he see her as a charity case, someone to be helped, such as Daisy Henderson, perhaps? She didn't want to be an object of his pity. Now that she had revealed her dreadful secret, would he try to pressure her into believing? She could not imagine Gil Chadwick acting like that, but wasn't it his responsibility to try to convert the nonbelievers in their midst?

He seemed surprised by the question. "Why? Because you have many admirable qualities, of course—compassion and dedication being only two of them."

She still felt wary. "What—what would it be like, our friendship?" she asked.

He considered the question. "Well, friends spend time together, enjoying experiences and sharing their thoughts, do they not?" he said.

He did not wish to shun her. Faith's heart surged with the realization that Gil found admirable qualities in her and thought her worthy of friendship. But she must not be selfish, she told herself. She could not take very much of his time.

"All right," she said, "but it must not appear as courting. You must be seen as available to any lady who would make you the proper Christian wife."

"Faith, why don't you let me and the Lord sort that out?" he suggested. "When He thinks it's the right time, He'll show me the woman to marry. Meanwhile, I want to assure you that what you tell me stays with me."

She wasn't sure what to make of his reply, but she needed to be alone so she could ponder this conversation, to examine it from every angle.

"All right, I accept," she said. Then, before he could respond, she added, "I...I have to go," and quickly ran out the back door.

He wasn't getting anything done. After the second time Gil left the front of the church sanctuary to go stand at the front door on the chance that he might catch a glimpse of Faith out on some errand, he returned to the parsonage and told Maude Harkey, who was caring for his father that day, that he was leaving for a couple of hours.

"Paying some calls?" she asked.

"No, I thought perhaps I'd get an early start on next Sunday's sermon," he said. "Sometimes a change of scenery helps." And he would do that, after he spent a good deal of time in prayer about Faith. He'd already lain awake for hours last night, seeking guidance on how best to help Faith believe again.

"Give me five minutes and I'll make you a sandwich to take with you, Reverend Gil," Maude said. "My father always said a man prays best when his stomach isn't growling."

He smiled. "Your father was a wise man."

The intense hue of April's bluebonnets was faded now that May had come, but it had been replaced by a carpet of gold and red—gaillardia, Mexican hat, Indian blanket, coreopsis.

"'Not even Solomon in all his glory was arrayed like one of these,'" he quoted aloud from Scripture. They were even prettier than the Bible's "lilies of the field," he reckoned. He'd learned the names of the flowers at his mother's knee, watching as she arranged bouquets for the table in a chipped crockery vase.

The bay gelding that the livery kept for his use flicked his ears at Gil's voice as he picked his way up the trail that wound into the hills. It had narrowed shortly after the horse had left the road and by this point was little more than a deer track at this point.

His eyes caught a flash of movement to his right as a golden eagle dropped like a stone, talons outstretched to catch a young jackrabbit nibbling on a bit of clover. But luck was with the jackrabbit that day, and he sensed his danger, bounding into a cleft in a limestone outcropping just in time to frustrate the predator of his meal. The eagle screamed in frustration.

I will put thee in the cleft of the rock and cover thee with My hand, it said in Exodus. But how could he help Faith see the Lord was her Rock, too?

In the shadow cast by the rock outcropping, Gil spotted a cluster of older mesquite trees. The place promised shade and peace, the ideal place to pray. He dismounted, dropping the gelding's reins to the ground. Well-trained, the horse would not wander far as he grazed amid the sparse grass. He thought about unsaddling the beast, but decided against it. He didn't figure to be here that long, and he needed to be able to remount quickly if danger threatened—danger such as a wandering band of Comanches. There hadn't been any reported sightings in San Saba County lately, but one never knew when they might reappear.

Patting the horse on the flank, Gil strode into the shade and lowered himself to the ground against one of the mesquites. Then his stomach growled, and he remembered the sandwich he had left in his saddlebag along with his Bible, and started to scramble back to his feet again to retrieve it.

No, first things first. He'd pray before he ate. That was why he'd ridden out here, wasn't it? To beseech Heaven to help Faith regain her faith? He bowed his head and clasped his hands.

"Heavenly Father, I—"

And then he heard the sound.

Chapter Eight

"**P**apa, I've brought your dinner," Faith called above the *clackety-clack* of the black Washington hand press to the man pulling ink-wet sheets off it and hanging them to dry on nearby cords stretched across the back of the office. Yesterday had been press day, but her father was always printing something such as handbills or "wanted" notices. The extra revenue coming in helped keep the *Simpson Creek Chronicle* profitable.

A bell over the door had tinkled the news of her arrival, but it was useless against the din of the monstrous black machine behind the counter. Nor had he heard her voice—she suspected the constant din of the press had rendered her father a little hard of hearing. She finally deposited the napkin-covered basket on the countertop and let herself through the swinging gate that separated the working area of the newspaper office from the front.

"Papa," she called again, and finally touched him on the shoulder. Startled, he flailed his arms and dropped the sheet he'd been about to hang up. It fluttered to the ground, and even as he bent to pick it up, Faith could see the still-wet print had blurred.

"Faith, I didn't hear you!" He had to shout to be heard over the din, but he looked pleased to see her.

"I'm sorry, Papa. Looks like that sheet is ruined."

Her father leaned over his beloved press and flipped a lever. After spitting out a final sheet, the press wheezed into silence. "No matter," he said. "I'll just run off another. Handbills for the mercantile, you see. Mrs. Patterson's having a big sale starting today." He reached in his vest pocket and offered her some coins. "Why don't you go see if there's some pretty hair ribbon or some other feminine frippery, now that you've got the young preacher's eye on you?"

Faith strove to hide her dismay. "Papa, but I'm afraid you're mistaken. We—we only sat together at the wedding party, that's all. We're just friends."

Her father snorted. "Hmmmphhh. I can tell if a fellow's eye is on my daughter, I think. So what brings you here, Faith? Not taking care of the old preacher today?"

"Not today, Papa. It's Maude's turn. Mama sent me over with some dinner for you. Come sit down now and eat it." She picked up the basket and carried it to his desk. She and her mother had learned that if they didn't insist he stop and eat right when they brought the food, he was liable to forget to do so and would shamefacedly bring the uneaten meal home with him in the late afternoon.

"Thanks," he said, obediently sitting down by the basket. "Guess I could eat a bite."

She sat down to keep him company, but she guessed he had already forgotten her presence, and wondered if he'd notice if she left. Then she remembered what she had tucked into her reticule. "There was a letter for you in the post office, Papa," she said, bringing it out.

"It's postmarked from Atlanta. Do you know some-one there?"

His gaze sharpened as he took the envelope and slit it open with the table knife her mother had packed. "If it's what I'm hoping it is…" Squinting down his spec-tacles, he studied the letter. "Yes! This may be the key to your mother's future, should anything happen to me."

"Anything happen—?" Faith echoed uncertainly. An icicle of apprehension trickled down her spine. "Papa, are you sick?"

Her father smiled a little too broadly. "No, nothing a man my age shouldn't expect. A few twinges in the chest, a bit of short-windedness every now and then. I'm not as young as I used t'be, after all. Doc Walker says my ticker should be fine long's I don't overdo things. Trouble is, I can't be trottin' all over San Saba County chasin' down news like I used to, *and* running the press."

"Papa, I've always said I could do more for you than just delivering the papers on Monday and sweeping out the office once a week," she reminded him, feeling the old remembered pain rise again when he said nothing and just continued to peruse the letter.

"Are you going to tell me what it's about?" Faith prompted, unwilling to be ignored today.

"It's a response to some inquiries I've been making to hire an assistant. He can serve as a reporter, writing up the stories he investigates, and help around here as needed," her father said, jerking his head toward the now-quiet printing press.

"But Papa, *I* could help you," she said, stung that he hadn't at least thought of her. She was right beneath his nose, and except for delivering his lunches and handbills he'd printed, she had nothing else to do but help her mother keep house.

"Faith, writing isn't your cup of tea," her father said dismissively. "I can't remember even seeing you read the paper. And from what I've seen, your spelling is… well, maybe we should call it creative? Nor do you know a comma from a colon."

Faith had to admit to herself that her father was right—reading and writing hadn't been her strengths in school. She'd been better at mathematics because she could see the logic in that. She'd always wanted and expected to be a wife and mother, but now she envied her cousin Louisa's skill in those areas.

"Now, Louisa could have done it, but she's the schoolmarm now," her father mused aloud, unaware how his words marched along with Faith's thoughts, and how they hurt.

"But I could write down the stories, and you could polish them up until they read right," she protested. "In time, I'm sure you'd have to help me less and less, and I could learn to run the press…"

"Thanks for offering, Faith, but it's all settled," her father said, taking a bite of her mother's peach pie. "Mind you, I won't be able to pay this fellow very much, so he can save board by living with us, and gradually work his way into being the editor."

Faith gazed at her father, dumbstruck. "He's going to live with us? Where will he sleep?" And then she knew.

Her father heaved a sigh. "I figured it's time we used Eddie's room, Faith," he said, not meeting her eyes.

She could agree with that at least. Her father had kept her brother's room like a shrine ever since his death, despite her mother's pleas to let her use it as a sewing room or for storage.

"And if this fellow takes over the paper someday, how is that going to take care of Mother?"

"Don't worry, Faith, if Yancey Merriwell makes it through his trial period, he'll sign a contract that entitles your mother to half the profit of the paper. And my will specifies she'll own the house."

Anxiety for him squeezed her heart, even as anger at him sparked. *He'd made a will? When? After the doctor had told him his heart wasn't strong?*

She couldn't stifle the question any longer. "And me, Father? What about me?"

He blinked in surprise. "You? But you'll be married to your young preacher, long before I ever pass on," he said. "You'll live in the parsonage."

"Papa, I told you Reverend Gil and I weren't courting," she said, trying to keep her distress from showing in her voice. He never thought of her. She was just a daughter. Daughters married, and it was their husbands' duty to take care of them. *Only sons mattered, and his had died.* "What if I never marry?"

"Horsefeathers, girl," her father said with a snort. "It's as plain as the nose on your face about you and Gil—unless you don't like the fellow, of course. And if you don't…" He shrugged. "I'm sure you'll find some other beau who suits your fancy. Now, don't you worry about this Merriwell fellow. He might not even cotton to Simpson Creek after being used to the big city of Atlanta. I reckon it's quite a place, even after that bluebelly General Sherman got done with it. Or you might even make a match with Merriwell. He sounds like a nice fellow. Dunno what he looks like, of course."

She'd listened to all she could without exploding. "Sure, Papa," she said, rising. "I'd better be going.

Mama needs me to pick up some thread at the mercantile. Be sure and finish your dinner now."

He put out a hand to stop her. "You don't need to worry, Faith. I'll add a codicil to my will that you *and* your mother own the house, all right? Thanks for bringing my vittles."

Faith's eyes stung and she knew she had to get out of the shop before she cried. If she could make it past the hotel to the alley—

But there was no privacy to be found in the alley. As soon as she stepped into it and pulled out her lace-edged hanky, she spotted Polly Shackleford entering from the other end which opened on Travis Street. She had already spotted Faith and was waving a hand in greeting, so it was too late to duck back out and escape into the mercantile.

"Hello, Polly," Faith said, hoping she didn't look as if she'd been about to weep. With any luck this would be a quick encounter.

"Faith, what's wrong?" Polly said, concern furrowing her brow as she came forward.

So much for hiding her distress. "Oh, nothing," Faith prevaricated. "A bit of dust blew into my eye." She made a great show of wiping it with her hanky before replacing it in her reticule.

"Oh, good," Polly said. "You looked upset. I was hoping you and Reverend Gil hadn't had a tiff or something." Her eyes searched Faith's face, clearly trying to find a clue.

Not you, too. "Reverend Gil and I have nothing to have a tiff about," she said, hoping she didn't sound snippy. "I'm only taking care of his father, as several of us are, nothing more."

"You could have fooled me, the way the two of you looked so cozy together at the wedding," Polly teased.

Faith wasn't about to go over the same ground she'd just plowed with her father. "Tomorrow's your day with Reverend Chadwick," she said, as if she hadn't heard the jab. "You're still planning on it, aren't you?"

"Of course," Polly said. "I believe I am as dependable as anyone in the group."

Why was Polly so defensive and prickly? "Are you out doing errands?" Faith asked.

Polly nodded. "I'm going to ask your father to make up a handbill for the box social, and then I'll check the post office for mail from bachelor candidates. You?"

"I have to go to the mercantile for my mother," Faith said. She hoped her father had finished eating—he'd never remember to eat once Polly interrupted him. She could have told Polly there wasn't any Spinsters' Club mail because Mr. Wallace had volunteered that fact when she'd been in the post office, but she was afraid the other girl would think she'd been poaching on Polly's chosen territory.

Polly seemed loath to move on. Faith cast about desperately for something else to talk about.

"You heard the news of Sarah's baby, didn't you?"

Polly nodded, her face wistful. "I wonder if I'll ever marry and have a child…"

Faith swallowed her exasperation. Couldn't Polly ever be happy for someone without making it into something about herself? "Of course you will," she said in a bracing tone. "Why, you and Anson had a good time at the wedding, didn't you?"

The other girl's face fell. "I *thought* we were, especially when he caught the garter… But then he went right back to his horse talk with those boys, as if I wasn't even there, and when it came time to leave, he said nothing about seeing me again. Oh, Faith, I'm truly going to be a spinster."

Faith smothered a sigh. The other girl certainly would be an old maid if she didn't abandon her poor-little-me air. "Oh, you never know. Anson may surprise you yet," she said, although she had little belief Prissy's cousin would ever spare a thought for Polly again.

Then she had an idea that might give Polly hope for a time, yet might also drive her father's potential successor away. Her father hadn't exactly said when Yancey Merriwell was coming, but he'd implied the man was single because he would be rooming at their house. She could tell Polly about Merriwell, giving her advance news of a possible bachelor candidate so that Polly could claim first dibs if she wanted to. And though she couldn't claim knowledge of the man's looks or manner, the news might intrigue Polly enough to cause her to rush toward the newcomer as soon as he set foot in Simpson Creek—which might make Merriwell flee the town on the next stage. Or could the Georgian find Polly Shackleford enchanting?

"You're looking like the cat that swallowed the canary, Faith," Polly said. "What are you thinking of?"

One look at her curious face and Faith knew she couldn't go through with it. A moral person didn't scheme that way, not when it might cause Polly yet more disappointment and her father more worry about the future.

"Oh, nothing, I was just thinking about something Papa said," Faith said. It was partly true at least. Even if she didn't tip her off about Merriwell, when Polly discovered the new bachelor in town, Faith's goal might be accomplished anyway. If Polly annoyed Merriwell so much that he left, Faith might have a chance to convince her father of her value as an assistant. Of course, she'd have to secure Louisa's help with writing copy that made sense and was spelled and punctuated correctly, but surely in time she would pick up the knack of it!

What had he heard? It sounded like a smothered groan. But surely he was the only human out here. Gil laid his Bible in the grass, stood and looked around, but saw no one. There was no more sound, not even the rustling of grass. Even the birds he'd heard calling from nearby hushed.

Had it been the cry of a wounded animal?

"Who's there? Are you hurt?"

Silence. But now it felt like a listening silence, as if he was not alone. As if whoever or whatever had made the sound was determined not to make that mistake again. Or was his mind playing tricks on him?

Then his horse, which had been grazing a few feet away, lifted his head, ears pricked and nickered—

—and was answered by the whinny of another horse.

Gil might have believed the other horse was wild if he hadn't been so sure he'd heard a human groan first. Was it possible the other person was no longer able to make a sound—perhaps because he had passed out? Because he was dying?

Could it be the trick of an outlaw, luring him into a trap? *Lord, please protect me,* he prayed as he moved cautiously through the brush. He had to take the chance. How could he live with himself if someone needed help, and he was the only one available but didn't provide it?

He moved around the base of the rock outcropping, dodging clumps of prickly pear and juniper, his ears straining for any sound.

And then he spotted the brown-and-white pinto, more of a pony than a horse, standing in front of a cedar brake. Its head was raised and nostrils flared as it watched Gil approach. Was it wild? No, it had a primitive sort of bridle with a feather dangling from the bottom of the nose piece. *An Indian pony.*

Gil froze. Had the groan been uttered by an injured Comanche? Or worse, one who lay in wait, planning to lure him closer in hope of taking his scalp? All the stories he'd ever heard of Comanche atrocities flooded his brain. He had no weapon, not even so much as a pocketknife. Perhaps if he backed up now, he could reach his horse before the unseen savage jumped him. Was the Indian even now poised to spring out at him or onto him from the rocks above?

Lord, save me!

There were plenty of loose rocks on the ground. Perhaps he could hurl one at the red man, disabling his attacker long enough so Gil could reach his own mount and escape.

Then he heard the groan again. This time it was less muffled, as if the person groaning could no longer fully stifle it.

And it didn't sound like a man's cry—it sounded *younger.* And full of real pain.

If someone was injured, he had a duty to try to help.

Inching warily forward, listening for any hint of movement, Gil peered into the shadowy midst of the cedar brake, and spotted an Indian boy lying on his back, dressed in buckskin leggings, breechclout and moccasins.

At the sight of Gil, the boy yelped in fear, and in a motion too quick for Gil's eyes to follow, yanked a knife from his belt and threw it at Gil.

The hastily thrown knife went wide to Gil's left, and clattered against a rock, and Gil picked it up to prevent the boy from using it on him again. But it seemed the movement had cost the young Indian, for he clenched his teeth over a moan and seized his lower leg with both hands. He kept his eyes open and trained on Gil, obviously fearing attack.

He *was* injured. Gil could see now that the leg was bent at an unnatural angle. Now that he was closer, Gil spotted a scraped cheek and hand, and a forehead beaded with sweat. Had he fallen from his horse? It didn't matter. What mattered was that Gil had to help him. But first he had to convince the boy, who was perhaps eight, that he meant him no harm. The boy's eyes remained wide, his hands curled into fists. He was ready to fight to the death.

"Easy, boy, I mean you no harm," Gil said. He threw the knife some distance away, then held both hands palm up. Would the Indian understand the gesture, or even if he did, would he believe Gil's sincerity?

The boy's eyes remained glowing black coals in the shade of the trees. He remained poised to defend himself, even though the tense way he held himself obviously cost him more pain.

How was he going to convince the boy he only wanted to help? The boy didn't understand English, and he sure didn't know any Comanche, nor even the sign language some men who'd dealt with Indians knew.

Lord, if You'd like to give me the gift of tongues right now, I'd appreciate it. Just one tongue—Comanche— that's all I really need.

He opened his mouth, but no Comanche words poured forth.

Did the young Comanche know about the symbol

of the Cross? Gil pulled on the silver chain beneath his shirt. His mother had given him that necklace years ago, and he had never stopped wearing it. He held out the Cross pendant, showing it to the boy. The little Indian's face remained suspicious.

Gil pointed to himself, then placed his hands together and bowed his head in an attitude of prayer.

Something flickered in the boy's eyes, but Gil could not be sure it betokened understanding.

Silence stretched between them. This wasn't getting anywhere. He could ride off, and hope the boy was found by his people. But the Indian was obviously in pain despite his attempts to put on a brave front, and what if his people didn't find him before some predator did? Coyotes roamed these hills, and worse, cougars.

Gil sighed. He could not abandon the boy, even if it meant fighting him to help him.

He looked around and saw no one. Yet the gesture he was about to make would make him even more vulnerable should there be any Indians hiding amidst the rocks, brush and mesquite.

Lord, protect me and help the boy understand, he prayed inwardly, and knelt on the ground, bowing his head and closing his eyes. With one hand he held up the Cross.

After an endless minute, he opened his eyes.

Gil couldn't tell for sure if the boy looked less on his guard, but maybe...

Perhaps introductions would help. "Gil," he said, pointing to himself.

"G-Geel," the boy mimicked. He turned his index finger toward himself and spoke, but the Comanche words were unintelligible to Gil.

"I'll just call you Tad," Gil said, making himself smile. *"Tad,"* he repeated, pointing at the boy.

The Indian boy wrinkled his nose, then shrugged. Apparently what the white man chose to call him didn't matter.

Turning his back and praying the boy didn't have a hidden tomahawk to throw, he walked slowly toward the Indian pony, who pricked his ears, but watched him come without alarm.

He took hold of the rawhide-thong bride and began to lead the pony forward. The boy let loose a spate of Comanche words. He pointed repeatedly to the pony, his eyes showing a different sort of distress.

Gil halted, looked back at the beast but couldn't understand. Watching the pony this time, he led him forward a few paces, and then he saw that the pony was favoring his off front leg. Every time the pony put weight on it, his head bobbed downward.

The pony was lame. Had he put his foreleg in a hole, causing the boy's fall? It was clear that he couldn't bear the boy's weight. Gil would have to put the boy up on his bay and ride behind him, letting the pony follow if he was able. Gil let go of the pinto's bridle, then led his own horse forward.

If only he had something flat to make a splint to stabilize the leg, but he didn't. There wasn't even a branch on any of the short, shrubby trees big enough for his purposes. He would have to pray the boy wouldn't pass out from the pain that moving his broken leg would cause. He prayed the bone wasn't protruding through the skin—he hadn't wanted to alarm the boy by cutting open the leggings to see.

He held out his arms, miming that he was going to lift the Comanche boy up onto the horse.

The boy nodded.

Gil steeled himself, then scooped his hands up under the boy, wincing inside as the boy gasped in pain. His shiny long black hair smelled of something pungent—hadn't Gil heard Indians used bear grease on their hair? As he lifted the boy closer to his bay, the horse snorted and stamped, his nostrils flaring at the scary scent. Gil prayed he wouldn't bolt, but his hands were full, so he couldn't grab the reins.

"*Steady,* fellow," Gil soothed. "The boy isn't part bear, he just smells like one."

The gelding stood obediently, although he rolled his eyes to indicate his displeasure.

As soon as Gil deposited the boy onto the saddle, Gil grabbed hold of the reins. Even though the little Comanche had his teeth clamped on his underlip to keep from crying out, Gil didn't trust him not to try to run off with his horse. The Comanches were horse thieves par excellence after all.

After picking up his Bible and stowing it in the saddle bag, Gil mounted behind "Tad." Then he wondered what he was going to do with the boy. His first instinct had been to return to town, but now he realized the impracticality of that. As kind as most of the townspeople were, how would they feel about the presence of a despised Indian in their midst? He didn't doubt that Nolan Walker would be willing to doctor him, but what if Tad himself thought he was a captive, and fought to free himself, possibly worsening his injuries, or hurting someone during an attempt to escape? Or the boy's tribe might come looking for him. Gil couldn't bring danger down on the Walker family. The boy's tribe might misinterpret the situation and take their wrath out on Walker and his family—even the whole town.

No, he had to return the boy to his tribe. Somewhere in these hills, the boy's family might even now be starting to worry about him. Gil pictured a mother fretting as the day faded into evening. Gil knew the right thing to do, but would he survive the attempt?

"Lord, protect me," he prayed aloud.

Tad swiveled in the saddle and eyed him quizzically.

"Just asking the Lord's blessing on my attempt to help you, Tad," he said, as if the boy could understand him. "Now, you're going to have to tell me where to take you." Gil pointed to the hills in all directions, then looked questioningly at the boy.

As he had hoped, the boy understood perfectly. He uttered something in his guttural tongue and pointed northwest.

Chapter Nine

Gil and the Indian boy wound through the hills for the next half hour across meandering, nearly dried-up creeks, around limestone outcroppings and thickets of scrub and cactus. There was no trail—Tad seemed to use some inner compass to navigate. *I'm never going to find my way home,* Gil thought, *if I'm even allowed to leave.*

The pinto had tried to follow them, but finally stopped and nickered plaintively as Gil's bay continued picking his way between the rocks and cactus. Tad called something back to his mount. Was he telling him to make his way back to camp when he was able? Gil was sure the jolting ride had to be painful to the boy as well, but he never uttered so much as a whimper.

Then suddenly the gelding stopped stock-still and snorted. A heartbeat later Gil knew why, as three mounted Comanche warriors materialized from behind a rock outcropping.

Ice encased Gil's backbone as the full force of their obsidian glares pierced him. In front of him, Tad called out in excited Comanche, pointing to his injured leg.

Gil could only pray the boy was telling the braves the true story of how he came to be sitting with the white man on his horse.

If he did, it wasn't evident from the way the murderous-looking savages jumped off their horses and ran to Gil and Tad. One warrior lifted Tad carefully from the saddle, then the other two lost no time in yanking Gil off his mount and onto the rock-strewn ground.

The Indians fell on him, fists flying, feet kicking. *Lord, help me!* he prayed, and then everything went black.

Sometime later, Gil was shaken roughly awake. He was still struggling to focus on their fierce faces when they hauled him to his feet.

There was pain in every bone of his body. His arms were bound tightly in front of him, the bindings linked to a rope held by one of the Indians. His feet were bare, his shoes having been appropriated by one of the warriors. The sight of the Indian wearing his shoes below long, bare legs would have been comical if Gil had dared to laugh.

He spotted his spectacles, amazingly unbroken, lying on the ground. Just then one of the Comanches saw them too and scooped them up. He perched them over his hawklike nose. Squinting through the lenses, he made faces that would have been comical to Gil if the situation had been different, but the others pointed and guffawed as if they found the sight hilarious.

Tad called out something, and the brave wearing his spectacles walked over to Gil and roughly shoved them into Gil's pocket while his companions mounted. Apparently not wanting the white man to get the idea all would be well because of this favor, however, he slapped Gil on the side of his head.

The blow stung, but Gil was so intent on keeping his balance that he hardly noticed the pain. Then the Indian whooped and vaulted onto a paint horse who looked like a full-grown version of Tad's pony.

I am with you always.

The words helped Gil temporarily stifle his fear. He searched for Tad, finding the Indian boy astride the bay and munching on Gil's sandwich. Gil thought he saw a hint of apology in Tad's eyes before the boy turned his face away.

So he would be walking while his captors rode, Gil thought grimly—*if they didn't get tired of his slow pace and drag him wherever they were headed.* He realized it was likely that before the next sunrise, his scalp would decorate one of these braves' lances, and his father and all the rest of the townspeople might never know what happened to him. Some would probably say he'd gotten tired of preaching and caring for his helpless old father and decided to light out for a fresh start far from Simpson Creek.

Would Faith think that, too?

Oh, Faith, I'm so sorry we never got to be together, he thought, regret stabbing his heart. *Please, Lord, help her believe again, in spite of my disappearance.*

Gil could not have said how long it took them to reach the Indian camp, for he was forced to run to keep up with the horses' trotting. Doggedly he placed one foot in front of the other and tried to ignoring the lacerating pain of his bare soles running over rocks. Once the Indian holding his rope tried to run him into a clump of prickly pear cactus, but he saw it in time to leap over it.

His agility evidently earned him a measure of respect, for the Indians slowed their mounts to a walk. But their action only gave Gil more time to feel how much his abraded feet hurt.

It was probably just a taste of what he would experience before he died, Gil thought. He wished he'd obeyed his first instinct to take the injured boy into town to Dr. Walker's instead of trying to take him home to his people.

No white man looking for the little encampment could have easily found it, nestled as it was in a deep arroyo.

A glad cry went up from the cluster of tepees as one of the inhabitants spotted the riders. In return the braves uttered shrill cries and brandished their lances, pointing at their captive. They broke into a trot again, forcing Gil to stumble after them, nearly blinded by the sweat pouring into his eyes.

Lord, be near me, whatever happens.

The horse whose rider held Gil's rope stopped so suddenly that Gil could not halt his forward momentum and crashed ignominiously into the dust. He heard the warriors whooping and dancing their horses around him, shrieking things in their incomprehensible tongue that probably didn't bode well for him. It probably counted as quite a show in the Comanche culture, though. Gil, from his position nose-down in the dust, saw Comanche women inching forward on moccasined feet.

The presence of females didn't make him feel any less doomed—it was known on the frontier that Comanche females tortured even more cruelly than their male counterparts. The women pointed at Gil and called back to the mounted braves.

In the midst of all the clamor, Tad was once more

lifted gently down from the bay. Gil saw an expression of distress twist the boy's face as the warrior began to carry him away; he pointed at Gil and let loose a flood of protest, pulling on the man's braid, but the latter ignored him. Then Gil was dragged toward an upright post, and he forgot all about the Indian boy as he was punched, elbowed and jabbed while a pair of the savages bound him securely.

Lord, this would be a good time to send some help...

A timid knock summoned Faith to the door just as she and her parents were about to go to bed. She found Maude standing on the front step, looking anxious and fearful in the light spilling from the doorway.

"Maude, what on earth? What's happened?" she demanded, hearing her father and mother come back down the hallway to stand behind her.

"Gil hasn't come home, Faith," the other woman said, plucking at the neckline of her dress. "He rode out about noon, saying he was going to work on his sermon in the hills..." She gulped air, then went on. "At first I assumed he'd decided to pay a call or two afterward and got invited to supper, but finally I commenced t' getting worried. I've tried not to let on to his father I was alarmed, and waited till he fell asleep to come tell you, but—oh, Faith, what if something's happened to Reverend Gil out there?"

Faith felt fear closing icy fingers around her throat.

Her father, who'd come to stand behind her, said, "Maude, he probably stopped for a drink of water at some ranch house and some lonely ranch family wouldn't take no for an answer about his staying for supper." His voice was encouraging. "Or maybe his horse went lame and he had to stop somewhere for the night to rest his mount."

"I imagine it's something like that," her mother put in.

Faith tried to look convinced for the sake of the frightened spinster in front of her. "You look tired, Maude. Go on home and I'll take over at the parsonage till Gil comes home."

Maude hesitated, but her shoulders sagged with weariness. "All right, but only if you'll tell me the moment you hear something."

Faith agreed and sent Maude on her way, then threw her shawl around her shoulders. "Something must have happened," she said to her parents. "I don't think Gil would linger at anyone's ranch, not with his father in the condition he is."

Her father sighed. "Maybe not, but it's full dark and there's only a sliver of a moon in the sky. It's not like we can send a search party out till morning."

Faith sighed, knowing he was right. "I'll come home as soon as I can," she told her parents, as she accepted the lantern her father handed her.

To Gil's surprise, the Indians left him tied upright to the post as they went about their business. Half-naked children stared at him curiously from a safe distance, pointing and whispering. Some eventually became emboldened enough to run up and pinch him, then run back to their playmates, laughing.

Nearby, squaws tended cooking pots. Savory aromas wafted toward Gil, tormenting him, but he was offered no food or water.

As the sun left its zenith in the sky, its rays found their scorching way to Gil's face. Salty sweat stung his cuts and abrasions. Did they mean to leave him here until he died or were they postponing the torture till later? The presence of a nearby stack of brush was not reassuring.

Thou wilt keep him in perfect peace, whose mind is stayed on thee. He'd learned the verse in his childhood, and now it encircled his heart. Incredibly, he dozed, exhausted by pain and apprehension, until the pain of his rawhide bindings cutting into his arms woke him.

Or was it the sound of horses trotting into the arroyo that had awakened him? As he opened bleary eyes, he attempted to focus on two Indians on horses pulling up in front of him. A pair of mangy-looking dogs barked at the new arrivals until they were hushed by a sharp command from a squaw.

The two men were older than the braves who had brought Gil here, and obviously important men, for one of the braves came at a run, his head bowed at a respectful angle. He called out something as he came.

Both men looked displeased at the younger man's words. The one closest to Gil gestured at him and peppered the brave with what sounded like questions. The other man leaped from his horse and disappeared among the cluster of tepees. Could this be Tad's father, going to see to the welfare of his injured son?

The man who remained looked stern, and snapped some command at the young brave.

The young brave pointed at Gil, looking indignant, and replied with spirit, but there was a certain element of respect in his tone, as well. Perhaps the mounted man was the chief?

The older man snapped something at him. Glaring at Gil, the brave approached, clutching a knife in one hand.

Did he just tell the brave to slit my throat? Gil wondered, and hoped his death would be quick, if so. He closed his eyes. *Lord, watch over Faith. And Papa.*

The young Indian didn't go for his throat, however, but bent behind the post to slice Gil's bonds.

His sudden freedom, coupled with exhaustion, sent Gil reeling toward the older Indian. Before he could commit such a trespass, though, he was yanked none-too-gently upright by the younger Indian.

The older man uttered another command, and the brave's hands gentled as he transferred Gil to him. Amazingly, Gil felt himself being encouraged to lean on the older Comanche as they walked between tepees until finally they stopped at one of them. He lifted up a flap in the tanned hide and gestured for Gil to go inside. Gil did as he was bid, but the other man did not follow him.

As soon as his eyes adjusted to the murky light within, he spotted Tad sitting on a pile of buffalo skins, being tended by the older Indian who had jumped from his horse. Gil saw that he had splinted Tad's leg with some flat pieces of stiff leather and was now tying the final knot to hold the splints in place.

Tad called some sort of greeting to him, then turned back to the man, gesturing first to Gil and then to the man whom Gil was becoming sure was the boy's father. Was he performing an introduction? Gil wasn't sure of that, but he figured he should not sit without being invited to do so, so he concentrated on keeping his balance as waves of dizziness washed over him.

Finally the Indian turned to Gil. "Sit, white man," he said.

Gil felt his jaw drop in astonishment at hearing English from the Comanche, but the other man made no move to explain. He made a clumsy job of lowering himself to the earthen floor, but the other man appeared not to notice as he called something in a voice designed to carry outside the tepee.

The Comanche turned back to him. "I am Makes Healing," the Comanche said. "I am the medicine man. I am grateful to you for trying to bring my son home. His name in your tongue would be Runs Like a Deer. Thanks to you that will still be true, after some moons have passed."

"I am Gil Chadwick," Gil said, following the other man's lead by giving his name first. "I was happy to help your son."

Makes Healing considered Gil's words, his black eyes unreadable. Then he said, "You took a great risk to help my son. You have not been rewarded for your kindness by our young warriors."

Gil nodded, resisting the urge to complain about it.

His restraint seemed to please the man, for he smiled faintly. "You will be better treated now. We will give you food and drink."

As if to prove the truth of what he said, a squaw entered the tepee then, carrying a crude wooden bowl full of chunks of meat that Gil had smelled cooking earlier. She set it before Gil, along with a hollowed gourd full of water.

"Eat. Drink," Makes Healing told him.

Gil lost no time in seizing the gourd and relieving the parched dryness of his throat. "Thank you," he said, before dipping into the stew with his fingers. He guessed the meat was buffalo, and it was seasoned with some unfamiliar flavoring, but the roasted chunks of meat were actually quite tasty.

How soon did he dare ask to leave? From the light

coming through the smoke hole at the top of the tepee, it was dusk. His father and Maude Harkey must be getting worried at the very least. Would Maude notify Faith? Then she'd be worried, too.

"What will you have as a reward, Gil Chadwick?" the Indian asked, while Gil chewed.

Would it be rude to ask to be allowed to leave immediately? Gil thought wryly, and said an inward prayer of thanks.

"I could offer you a beautiful Comanche woman for a wife."

Gil almost choked on his meat. Was the man serious or merely toying with him? The black eyes gave no clue, but Runs Like a Deer chuckled out loud.

Gil reckoned it was best to use diplomacy. "Thank you for that honor," he said with all the solemnity he could manage, "but I am a minister of the Christian faith—"

"You are a holy man?" the medicine man interrupted, clearly impressed.

Not nearly holy enough, Gil thought, remembering his past, but he knew what the Indian man meant, and merely nodded. "A holy man of my people must marry a woman who is a Christian."

"You take a wife, you tell her what to believe," the other man countered, but there was a twinkle in the obsidian depths of his gaze. "You are a holy man—she must respect you."

Gil took a deep breath, hoping he could trust that twinkle. "Again, I thank you, but there is a woman among my people that I wish to marry." *If Faith comes to believe,* he added to himself.

"The only reward I would ask of you, Makes Healing," Gil said, "is to be allowed to return home now."

"Now you are tired. You will return home when the sun rises again. You should eat more, then rest."

Gil could only imagine how anxious his father would be if he was gone all night. And Faith—she'd know he would never willingly be gone so long. Would she be anxious for him, fearing the worst?

"My father is old and has been very sick," he countered. "He and the people who care about us must be very worried at my absence, for I had planned to return home hours ago. Please, with your permission, I must leave soon—tonight."

The medicine man eyed him for what seemed like an eternity. Finally, he nodded. "Your horse will be brought. You will be guided to the white man's road."

Thank you, Lord! Gil prayed in relief.

"You will be blindfolded until you reach the road, holy man," Makes Healing went on. "You must never try to find this camp again or tell your people of it. I have forbidden our young braves to harm you further because of your goodness in helping my son, but I would not be able to restrain them a second time. If you come to the camp again or if the bluecoats come looking here because of your words, I could not stop them from taking vengeance on you and on your people."

Gil swallowed. "I understand," he said, knowing he would never be able to find his way back here even without the blindfold. He wondered how he was going to explain his absence and his obvious injuries, but he would have to find a way, for endangering the boy and his people would be poor thanks for the mercy he had been shown.

Could he trust the braves' obedience to the medicine man's order not to harm him? They'd had a blood-thirsty glint in their eyes, and who would know if they murdered him somewhere beyond earshot of the camp?

Chapter Ten

$\backsim\!\!\!\sim$

Gil walked quietly into his house, using the back door that led into the kitchen. He'd already untacked and stalled his horse at the livery, not wanting to wake the proprietor to do it at an hour he reckoned to be some-time after midnight.

The flickering light of a lamp illuminated a figure in a dress, her head on her hands on the table. From her regular breathing, it was obvious she slept, yet as he drew closer, he saw the figure was too slight to be Maude Harkey's, and her hair was auburn, rather than Maude's bright red. *What was Faith doing here?*

He stepped closer, and became sure it was. But how to wake her without frightening her?

"Faith?" he called softly, then, when she only stirred and mumbled something in her sleep, called more loudly, *"Faith?"*

She came awake so suddenly that she nearly tipped over the chair. Blinking, she focused on him, then jumped to her feet.

"Gil Chadwick! Where in tarnation have you been?" she whispered. "Maude was worried sick when you never came home—" Suddenly she stared at him, then lifted the lamp to illuminate his face. "What *happened* to you? Have you—have you been in a *fight?*" She leaned closer.

She thought he'd been in a saloon altercation and was sniffing for the smell of liquor! The thought that he'd been brawling in a saloon was so vastly different from what had really happened that he couldn't help chuckling.

"I'm glad *you* think it's funny, Gil!" she hissed indignantly, pointing at him. "While you were out gallivanting around, we were just waiting for dawn to organize a search party!"

"I'm sorry." He held up his hands in a gesture for peace, knowing she would see they were badly scraped and cut, too. "I didn't mean to make light of it, and I'm sorry I worried you. Does everyone in town think I'm missing?"

"Only Maude, my parents and I," she admitted. "We couldn't see waking everyone else when there was nothing anyone could do till first light."

"I'll apologize to them personally," he said. "I wasn't in a fight, I…well, I accidentally came upon some Comanche braves. I managed to outrun them, but then… uh, my horse spooked at a jackrabbit and I fell off. I must have hit my head on something, because when I came to my senses, it was dark."

His throat tightened as he uttered the half-truth. *It wasn't completely a lie,* he told himself. It *had* been completely accidental that he'd found Runs Like a Deer, then the three Comanche braves. And his interaction with the braves couldn't properly be termed a fight— he hadn't been able to throw even one punch.

"You were unconscious?" she asked, her hands over

her lips. She looked alarmed, but the disapproving glint had left her eyes. "It's fortunate you were able to make it home, then."

"I'll be all right, just a little sore," he said, feeling guilty at allowing her to jump to the wrong conclusion. "Is my father asleep? Was he worried? Where's Miss Maude?"

"I sent Maude home. I planned to tell your father we thought you'd stayed over for supper at some ranch so he wouldn't be anxious. He was asleep when Maude left to come tell us, and he was still asleep when I looked in on him," she said, still whispering.

Once again, Faith had seen a need and taken care of it, he thought, touched, even though she'd been willing to tell a little lie just as he had. He was conscious of an overpowering wish to kiss her, but he couldn't cross that line. Not as long as his soul and hers resided on different sides.

He let out a breath, feeling the weight of worry about his father slipping off his shoulders. With any luck, the old man would never have to know his son had been in danger today—although that meant repeating the lie to his father.

Or perhaps his father was the one person he could safely tell the truth, he thought.

"Thank you for staying with Papa," he said to Faith. "Let me just look in on him, and then I'll walk you home."

"I'm not leaving until I wash those cuts and scrapes," she told him tartly. "You look like you've been tied up in a sack with a wild cat. Sit down there," she commanded, pointing to the chair she'd just vacated.

He watched as she moved efficiently around his kitchen, lifting a big bowl from the shelves into which she pumped some water. She got a cake of soap and some clean rags, then began to gingerly clean his wounds.

The soap stung like a battalion of wasps on his broken skin, but he bore her ministrations meekly, wishing he could tell her his feet looked worse. Faith would never believe he'd fallen from his horse, as he'd implied, if she saw them. He'd just have to tend to those wounds himself, and make sure she didn't catch him wincing when he walked her home. It served him right. He hoped she didn't smell the pungent green poultice the medicine man had anointed his feet with before wrapping thin strips of cloth around them. The bandages made for a tight fit when Gil had put his newly returned shoes back on, but that hadn't bothered him until he'd dismounted and walked from the livery stable. He was sure he had bruises blossoming all over his chest and abdomen, as well.

When she was done, Gil looked in on his father to assure himself the old man was still asleep before he kept his promise to walk Faith home.

"I'll let Maude know you're all right in the morning," she told him, as they walked down Fannin Street from the parsonage to the Bennetts' house. "She lives in the boarding house, and I don't want to wake the whole place."

"Thank you," he told her. "And again, I'm sor—"

She surprised him into silence by reaching up and placing a finger on his lips. "No more apologizing," she told him.

The urge to kiss the finger, then her sweetly curved lips, came over him again, and once more, he had to suppress it.

It seemed as if her action had startled her, for she

shoved her hand back down at her side again. "I'm just glad you're all right," she said quickly.

I'm glad you're glad, he thought, *although you don't know half of the story.*

By now they had reached the Bennetts' house, but he wasn't in a hurry to bid her good night. "I went up into the hills to pray about you today," he said, as she placed her foot on her porch. "That was the reason I rode out."

She blushed, then said, "And?" her voice carefully neutral.

"When will you be taking care of Papa again?"

"Tomorrow morning," she said.

He eyed the low-hanging moon ruefully. "*This* morning, you mean, so I must not keep you up much longer. I've already robbed you of some of your sleep. Come later in the morning, if you like. Papa and I will be fine. But perhaps when he takes a nap, we could take some lemonade and some of those cookies Mrs. Detwiler keeps bringing, and spend some time talking on the riverbank?"

She hesitated. "I'm afraid it might be misconstrued by someone passing by." Faith avoided his gaze.

He started to argue, but realized she was right. Sitting alone together by Simpson Creek could look like they were having a picnic, and therefore courting.

"All right, then," he said. "Perhaps we could talk in the sanctuary? Surely no one could get the wrong idea if you did that."

"I suppose that would be all right. Good night."

Gil watched her as she walked up the porch steps, and quietly entered her house.

Faith sprang out of bed, full of anticipation, as if she had not been up late the night before. She found herself picking out one of her favorite dresses in her wardrobe, one of orange blossom-sprigged cotton with a green sash at the waist that tied in a bow over her bustle. Both colors complemented her auburn hair and green eyes, she knew. She couldn't seem to resist taking special care with her hair, either.

It was as if she were two different people, one a sensible person who knew she must not start something she could not in good conscience complete, the other a girl who could not stop smiling into the mirror at the thought of spending time with a man whose hazel eyes had flecks of gold in them, and whose voice caressed her heart every time he spoke.

"How pretty you look, dear," her mother said as she came downstairs. "Going to take care of Reverend Chadwick?"

She nodded. "And to see if his son is all right after his spill yesterday." When she'd returned home last night, she'd told her parents what had happened to Gil.

"He'll likely be more sore and stiff today than he was last night," her mother said. "Not that he'll admit it, mind you, if he's like most men," she added with a laugh and a roll of the eyes.

"He didn't seem to want to talk about it last night," Faith said. "I suppose he's embarrassed that he fell from his horse. All men seem to think they should ride like they were born in the saddle, don't they?"

Her mother nodded. "It's God's own mercy he was able to escape those Indians! And that he didn't break a leg or crack his skull, alone out there in the hills, isn't it?"

Faith nodded, although privately she thought it was just pure luck. It was not as if Gil was a cowboy, always in the saddle, after all.

"Why don't you take some of my willow bark and brew a tea for him?" her mother said, moving toward one of her glass jars in which she kept a number of home remedies. "That'll take away the aches."

"I'll take it, Ma. But you're right, he probably won't admit needing anything," Faith said, and sailed out the door.

Breakfast was over, and Faith had started a pot of soup simmering on the stove for dinner. Gil had gone off to his study to work on Sunday's sermon, and the old preacher had seemed content to sit in the kitchen and watch the birds flit about from tree to tree from his window. But now he put a gnarled hand on her sleeve as she passed by, and when she paused to see what he wanted, he pointed in the direction of the back door.

"Did you want to go outside, Reverend?" she asked. "It's a little hot, but I suppose if you sit in the shade of that live oak, it'd be all right for a while."

He shook his head vigorously and pointed again.

She realized he was pointing at the hat rack by the door, rather than at the door. "Yes, you'll need your hat to keep the sun out of your eyes."

Again, he shook his head. *"C-c-caaannh..."*

He was pointing, not at his hat, but at the cane which also hung from the row of knobs along with his and Gil's hats.

"You want your cane?"

The old preacher nodded, then made motions with the first two fingers of his good hand to indicate walking.

Faith stared at him. He'd been able to tolerate pivoting from a somewhat shaky standing position when transferring from the bed to the wheeled chair, but now, it seemed, he'd decided he was ready to take the next step. Literally.

Moments later, she called to Gil in the study. "Gil, could you come here for a moment please?"

He was still placing his folded spectacles in his pocket when he reached the kitchen. "Do you need help with—"

Faith watched as Gil stopped, dumbstruck at the sight of his father standing a few feet from the wheelchair, leaning on his cane. Then the old man took a wobbling step toward him. Then another and another.

"Papa! You're *walking! God be praised!*" He turned to Faith, tears of joy standing in his eyes. "Faith, it's a miracle!"

Faith couldn't stop grinning. "You can't keep a good man down, that's for sure," she said. Her grin broadened as Gil swept them both in an exuberant hug, although he was careful not to knock his father down.

"Dr. Walker said he thought he might eventually walk again, but I hadn't dared to hope," Gil told her, "at least not this soon. Papa, you're amazing!"

His father grinned crookedly, then mumbled, "Don' be...dourrrr."

Faith turned to Gil for a translation.

"I think he told me not to be a doubter," Gil told her. "I won't, Papa. Never again!"

Then the old preacher pointed outside, and it was clear he wanted to get there with his newly regained ability to walk. They spent a happy hour sitting in the shade with him, not talking much, just rejoicing in the moment.

The effort had tired him, though, and when they brought him back inside, he indicated a desire to go to his bedroom and nap.

By unspoken mutual consent, Faith and Gil quietly left the house and went into the church sanctuary.

"Tell me if I'm wrong, Faith," Gil said, as they settled themselves on the front-row pew. "But I get the idea you don't think what happened to Papa this morning was a miracle."

Faith stiffened. She'd not expected Gil to be so direct. She shrugged. "I don't know, Gil. But Dr. Walker had already said he *might* learn to walk again."

"That's true enough. But I was thinking of a verse in the Bible that might help you. It's in the ninth chapter of Mark. The father of a child having convulsions asked Jesus for help, and yet he could hardly bring himself to believe Jesus could help him. Jesus told him, 'All things are possible to him that believes.' Then the father said, 'Lord, I believe, help Thou my unbelief.'"

Help thou my unbelief.

"You mean if I'm willing to believe enough to pray 'help me to believe,' I might regain my faith?" she asked.

He nodded, his eyes full of reflected light as he watched her.

"Why would that work, praying when I'm full of doubt, if it didn't work to pray with all my heart, after that snake bit Eddie?"

He sighed. "I don't know, Faith. Why your brother died is something we won't know till we get to Heaven," he admitted. "I *do* know God was with you when you prayed, and He felt your heartache."

His certainty made her feel contrary and rebellious. "I'd have settled for Him healing Eddie—wouldn't that have been better?"

The words hung on the air, heavy between them.

After a moment, Gil opened his mouth to speak,

but before he could form a word, they heard boot heels coming up the aisle.

"Thought I might find you in here, Reverend," Sheriff Bishop said. "Oh, Miss Faith, I didn't see you right off. Am I interrupting something?"

"We were just talking about miracles, Sheriff. My father walked this morning," Gil told him.

The sheriff's guarded, taut features relaxed somewhat. "That's real fine, Reverend Gil. Glad to hear it."

"Was there something I could help you with, Sheriff?" Gil asked.

"Maybe," Bishop said, and glanced at Faith, seemingly hesitant.

Faith rose. "If you need to talk to Reverend Gil privately, Sheriff, I could go back to the parsonage—"

"There's no need," Bishop said, "because I'm told you already know about this, Miss Faith. Gil, Miss Maude came to see me bright and early this morning. She was pale as bleached bones—said Faith had just told her you'd had a run-in with some Comanches, Reverend Gil. And because you look like the loser in a fight," he added, indicating Gil's face, "seems she was telling the truth."

"Oh, dear…I didn't think how much any talk of Comanches would upset Maude," she said, twisting a fold of her skirt. She turned to Gil. "I stopped at the boarding house this morning before I came to the parsonage, just to tell her you'd gotten home because she was worried about you, too."

Maude's eyes had widened when Faith told her about Gil encountering Indians, but Faith had been in a hurry to get to the parsonage and she hadn't thought any more about it. Now, too late, she realized how upsetting her news must have been. "Neither of you were living here when the Comanches raided Simpson Creek a couple of years back, but Doc Harkey, her father, was one of those killed in the attack."

Gil nodded, his face somber. "Yes, I remember my father telling me about it."

"Where were you when you came upon the Comanches?" Sheriff Bishop asked.

"I started out going north, but after encountering those braves, I gave the horse his head and let him run wherever he would, just to escape. I actually got a bit lost," Gil said with a shrug.

"How many Comanches?"

Gil told him.

"Three? Probably just a hunting party," Bishop said. "Still, I reckon we ought to get word of this incident to the cavalry, so they can step up their patrols of the area."

Was she imagining it or did she see Gil tense next to her? *Why?*

"I'm sure you're right, Sheriff, but those braves are more than likely many miles from here by now," Gil said.

"Their camp could be nearby," Bishop countered. "They're a nomadic people, but they frequently stay in one place for a season. The young men go out in small hunting parties to bring meat back to the camp. But sometimes they get greedy and go after livestock and—" He glanced at Faith and seemed to think better of what he'd been about to say. "Anyway, I'll pass the word around so everyone's on guard."

Faith couldn't suppress a shiver, remembering the terrifying day of the raid. Out of the corner of her eye, she saw Gil glance at her in concern.

"I think I was just in the wrong place at the wrong

time," Gil said. "But the Lord saved me from any worse harm than a few bruises and cuts."

"Thank God," the sheriff responded. "I'll be going now. Good day, Miss Faith. You take care of yourself, Reverend."

Of course they would give God the credit for Gil's safe return, but Faith thought he'd merely been very lucky. *But why did Gil seem to visibly relax once Bishop had gone?*

Chapter Eleven

"Now that it's just us men again," Gil said to his father when Faith left for the day, "do you want to sit and read your Bible while I work on my sermon some more, Papa?" Gil wasn't sure if his father could actually read since he'd had his stroke, but it seemed to comfort him to hold his Bible and look at it at least.

But his father beckoned for him to come and sit beside him at the kitchen table. Then the old man pointed at Gil's face.

He'd known his father's inquiry was coming. This morning, when Gil had helped him get out of bed, he'd peered at Gil curiously, but perhaps he'd held off trying to ask because he knew his nurse for the day would arrive at any moment.

Gil took a deep breath. "You're the only one I can tell the whole story to, Papa," he said, and told him the entire tale of his ride into the hills, his discovery of the Comanche boy and subsequent capture by the Comanche warriors, and his certainty, for a time, that he wouldn't survive the adventure. He showed him the wounds Faith hadn't seen because his shirt and shoes had covered them.

"So you see why I can't tell everything, Papa," he concluded. "I wouldn't want anything to happen to that boy after his father made them release me."

The old man nodded, but his eyes looked troubled.

"I know, I'm not entirely at peace with it, either," Gil confessed. After what had happened in his seminary days, he'd promised the Lord—and himself—that he'd never lie again. But by not telling Faith the whole truth, he'd as good as lied to her.

Should he tell her exactly what had happened, but request that she keep silent about the Comanche camp for the sake of Runs Like a Deer? A preacher had to be discreet about personal information he was entrusted with. Wasn't this a similar situation?

And what about the larger secret he'd been keeping, about the time he had lost his own faith for a while? He'd never even told his father about that. Would it help Faith to know that he had once gone through a time when tragedy had caused him to question the very existence of the Lord? The sin that had preceded the tragedy certainly didn't show him in a very good light.

His mind shrank from the thought of admitting what he had done while he was a callow seminary student. Yet might it not help Faith to know that he, too, had had to struggle to regain his belief in God?

He'd have to pray about it for sure.

Since all the members of the Spinsters' Club would be at church on Sunday, even Milly Brookfield and Caroline Collier from their outlying ranches, it had been decided to hold the tea in honor of the birth of Sarah

Walker's baby daughter at the church social hall that afternoon.

They had also invited Daisy Henderson to join them because the woman had seemed lonely. Now, sitting with the others, she seemed shyly happy to be included.

"Jack wanted to know why we were calling it a 'tea' because he saw us carrying in so many delicious-smelling covered dishes," Caroline Wallace remarked wryly, nodding toward the overladen table.

"I'm serving tea, aren't I?" Prissy Bishop responded with a grin, pouring the beverage into flower-painted china cups that had been her mother's legacy. "And we're having cucumber and watercress sandwiches as well as everything else. That makes it a tea, doesn't it?"

"Oh, he was just hoping for an invitation to come help himself to a plateful," Caroline responded wryly, and the others chuckled.

Faith had to smile at the image of Caroline's rancher husband holding one of the delicate tea cups in his work-roughened rancher's hands and taking his turn admiring Elizabeth, Sarah's infant daughter, who was being passed around and admired.

"No one has to worry that he'll starve, though," Milly put in. "My husband invited Jack to join him, Sarah's and Prissy's husbands to dinner at the hotel while we're having the party. They included Reverend Gil and his father, too," she added, looking at Faith.

Faith felt herself flushing as others turned in her direction, too. She was aware that Polly's eyes had narrowed. "It's such a blessing the old reverend is feeling well enough to go, isn't it?" Faith remarked to the group.

"Yes, I imagine the five of them are keeping Ella hopping, providing second and third helpings," Prissy said, referring to the only spinster who'd been unable to attend the party because she waitressed at the hotel restaurant. "Poor Ella, always working so hard. We'll have to make sure she's able to attend the next spinsters event—"

"Which would be the box social," Polly said, inserting herself into the conversation, "which is actually more in keeping with the real purpose for which we set up the Spinsters' Club in the first place—as I'm sure Milly will confirm, won't you?" she asked, turning to the group's founder.

For a moment, it was so quiet in the social hall that little Elizabeth's baby noises seemed abnormally loud. Everyone stared at Polly. Faith was dismayed to see Daisy Henderson looking distinctly uneasy. Did she now feel unwelcome, thanks to Polly's pushy and condescending attitude? Faith tore her gaze away from Daisy and back toward Milly, hoping the plucky woman who had been the first Spinsters' Club bride would give Polly the comeuppance she so richly deserved. But Milly seemed too shocked to form a reply.

"That was indeed our primary purpose in starting this group," Faith heard herself say.

Polly looked surprised at Faith's sudden apparent support and smiled triumphantly—but prematurely.

"But I believe everyone would agree that we've become so much more," Faith went on. "We've grown into a group of ladies whose purpose is fellowship, whether that purpose involves matchmaking, or celebrating the birth of the offspring of our members, such as sweet little Elizabeth there," she said, gesturing toward Sarah's baby. For a moment she couldn't help wondering what it would be like to have a baby of her own. *But no, she mustn't think about that.*

There were murmurs of support around the circle

of ladies, and the tense, anxious expression on Daisy Henderson's face relaxed.

But Polly was not to be deterred. "Of course we enjoy each other's company. I'm certainly not saying anything contrary to that. But did you notice the poster for the box social on the door of the social hall, ladies? Your father was so kind to do them for us gratis, Faith," she said, fluttering her eyelashes at her. "I've also put up posters in the mercantile and the post office, and Caroline's brother has ridden over to San Saba, Lampasas and other nearby towns and posted them in similar places there. I'm expecting each of us to use our creativity to decorate our supper boxes. Each box will go to the highest bidder, so I know you ladies will make each one as pretty and appealing as possible."

Faith saw wary nods.

"And what becomes of the money we raise?" Louisa Wheeler asked.

Before Polly could speak, Maude did. "We usually donate to the town's Society for the Deserving Poor."

Polly gave a gusty, put-upon sigh. "I wish we could keep it to fund more elaborate Spinsters' Club events to attract a more *affluent* sort of bachelor..."

Milly rolled her eyes at this pronouncement, which Polly fortunately missed because she was looking at Maude. Faith stifled a giggle.

"But I suppose that would be *frowned* upon," Polly went on. "Very well, we'll give the proceeds to the poor."

Kate Patterson, one of the newer members, asked, "This event is open to the rest of the town, too, isn't it?"

"Of course. We'll raise more money for the deserving poor that way," Polly said. "Husbands will bid for their wives' supper boxes, so the married ladies certainly won't be any competition for us spinsters," she said with an airy wave. "Are there any other questions, ladies?"

"I think it's time we presented Sarah and Elizabeth with the gifts we've brought, don't you, ladies?" Milly said, and the next hour was spent admiring the dainty clothes, crocheted blankets and embroidered bibs brought for Sarah and the doctor's new daughter.

"Thanks for speaking up when Polly was being so rude and pushy, Faith," Prissy said as Faith, Milly and Caroline helped Prissy load dishes, glassware and silverware onto Milly's buckboard to be carried to Prissy's house. "I wanted to, but I couldn't possibly have responded in a Christian way just then, as you did."

"I—I did?" Faith found the idea that she had done anything in a Christ-like way startling. *If they only knew.*

"Of course you did," Milly agreed. "You reminded her that fellowship with our sisters in Christ is even more important than finding husbands."

"Thank you, but you ladies are probably giving me too much credit," Faith said uneasily. "I was just afraid she was making Sarah uncomfortable, because we were celebrating the birth of her baby rather than plotting to lure bachelors to Simpson Creek, and Daisy, too, because she's just lost her husband."

"And you steered her very diplomatically but firmly," Caroline put in. "Well done, Faith." She glanced at the small gold watch pinned to the bodice of her dress. "Milly, we'd better get these things over to Prissy's, so we'll be back here to meet Isaiah when he comes to take us back home."

"Oh, good, I'm glad you two will have one of the

hands with you," Faith said, "after Reverend Gil met up with those Comanches the other day. I think you're so brave being out there on the ranch with your husband gone, Milly, even if Caroline and Jack are your neighbors. Aren't you afraid sometimes?"

"Oh, the Lord will protect me and our son," Milly said. "With the help of the cowhands Nick left at the ranch."

"My Sam says those braves that attacked Reverend Gil were probably just a hunting party that's long gone from the area anyway," Prissy said.

"Besides, our ranch is completely the other direction from where Reverend Gil encountered the Comanches, from what I heard," Milly added. "And I've become a crack shot with a Winchester, if I do say so myself. But I would welcome some company. Faith, why don't you and Reverend Gil drive out to see us sometime, now that his father's doing so well? That would give you two a nice long ride together out there and back."

"Reverend Gil and I aren't courting," Faith insisted, uncomfortable again.

"Whyever not?" Prissy asked. "He's so nice, and I can tell he's sweet on you."

Faith shrugged and looked away. "I'm not sure I'd make the best preacher's wife."

"Horsefeathers," Milly scoffed. "It's as plain as a white cat in a mud puddle that you two are meant for each other."

"I certainly never thought I'd marry Pete's brother, not after he just showed up with his twins like he did," Caroline added. "But when the Lord selects our spouses, He has a way of changing our minds to suit His plans for us."

Faith was very sure she was in charge of her own

fate, rather than some invisible, unknowable deity, but she wasn't about to argue.

"Ladies, did you have a nice party?" Gil asked, and the four women whirled around to face him from the back of a buckboard. They'd been so intent on lifting an ornate crystal punchbowl into a large padded basket at the back of the wagon that they hadn't heard him approach. Now he saw smiles on all four faces, but only one of them had a blush blossoming on both cheeks as she recognized him. Faith.

Milly Brookfield found her voice first. "Yes, it was a lot of fun, Reverend Gil. If you were hoping for leftovers, I'm afraid we only had crumbs left," she teased.

Gil grinned and patted the front of his vest. "No, I'm way too full of roast beef from the hotel. Thank you just the same."

"Did you and the rest of the men enjoy your meal?" Faith asked him, wishing she could control the heat she'd felt rushing to her cheeks and the way her heart sped up, even while she tried to sound casual.

"Very much so," he murmured, noting the way the willow-green dress with darker green piping complemented her lovely eyes. "Once they stopped teasing me about my battered face at least. Jack Collier told me I looked like a prizefighter who'd lost his match. It was good seeing Papa laugh. I left him at home dozing, and thought I'd see if you needed help carrying anything. And I see you do," he said, as she lifted a large pewter platter from the grass where she'd left it while helping the others load the buckboard. "Here, let me help you with that."

Apparently sensing he'd insist if she tried to decline, she handed it to him, ignoring the chuckles from the others as they drove off. "You know, no one's going to believe we're not courting if you do things like that," she told him. "Prissy winked at me just now as they left."

"Things like what? I came to see if I could help any or all of you. You were the only one left."

She gave him a skeptical look.

"Well, I suppose you could say that was a fib," he admitted. "I was certainly willing to help any of the ladies, but you're the one I feel most willing to assist."

Why had he said that? Gil wondered. Hadn't he agreed with her that unless she shared his faith, they could not court? Yet he couldn't seem to keep himself from feeling attracted to her, and from saying things such as he had just said. Her cheeks were pink again and she seemed to be struggling to hide a smile.

Surprisingly, he didn't feel any sense that his flirting with this woman wasn't pleasing the Lord. *Could that mean she would regain her faith at some future time?*

Perhaps Faith was fighting similar feelings, for her face grew serious. Her eyes met his and she said, "A fib is a little lie, isn't it? I thought Christians weren't supposed to lie."

She wasn't teasing him back. Was she trying to put distance between them? Yet she hadn't said it as a taunt, either.

Could this be the very opening he'd been looking for to ease into a discussion of spiritual things?

"No, Christians aren't supposed to lie," he said. "But this side of Heaven, we remain fallible beings who merely try our best to do the right thing with God's help. No one is perfect but God."

Her eyes were troubled, and he wondered if Faith

was thinking God wasn't so perfect, either, because He'd let her brother die.

By mutual, unspoken consent they drifted over to the bench that sat beneath the big live oak tree at the back of the churchyard, and sat down.

"Christians are called on to show the world God's love," he said. "Yet sometimes, speaking the truth could hurt someone's feelings to no good purpose. So if it isn't a truth that must be said, I don't think the Lord wants us to say some things."

She looked at him quizzically. "What do you mean?"

"Here's an example. Just between you and me, I don't find a certain female appealing, and it's completely unlikely that I would ever want to court that particular female. But I wouldn't be showing Christian behavior to tell her that if it could be avoided, would I? To hurt her feelings, just so I could claim I was honest. Do you see?"

He thought from a certain look of knowing in those green eyes that she had guessed he was speaking to her of Polly. A glint of amusement sparkled in her eyes.

"That's the 'Golden Rule,' isn't it? 'Do unto others, as you would have them do unto you.' But I do that, too. It's basically just being kind."

He nodded.

They were both silent for a few moments, and then, staring straight ahead, she asked, "I understand why God—if there *is* such a being—didn't answer my prayers, or my parents', when we prayed for my brother. We're just ordinary folks. But why didn't he answer your father's? He's a preacher, and there's no more righteous man than your father. But even his prayers couldn't save Eddie."

"Faith, God says in the Bible, 'My ways aren't your

ways,' so I don't understand what His reason is for taking your brother any more than why my mother died years ago, leaving my father alone. But a preacher's prayers have no magic in them. A preacher's just as much in need of a Savior as anyone else."

Once again, she looked doubtful, and for a moment, he was tempted to tell her just what a big sinner he truly had been, when he'd been away at seminary, lonely and unused to worldly women, he had fallen in love with a woman so unsuitable to being the wife of a preacher that she made Faith look like a saint by comparison. When she died, their unborn baby had perished with her.

Yet he dared not tell her. If he did, she would question what right he had to get up before the congregation every Sunday and tell anyone how to live. She would never understand how a preacher could sin so much and still call himself a preacher. And if his father heard of it, he might be so devastated by his son's failings that he could have another stroke.

But maybe he could tell her a part of the truth, Gil thought, enough so she could understand the point he was trying to make.

"I'm sure *you* never doubted that God exists," Faith said now, a note of challenge in her tone.

He took a deep breath. "Faith, once, while I was away at seminary, I prayed desperately for the life of an unborn baby...and his mother who'd been shot," he said, looking down at his hands. "I prayed so hard I understood what the Bible meant when it said Jesus prayed so hard He sweated blood." He closed his eyes, remembering those hours on his knees, his frantic pleading.

When he looked up, she was watching him. And waiting.

"They died anyway," he said dully. "And for a long

time, Faith, I doubted that God existed. How could He, when He could let a sinless baby die? I came so close to packing my valise and heading home. Of course I had no idea what I'd be if I wasn't going to follow in Papa's footsteps…"

"But you got your faith back," she said. "How? The next time you prayed, you got what you asked for?"

He steepled his fingers and looked at her. "No, Faith, because talking to God isn't like a magic spell we utter. Getting my faith back wasn't that simple, and it took time. One of my seminary professors urged me to consider my presence at the seminary one day at a time— even one hour at a time. For a while, it seemed like the time I spent in prayer was just like talking to a wall, like there was no one there. But I kept trying—and He kept trying, too, I guess, and one day I felt His presence in my heart again." *And the promise of a better life ahead of me,* he thought, but he couldn't tell her that without revealing who the woman had been to him.

She was silent, staring unseeingly ahead of her at the tombstones that now cast long shadows across the lawn. Had his words made any dent in the hard shell that imprisoned her soul?

Chapter Twelve

Drowsiness ebbed as Faith entered the newspaper office the next morning. It was Monday, press day, and by now her father would have a stack of newspapers to be delivered to the local businesses that advertised in the paper. She'd deliver them, and by the time she returned, he'd have another armful to be taken to those residents who subscribed. Those subscribers who lived on outlying ranches had their papers delivered to the post office, to be claimed when they ventured to town.

She'd lain awake a long time last night thinking about what Gil had said. If there was a God, had He really stayed with Gil during his crisis of faith after the tragedy, or was that just wishful thinking on Gil's part? And who was the woman he had mentioned, the woman who'd been fatally shot, and her unborn child with her? Had she been important to Gil somehow, or just an acquaintance from the local church? Why had she been shot? How awful that when she died, two lives were lost instead of just one.

The sound of the printing press clacking away dissolved the remaining cobwebs in Faith's mind, helped by the strong cup of coffee she'd downed before she'd left home. She always felt such a sense of purpose when she could help her father; she wasn't just a grown woman still living at home assisting her mother as needed while she waited to meet a suitable man and make a home of her own—she was Faith Bennett, assistant to the newspaper editor.

"There you are at last," said her father, taking a sheet of newspaper off the cords stretched from one wall to the other and folding it. "I sure didn't want to have another Monday like the last one, printing *and* delivering the papers myself," he groused.

Had he forgotten what she'd been doing that day? "But Papa, Reverend Chadwick—"

"Yes, I know, you were nursing the preacher," he said quickly. "I just can't do it all myself, that's all. Now that you're here, let's get busy."

Her father was always grumpy and impatient on press day. But maybe he had begun to see how essential she was. Perhaps after her deliveries were done, she should go home and try writing a piece on some bit of news she encountered around town. She would show it to Louisa secretly after her cousin was done with her school day, and make sure it was polished and grammar-perfect, then present it to her father. If she did well enough he might come to see that he didn't really need to hire that fellow from Georgia…

Minutes later, she left the office with her printed cargo and headed for her first stop, the hotel. Its proprietor had bought a particularly large advertisement this week and her father had instructed her to be sure and show him its prominent placement on page two, right next to her father's editorial about the need for vigilance on everyone's part now that Reverend Gil had been attacked by Comanches and only escaped by the "grace of God," as he had written it.

What did "grace" mean in this instance? She'd have to ask Gil, but be careful to do so casually, and when he could only give her a brief, to-the-point answer. He'd given her far too much to think about yesterday afternoon.

Now she was thinking about Gil yet again, and the earnest light in his hazel eyes when he'd tried to answer her question about Eddie's death. There could be no real answer, of course. Before the conversation had turned serious, though, his talk had been too much like the bantering between a suitor and the object of his interest. She had to find a way to spend less time with him.

That would soon come naturally, now that his father was doing so much better. Before Faith had gone home yesterday, she and Gil had even talked about the fact that eventually, his father would probably be able to see to his own needs well enough that the presence of a spinster nurse wouldn't be necessary unless Gil had to spend any extended time away from the parsonage.

Faith had one more shift with old Reverend Chadwick this week, and perhaps it would be a good idea to get one of the other ladies to take it, so she could avoid situations where she and Gil spent too much time together. They dare not continue to nurture the inappropriate affection that had been growing between them.

Which of the other spinsters could she ask to take her place? Anyone but Polly, she thought wryly, for the other girl was probably still irked by what Faith had said to her yesterday at the party. And in any case Gil would want to avoid that young lady's company as much as possible.

What might be best for her, Faith realized, would be

meeting another gentleman who was more of a free-thinker like herself. Then it would be very clear to Gil that he needed to look elsewhere for a wife. She would be doing the right thing for Gil as well as herself.

Yet it was unlikely such a thing would happen before the box social supper, if it even happened then. If Gil found out what boxed meal was hers, and won the bid for it—and who would try to top the well-liked young preacher's bid after all?—there was no way she could convince anyone that Gil and she weren't courting.

Just as she was leaving the hotel, her first paper delivered, she saw the stagecoach pulling up on its regular run from Austin. She halted, always interested to see the variety of men and women emerging from the interior of the coach. Sometimes they were all strangers; other times, she recognized townspeople returning from a journey. She wasn't aware of anyone from Simpson Creek who'd been away, but if there were any of the latter group, she knew her father would be interested in hearing of it so he could include the tidbit in his regular column "Doings about Town."

None of the half-dozen people who emerged were familiar to her, however. There was a weary-looking middle-age couple who lost no time in disappearing into the hotel, then a pair of fellows who jumped out and gazed with interest, not at her, but at the saloon across the street. Next came an elderly female clutching the hand of a small wiggly boy, who was assisted in her descent by the driver. Last of all emerged a young man, perhaps only a year or two older than the other two, but as different from them as night and day.

Even standing in profile to her, the man had a certain grandeur to him, she thought, remembering a time her father had used the term when writing about a long-ago time when he'd met a prominent thespian on tour from New York.

The man standing by the stagecoach stretched his arms now as if his muscles had been cramped by the long journey, raising a black bowler he'd been clutching in one hand to the sky, as if announcing his arrival. He was of middle height, but carried himself as if he were the tallest man in Texas.

He wore a sack coat of pearl-gray with matching trousers and a vest of black and silver brocade. As Faith watched, he clapped the bowler on his head, covering a head full of thick wheat-colored hair, then smoothed both sides of a luxuriant moustache absently with a thumb and forefinger.

"You boys remember we're takin' off in an hour," the stagecoach driver called to the pair of gents who were making their way across the dusty street to the saloon. "We gotta make tracks if we're gonna keep to th' schedule, and I ain't comin' along to pull yore heads out of a whiskey bottle iffen ya don't show up once the team is watered an' the other folks've et their grub." The pair ignored him, so he turned to the man Faith had been studying and said, "I'll fetch yore trunk down now, sir, because you're the only one not goin' on to th' next stop."

"Obliged to you, sir," the man said in a voice as thick with a Deep South drawl as molasses trickling from an overturned pitcher. He turned so his back was to Faith, peering down the street with eyes shaded by his gloved hand. Then, apparently not spotting what he was looking for, he turned back to the stagecoach driver, who had climbed up to reach under the leather flap covering the passengers' luggage. "By any chance, would you know where the newspaper office is, Driver?"

The combination of the thick southern drawl and his question told Faith who he was. When the driver called him by name in his next breath, it only confirmed her sickening realization.

"On th' other side of the hotel, Mr. Merriwell," Turner said, pointing a thumb behind him in Faith's direction. "I'll leave your trunk here on the boardwalk. No one'll bother it."

As Yancey Merriwell stepped around the coach to see where the driver was pointing, his eyes lit on Faith. And widened appreciatively.

"Good day, Miss," he said, sweeping his bowler off and bowing.

"I can take you there, Mr. Merriwell. As it happens, I'm the daughter of the editor. We…we weren't expecting your arrival so soon," she stammered, hoping her face didn't reflect her dismay. "My father just got your letter the other day."

"You must be Miss Bennett, then," he said, straightening. "I'm honored to meet you. I'm afraid I've acted a little impulsively," he confessed, with a smile that was both sheepish and sure of its effect. "As soon as I sent off the letter, I set off by train for Texas, and when I could come no nearer to Simpson Creek by that mode of transportation, I boarded the stagecoach, so eager was I to assume my new position. I hope I didn't act rashly. He hasn't given the position to someone else, has he?"

"Oh, no," she assured him. "Because you're here, allow me to introduce you to my father." She gestured for him to cross the narrow alley between the hotel and the newspaper office, and saw that he moved with an elegant grace. "I'm sure he'll be pleased you've seized the initiative and come on ahead." *As pleased as I am disappointed that I won't have a chance to prove myself before your arrival.* She tried to tell herself the man had exhibited an amazing amount of gall by not waiting for her father's letter of invitation, but it was impossible to do so under the force of the man's golden charm. Her father *would* be pleased, she thought. *I was only fooling myself to think I ever really had a chance, anyway.*

Just as she had suspected, her father was pleased. *Exuberant* was more the word Faith would use to describe the excitement lighting her father's face after she'd identified Merriwell. He was so transported by Yancey Merriwell's arrival that he didn't even hear Faith announcing she was leaving to resume her newspaper delivering. She thought her departure would go unnoticed, but just as she reached the door, Merriwell looked up.

"I'm certain I'll see you later, Miss Bennett," he said in his courtly drawl. "Thank you so much for escorting me here and making the introduction. It was most kind of you."

I'm sure you would have found your way to the right building, because you were in spitting distance of it, she thought waspishly, but aloud she only said, "It was my pleasure to assist you, Mr. Merriwell."

She'd better stop at the house and alert her mother they would have another place to set at the supper table tonight. As soon as she finished her rounds, she'd need to help her prepare Eddie's—no, she should probably call it the guest room now, she supposed. She wondered if this would be her last time to deliver the newspapers. Would Merriwell take even that little pleasure from her?

The next morning Gil had just finished paying a call on Mrs. Henderson to check on the widow's well-being when he spotted a man and woman making their way down the boardwalk toward him. It was Faith, but who was the man walking alongside her? He wasn't touching her in any way, but she seemed to know him, for she was talking to him and pointing to the establishments as they passed them. The stranger was quite the dandy, Gil thought, studying the other man's stylish garments. Not a Texan, he thought, but someone from the east and he possessed attractive features to go with his clothes.

What was it about the way the man smiled down at her that raised Gil's hackles?

Faith caught sight of him and smiled, urging the other man forward.

"Good morning, Reverend Gil," she called. "I'd like to introduce you to someone."

"Good morning, Miss Faith. You're looking very pretty today." She was, in fact—was there a color that did not look well on Faith Bennett? By complimenting her in front of this man, had he been unconsciously trying to stake a claim of sorts on her?

"Thank you, Reverend," she said formally, and Gil found himself wishing she would call him by his Christian name as she did at other times. "May I present Mr. Yancey Merriwell? Mr. Merriwell, this is Reverend Gil Chadwick, the younger of our church's two preachers."

"My very great pleasure, sir," the other man said, bowing and shaking Gil's hand with restrained enthusiasm. "My" came out *"mah"* and Merriwell's *r*'s were all slurred, but without a Texan's twang.

"Welcome to Simpson Creek, Mr. Merriwell," Gil said, hoping Faith would enlighten him further.

"Mr. Merriwell is from Georgia," Faith went on. "He's come to take on the position of my father's assistant at the newspaper." Her tone was informative, but Gil caught a quick flash of pain in Faith's eyes.

"I see."

"Yes, he'll be staying with us, at least for the time being," Faith said. "We had a…a spare room, and until he finds lodging of his own…"

Gil didn't like that news. At all. The idea of this sleek, fashionable man in such close proximity to Faith—*what was her father thinking?* He looked closely, but he couldn't see any flash of triumph in the other man's eyes. Gil thought of mentioning the vacancy at Mrs. Meyer's boardinghouse its proprietress had mentioned to him in passing, but thought he'd save his breath. This man looked as if he'd disdain such lodgings.

"We've been taking a tour of Simpson Creek," Faith explained. "Papa asked me to show Mr. Merriwell around, point out where all the businesses are. He's been meeting some of the proprietors," Faith went on.

"Then I'd best not hold you up," Gil said, suddenly eager to get away from the Georgian. "I hope I'll be seeing you at Sunday services, Mr. Merriwell."

Something flickered in the other man's eyes. "Unlikely. I admit I'm something of a…a doubting Thomas, you might say—a freethinker."

Gil was startled by the bold way Merriwell admitted it, and his gaze darted quickly to Faith's face. What did she think of the Georgian's blunt announcement? Had they already discussed it? Was she pleased to find a like-minded fellow, just when Gil had been thinking he might be making progress in bringing her closer to the Lord? Would Merriwell's coming only stiffen her resistance to belief in God?

"But perhaps you should reconsider, Mr. Merriwell," Faith said then. "The church is the center of Simpson Creek life. The easiest way to get to know its people is to converse with them at church. And Reverend Gil is a most eloquent speaker."

Her defense of church attendance surprised Gil, but was that the only reason she came—for the sake of her social life, and because he was an eloquent speaker, as his father had been before him?

The man smiled slowly as if impressed by her suggestion. "Perhaps I will, then. You are probably right, Miss Faith."

Had Faith already granted the upstart the right to use her first name, even with "Miss" in front of it, or was he just hoping Faith wouldn't object?

"I'm sure of it," Faith said. "And perhaps one of your first interviews should be with Reverend Chadwick here. He has a most interesting story to tell, having been accosted by Comanches only days ago. The fading cuts and scrapes on his face are a result of that dreadful encounter."

Merriwell looked intrigued. "Is that right, Reverend? Fascinating. I would indeed like to speak to you. It would be most interesting to me."

Gil wished Faith had not mentioned it. There was nothing he wanted less than to relive the event for Yancey Merriwell so this man could write his first newspaper column about it, spreading the tale to the farthest reaches of San Saba County—a tale that was only partly true. But of course Faith did not know the reason for his preference.

"Perhaps later," Gil said stiffly. "Right now I need to check on my father. Good day to you, Mr. Merriwell."

"I don't believe your reverend likes me, Miss Faith," Merriwell said when they were out of earshot.

His words startled Faith. "I—I'm sure you're mistaken," she said. "What would make you think such a thing? A preacher likes everyone."

He chuckled. "Preachers are human, Miss Faith. They have likes and dislikes just as the rest of us mortals do. And it's only a feeling I had about him. If you will allow me to be shockingly plain-spoken for such a new acquaintance, Miss Faith, I believe it's because he's interested in you."

Despite the way his accent softened his words, what he said was so dismaying that Faith stopped stock-still, then turned to face her father's new assistant. *Was Gil's feeling for her it so obvious that even a stranger could sense it?*

"You are entitled to your opinion, sir, of course, but I'll say it again—you're mistaken," she said, staring straight ahead as she began walking again. She couldn't decide how she felt about Merriwell's remarks about Gil. Voicing such an opinion on such short acquaintance was brash of the man, possibly even impertinent, but he'd said it in such a charming, teasing way she found it hard to be offended.

"And why wouldn't you want the preacher to be interested in you?" Merriwell asked. "Have you another beau, perhaps?" He stopped and clapped a hand over his mouth. "I'm sorry, I don't know what possessed me to ask such a rude question. It's none of my business, of course."

No, it isn't, she thought, but somehow she felt compelled to answer. His admission to Gil that he was a nonbeliever like herself had stunned her. Perhaps this was a man she *should* be interested in because they shared the same philosophy.

"I like Reverend Gil—we call him that to differentiate him from his father, Reverend Chadwick—we are only friends. I helped care for his father after he was stricken by apoplexy recently. But he and I would not make a good match, for like yourself, Mr. Merriwell, I am a freethinker."

Now it was the Georgian's turn to appear startled.

"You don't say, Miss Faith! Now, that is interesting that we hold that opinion in common," he said. His eyes warmed.

Why had she made such an impulsive admission?

Merriwell leaned closer. "Perhaps there are other things we have in common, as well," he said. "You are a most surprising lady, Miss Faith."

"I should not have said what I did, sir, and I would beg you not mention it to anyone," Faith said. "It is not anything I would want known, for it would hurt my parents immensely if they found out."

He responded by taking her hand and placing it over his forearm. "I am the soul of discretion, if a nonbeliever may claim he has a soul. Rest assured, your secret is safe with me, Miss Faith. Our feelings are unshackled by the bondage of religion, but we must often keep them to ourselves for fear of public censure, must we not?"

His forwardness in touching her irritated her, as did his attempt to make it seem as if they were two against a world that would persecute them. She wanted to yank her arm away, but instead she gently disengaged herself. "You exaggerate the situation, Mr. Merriwell," she said coolly. "I believe in being a moral person and keep my beliefs, or lack of them, to myself out of love for my parents and friends. Now, here we are at the mercantile," she said, pointing at the sign over the door. "We should really go in and introduce you to Mrs. Patterson, its proprietress. She's one of our best customers."

As they waited politely to speak to Mrs. Patterson,

who was helping a customer, she examined her mixed feelings about Merriwell.

Last night her father had beamed at him as if the Georgian was a newfound son. Even her mother seemed to find him fascinating as he told tales over the supper table of the gallant but defeated Old South. He'd been the son of a well-to-do owner and editor of a prominent newspaper there before Fort Sumter fell, he said, and had become a war correspondent with the intention of reporting the glorious Confederate victories. But after the South was beaten, he returned to find his father had died and the newspaper office had been reduced to charred timbers. To hear him tell it, there was no longer any way to publish an honest newspaper with the Federals still overrunning the state. After trying for three years to make a go of it in Atlanta, he had finally come west to recoup his fortune where the air was less thick with the stench of Yankees.

He hadn't mentioned anything about his lack of faith in front of her parents, Faith remembered. How had he sensed it was safe to say it in front of her?

Well, she'd barely known the man twenty-four hours, and it was way too soon to say if Merriwell was a better man for her. Certainly there needed to be more reasons to like him than merely because he was a fellow nonbeliever. He was certainly charming and good-looking, if one was willing to ignore the feeling that he seemed to feel entitled to her regard.

But a voice within her protested the very notion of giving away that place in her heart that Gil occupied, even though she'd never willingly given it to the preacher.

Chapter Thirteen

"Mr. Merriwell, I run the only mercantile in Simpson Creek. When the townsfolk need dry goods or what have you, where else are they going to go? Why would I need to do more advertising? I really only advertise now and then to support our local newspaper. I'm a widow, you see, and not wealthy," Mrs. Patterson said, when Yancey tried to persuade her to buy a larger advertisement in the *Simpson Creek Chronicle*.

"I understand, ma'am," he responded smoothly, "but have you considered that by placing one item—any item you choose, ma'am, perhaps something that's been slow to move off your shelves—at a special sale price, you encourage your customers to come in to buy that item while they may do so inexpensively. Once inside your door, they may well impulsively buy other things. The result is increased profit for you," Yancey Merriwell concluded convincingly, giving the proprietress the full force of his winning smile.

"I don't know…" Mrs. Patterson murmured, and glanced at Faith as if seeking direction.

Faith only smiled. Merriwell would need to make this sale entirely on his own, if he could.

"Mrs. Patterson, I admit I'm a newcomer," Yancey admitted, "but I'm told Simpson Creek is growing. Some day you may not own the only mercantile. And when that day comes, you want to be sure that your store owns the loyalty of the townspeople of Simpson Creek. You can do that by regular advertising, which keeps your store prominent in the townspeople's minds, and by constantly reminding them of merchandise you sell which they might need."

"Another mercantile in Simpson Creek? Just let them try to open one!" Mrs. Patterson exclaimed, and promptly bought a large advertisement to be placed on the front page of the next edition, with yellow gingham fabric being featured as the sale item. What was more, she agreed to place an advertisement every week for the next two months, with a promise to buy more if Mr. Merriwell's strategy worked.

"I do believe you could sell ice at the North Pole, Mr. Merriwell," Faith remarked as they left the store, cha-grinned because she had never been able to persuade the shopkeeper to buy more than the most minuscule advertisement on the back page. Her father would no doubt be even more pleased than ever with his new em-ployee when he heard the news.

She watched for any sign of smugness, but Merri-well only looked pleased by the compliment. "Please, call me Yancey, Miss Faith," he said. "I'm just trying to prove to your father he did the right thing by hir-ing me," he said with a modest shrug of his shoulders.

Oh, he's already persuaded of that, Faith thought, remembering the way her father had beamed at the Georgian over supper last night. She admitted to herself that it hurt to think of the way her father and Merriwell had talked nonstop in the parlor last night after dinner, making plans for new features in the newspaper. Faith and her mother might as well have not even been present.

What was the real reason Yancey Merriwell had left Atlanta? If it was truly the Yankee occupation of Georgia, wouldn't he have found it difficult to run his newspaper sooner? Faith wished she dared ask. There was something about the Georgian that seemed too good to be true.

She supposed she should take Merriwell back to the newspaper office. Her father had planned to show his new employee how to run the press this afternoon, for Merriwell had claimed to use a different model back in Atlanta. Her father had always claimed his trusty old Washington press had certain crotchets its operator had to be aware of.

"Well, we've visited every business establishment in Simpson Creek," she said brightly. "Perhaps you should return to the office now. I'll go home and bring back the dinner that Mama's doubtless got ready for you both."

"Actually, Miss Faith, your father suggested I take you to dinner at the hotel when we were finished with our little tour," Merriwell told her. "A treat to thank you for showing me around."

The Georgian's bland announcement rendered Faith speechless. She struggled to keep her features expressionless while inwardly, fury raged. After knowing him for such a brief time, her father was giving Merriwell encouragement to court his daughter? Wouldn't that be a neat solution to worry about the future, if Merriwell became not only his future successor, but also his son-in-law?

Hadn't her father been pleased, only days ago, when he was sure Gil was interested in her? Had he been so eager to have her off his hands that he didn't care who the man was who did the taking?

"Why, hello, Faith!" a voice trilled in front of them. "I just heard from Mrs. Detwiler about your father's new employee. This must be the man himself, eh?"

She should never be surprised at the speed at which Mrs. Detwiler managed to pass on the latest news. They had only run into the old woman minutes ago at the bank. And while she was not usually pleased to run into Polly Shackleford, this time she practically kissed the other woman's cheeks in gratitude. She'd thought before that it would not be the right thing to sic Polly on Merriwell, but after what her father had done, it now seemed not only fair but just.

"It's good to see you, Polly! Yes, this is Mr. Yancey Merriwell, late of Atlanta, Georgia, who has just become my father's associate editor," she said. "Mr. Yancey, Miss Polly Shackleford, the current president of the Simpson Creek Spinsters' Club."

The Georgian bowed low. "Miss Shackleford, it's my pleasure to meet you. What organization did you say she was president of, Miss Faith?"

"The Simpson Creek Spinsters' Club," Faith repeated. "Why, this might be another good story for you, Mr. Merriwell! Polly, Mr. Merriwell was just about to take me to dinner at the hotel. You simply must come along and tell him all about our wonderful club."

Polly blinked, probably surprised by Faith's sudden effusiveness, but she didn't waste time demurring politely. "Why, how nice of you to include me," she gushed.

If he was disappointed he would not have his employer's daughter all to himself, Merriwell was too much the gentleman to say so.

"I cannot imagine anything that would please me more than to have the company of not one but two pretty ladies while dining," Merriwell said. "And I do indeed wish to hear all about this Spinsters' Club you speak of, although I cannot imagine either of y'all belonging to a group by that name," he said, the personification of gallantry. He offered each of them an arm and turned toward the hotel. "Shall we, ladies?"

Over the next hour Faith watched in amusement as Polly monopolized the conversation at their table in the hotel restaurant, telling Yancey Merriwell in minute detail about the founding of the Spinsters' Club, every match made and all about the coming box social, making it sound like that while the Society for the Promotion of Marriage had not actually been Polly's idea, she had been the driving force behind the continued success of the group. By the end of dinner, Yancey Merriwell's eyes were glazing over, but Polly had secured his agreement to come to the box social, not only to cover it for the newspaper, but also as a participant. Faith could even find it in her to feel sorry for the Georgian, whose polite, courtly facade had begun to show signs of strain by the time dessert was offered.

Perhaps Polly had talked too much for Merriwell to want to flirt with *her* rather than herself, Faith thought, but by bringing Polly along, at least Faith had not had to sit alone with the Georgian and politely fend off his advances. She was still going to have a talk with her father, however, and make sure he understood in no uncertain terms how angry she was about him apparently giving his new employee his blessing to court her.

Now she couldn't believe she had ever considered,

even for a moment, that Yancey Merriwell might be a man to consider as a match. Gil was ten times the man Merriwell was, even if he did believe in a deity she could not. She longed to tell him about her father's perfidy, but surely it wasn't right to go running to Gil when she was hurt after they had agreed it wasn't right for them to court?

No, she could stand on her own two feet and handle her hurt feelings herself, thank you very much, even if she did long to fly into Gil's comforting embrace.

Faith's anger simmered during supper, another mealtime which her father spent sharing newspapering anecdotes with Merriwell, when he was not boasting to Faith and his wife and daughter of Merriwell's knack with the old Washington press.

"Mama, would you mind if I didn't help you with the dishes tonight? I would like to talk to Papa for a few minutes—privately."

Her father looked up, surprised. "Well...I *had* planned to discuss Yancey's first editorial with him, and see what suggestions he might have for future articles..."

Her father's hesitation only caused her smoldering anger to fan itself into crackling flames again. "This won't take long, Papa," she said, tight-lipped. She darted a glance across the pecanwood table at Merriwell. The Georgian looked distinctly uncomfortable. Did he know that she was furious? Good! At least the man had *some* perception to go along with his audacity.

"Robert, surely you could spare a few minutes for your daughter," Lydia Bennett snapped, taking Faith completely by surprise. "You don't mind, do you, Yancey?" her mother added in a kinder, but still firm, tone.

"Of course, Mrs. Bennett. It's only proper that your family concerns come first. I'll just go to my room and work on polishing the editorial, all right, Mr. Bennett? I won't come out until I'm summoned."

"Shall we go into the parlor, Faith?" her father asked, his face wary.

"Oh, why don't we go for a walk instead?" she asked, going to pick up her paisley shawl from its hook by the door. She did not want to be anywhere where her mother or Merriwell might overhear their conversation, for she rather thought she would be raising her voice. Perhaps they should head for the creek. If she was lucky, no one else would be fishing there or splashing in its shallow depths.

"What's this about, Faith?" her father asked when they stood looking down into the clear green water. A dragonfly flitted along the bank, skimmed along the surface of the water, then flew higher to avoid the gaping mouth of a bluegill that had jumped at it. Somewhere in the underbrush, a pair of crickets chirped.

Faith gathered her courage. She had never spoken to her father in anger, never even talked back to him since she'd been old enough to put her hair up.

"Papa, I—I'm sure you meant well," she began, feeling her heart thudding within her, "but I will not be treated like a prize to be bestowed."

"Whatever are you talking about?" Robert Bennett asked.

Apparently his puzzlement was honest, but she must not let that dissuade her from her chosen course, or it would only keep happening. "These are modern times, Papa, not the Middle Ages," Faith said. "You must stop dangling me in front of your precious Yancey Merriwell like a reward for being a good employee."

Her father took a step back. "You're upset because I told Yancey he could take you to the hotel for dinner? I didn't mean anything by it. I thought you liked Merriwell, and it would be an enjoyable outing. He seems like a decent fellow to me," he protested. "But you can step out with him or not—it's *your* choice."

She felt her hands clench into fists at her side as she leaned forward, jabbing a finger at him. "Just a few days ago you were telling me you were certain Reverend Gil was sweet on me—what of that? You've known Merriwell for a couple of days, and what do you really know of him? Only what he's told you, that's what. I don't know why, but I don't trust him."

Her father crossed his hands over his chest. "When did you develop this suspicious nature, Faith? I have no reason to think Merriwell is anything less than—"

"Perfect," Faith finished for him, feeling tears welling up and stinging her eyes. "You've practically adopted him already! When will you start calling him 'son'?"

"Faith!" her father cried. "What a thing to say! I never—"

"You might have asked me how I felt before having him ask me to have a meal with him."

Her father had the grace to look ashamed. "I'm sorry you felt that way about it. If I made the wrong assumption, I'm—"

She interrupted him, a thing she had never done before. "Don't worry, I managed to scotch any notion he might have that this was our first outing as a couple by inviting Polly Shackleford to come along."

Her father rolled his eyes. "That's enough punishment for any man to have to endure," he said. "I'm lucky Merriwell hasn't fled town already."

She saw that her father thought she was ready to make a joke of it. "Oh, that would be too bad, wouldn't it, if Merriwell suddenly disappeared? You'd be back to depending on your daughter for assistance, wouldn't you? A very poor second choice, I know!"

Tears flooded down her face now, unchecked—tears she'd been holding inside for far too long. "You never appreciated what was standing right in front of you, Papa—me! I may not be as perfect as Yancey Merriwell, but you could have at least tried to teach me," she said bitterly. "You never even considered that *I* could follow in your footsteps, after Eddie died."

Her father's face went white. For a long time he said nothing, just stared down at his shoes. Then he swallowed hard. "Faith, I suppose I'm rather traditional in how I see a woman's role in life. I thought you'd want what most women want, a husband and a family…"

"I do, Papa, I do. But until that man comes along—if he ever does—I could do something besides just helping Mama around the house, couldn't I? Milly Brookfield ran a ranch, and Sarah helped her. Caroline Wallace was a schoolteacher, until she met Jack—"

"What of your friend Prissy? Far as I could see, she was just a useless flibbertigibett until she met Sheriff Bishop," her father pointed out.

"But her father is wealthy, Papa, and even she wasn't content to be merely a decoration around the house. She got Sarah to teach her how to cook, and she administers funds for the Society for the Deserving Poor now…"

"All right, you want to be more useful, I understand that, but newspapering is a man's job. And I've already told you why I didn't consider having you assist me—"

"Oh, yes, my lack of grammar skills," she retorted. "Fine, treat Yancey Merriwell like he's your new son.

Just be sure and lock your cash drawer until you've known him a few more days, would you?"

"Faith Letticia Bennett!" her father roared. "That's enough! You have no reason to make such an outrageous slander!"

She'd never seen her father so angry—red-faced and shaking, a vein bulging in his temple. And then she remembered why he'd sought to hire an assistant in the first place. *What if their angry confrontation caused him to have a heart attack or an apoplexy such as Gil's father had suffered?*

"I—I'm sorry, Papa!" she cried, rushing forward, searching his face for any hint he was about to collapse. "I'm sorry," she repeated, reaching out a shaking hand. "I apologize. You're right. I had no basis for my accusations, just…" *Just jealousy that you care so much for a stranger, and can't see I need to feel important to you.*

Her father looked weary and a score of years older suddenly, but the high color was fading from his cheeks and his breathing slowing. "I forgive you, Faith," he said slowly. "I'm sorry if I…have seemed…overenthusiastic about Merriwell. I—I'm just trying to do the right thing by you and your mother, to assure your future…"

"I know… Are you all right, Papa? Not having any chest pains, are you?"

"I'm all right," he assured her. "The medicine Doc Walker gave me seems to be helping. Don't worry about me. Are you ready to go back home?"

And have her mother—or worse yet Merriwell—see her tear-swollen face?

"I think I'll stay here awhile, Papa," she murmured, and watched as he trudged away, his shoulders sagging.

Some moral, upright woman she was! What kind of loving daughter raged at a parent with a bad heart, even after what her father had done? Suddenly she felt guilt washing over her like flood waters, each wave swamping her with despair. *She was a selfish, horrible person—no wonder her father didn't love her!*

Then suddenly she was enfolded in warm, strong arms, and a familiar voice asked, "Faith? Faith, what's wrong? I heard you weeping… Please, sweetheart, don't cry…"

Gil. He had heard her weeping, and he had called her *sweetheart.* In a moment she would have to pull herself out of his arms and remind him of the reasons why he must not be holding her like this, but right now she just couldn't. It felt too comforting.

Chapter Fourteen

Gil was sure nothing he'd ever experienced felt as good as holding this woman in his arms, stroking her hair, feeling the deep shuddering sobs gradually subside into regular breathing. But he needed to find out why she had been keening like her heart was breaking within her. *Had someone died?* Dr. Walker had confided that Mr. Bennett's heart wasn't strong, and had asked him to pray for the man, but Gil thought he'd seen Faith's father walking away from the creek moments ago as Gil had left the parsonage and descended the creek bank.

He thought back to his encounter with Faith and that new employee of Mr. Bennett, Yancey Merriwell, earlier in the day—of the mocking smile on Merriwell's face as he'd proudly proclaimed himself a "free-thinker"—which was another word for pagan as far as Gil could see. He hadn't missed the gleam in the Georgian's eyes as he'd gazed at Faith, either, and it had made him sick at heart. *Had Merriwell—*

"Was it your father's new employee, Faith? Did that man hurt you somehow? He didn't—"

"No, Merriwell didn't do anything..." she wailed, crying again, and he held her while the storm raged, relieved that at least he wasn't going to have to pound Merriwell into a bloody pulp.

"Then what has you so upset, Faith?"

Then it all tumbled out, what she'd said to her father, how her father had asked Merriwell to take Faith to dinner at the hotel without consulting her on the matter, how she'd accused her father of favoring his new employee over his own daughter, how Faith felt her father had never valued her. How she'd feared her anger would make her father keel over dead because of his weak heart.

"Mr. Bennett seemed all right to me, Faith," he said. Then when her gaze sharpened, he said, "I didn't eavesdrop on your conversation. I happened to step outside the parsonage and spotted him walking away toward your house."

Faith seemed somewhat reassured by that, so he gathered his courage and went on, selecting his words with care. The last thing he wanted to do was help widen the rift between father and daughter, even though he thought Mr. Bennett had been clumsy with Faith's feelings and foolish not to use her help when she was so eager to give it.

"I'm sure your father forgives you for what you said, just as you forgive him for telling Merriwell to take you to dinner without asking you, don't you? It was clever of you to make use of Polly's sudden appearance, though. I'll bet she's never thought of herself as a chaperone, did she?"

That coaxed a smile from Faith, as he'd been hoping. "The poor man hardly got a word in edgewise after Polly started talking," she told him. "Poor Polly. She seemed to like the man, but I'm sure he'll steer clear of her now."

They were quiet for a time, the only sounds coming from the chirping of crickets and the occasional splash of a fish below.

"I—I violated one of the Commandments, didn't I?" she asked suddenly, startling him. "The one about honoring one's father and mother?"

"The fifth Commandment," he murmured automatically. He wondered why she cared, if she didn't believe in the Giver of the Commandments, but even nonbelievers had consciences.

"Yes, by speaking angrily to your father, I suppose you did, but on the other hand, you wouldn't have been 'honoring' him by going along with something you feel to be wrong, or turning a blind eye to his trusting a man who may or may not be worthy of that trust. And in Ephesians the Lord tells fathers not to 'provoke their children to wrath,'" he told her. "Would you like me to talk to him about Merriwell, see if I could help?" Gil wasn't at all sure how Faith's father would feel about a man scarcely older than his daughter counseling him, but he *was* the town's pastor.

"No, I don't think Papa will steer Merriwell toward me again, now that I've made my feelings clear," she said. "But thanks. I suppose I ought to tell Papa again I'm sorry for yelling at him, though."

"You'll sleep better if you do," he agreed. "But, Faith, none of us gets through life without making mistakes—violations of the Commandments, if you will. That's why we need a Savior."

Faith's face took on a guarded look and she turned away.

I've gone too far, Gil thought. He didn't want her to leave, even if it was getting dark.

"I—I'd better go," she said. "I—I'm sorry for wetting your shirt," she added, pointing to his damp shirt front with an attempt at a smile.

"I'm not sorry," he assured her. "Anytime you want to talk—or cry—I'll be here for you, Faith."

Faith was full of conflicting emotions as she walked in the gathering darkness the short distance from the creek to her home. While he'd been comforting her as she wept, Gil had called her sweetheart.

Did he regret saying it, the moment the word had passed his lips, knowing it contradicted the stance he had taken about a relationship between the two of them?

Yet despite that, she had reveled in the word. *Sweetheart.* No matter how little sense it made in light of their conflicting philosophies, she would not have him unsay it for the world.

Because she loved him.

It was as simple as that, and as complex. Because what was she going to do about it, knowing he believed in a God that cared about humankind, while she had believed if there was a God, He didn't care about the people He'd supposedly created?

She wanted to believe, if only to be worthy of Gil. But that wasn't enough, was it?

What was that Scripture verse he had quoted? *Lord, I believe. Help thou mine unbelief.*

What would happen if she prayed that prayer, not knowing if there was anyone up there to hear it? Was it a lie to say she believed when the strength of her belief was so tiny it almost didn't exist at all?

With God, all things are possible.

Where had that *come from?* She'd learned the verse at her mother's knee long ago.

If nothing was impossible, why hadn't Eddie lived? a voice hissed within her.

She didn't know, she couldn't know, and for once, for this moment, it was all right. Peace settled over her as she reached the front porch of her house. Peace, and assurance that somehow, she and Gil would find a way.

"Oh, there you are, Faith. I was beginning to get worried," her mother said at the door, her familiar figure backlit by the lamp still burning in the parlor. "Are you all right, dear? Your papa said you were upset, but that you were going to stay by the creek a few minutes…"

"Is he…okay?"

Her mother nodded. "He was tired and he went to bed, but he seemed all right. Maybe a little worried about you, that's all."

Faith winced inwardly. "I—I said some things I shouldn't have said," she admitted. "I told him I was sorry, but…" She felt tears threatening to spill again, but she willed them away with steely resolve. She had cried enough for one night.

"Faith, I know why you were angry and I understand," her mother said. "To some extent, I agree with you about how your father's been acting about Mr. Merriwell. I don't think he realized it, Faith, but he does now."

"He—he does?" That he had talked to her mother about it spoke volumes.

Lydia Bennett nodded. "He never meant to hurt you by it, Faith. Oh, men can be oblivious sometimes to the way their actions affect their women, sure enough, and sometimes they underestimate what we can do, but when it comes right down to it, he's motivated by his love for us. He's worried about the future, Faith. He doesn't think I know about his visit with Dr. Walker, but I do."

Faith stared at her mother, startled by the quiet words. The woman had betrayed no hint of her knowledge before.

"Dr. Walker thought I should know," her mother went on, "so I could be alert for symptoms that might indicate his heart is getting worse—shortness of breath, chest pains, swelling in his feet… So I can make sure he doesn't get too tired, without his knowing I'm being watchful." She sighed. "Men do have their pride, you know."

Faith glanced into the parlor before speaking again. It was empty, but she lowered her voice a notch nevertheless. "Mama, what do *you* think about Yancey Merriwell?"

Her mother studied Faith before replying. "I'm still making up my mind. Oh, he's a little full of himself, right enough, but that may be all it is. Until I know one way or another, though, I've moved the household money your papa gives me, and that gold pocket watch your papa never remembers to wear, to a safe place." Her mother winked.

Her commonsense approach was so comforting, so typical of her mother, that Faith impulsively hugged her. "I love you, Mama."

"I love you, too, dear. Did you get things all settled in your head, down by the creek?"

Faith found herself smiling. "Gil helped a bit," she said. "He…happened to see me down at the creek after Papa left, so he came down and we talked," she said.

"He's a good man, Faith."

"Yes…" Faith sighed. "But…"

"But?"

"How do you know if a man is…is the right one? And please don't tell me 'you just know,'" Faith said.

"All right, I won't," her mother said, smiling a little at Faith's vehemence. "I know that's not helpful when a body's trying to decide, even if it is true. But I will say in the end it's a leap of faith somewhat. You just have to jump, with enough confidence that you've made the right choice and that man will catch you."

Faith groaned. Did everything come down to faith in the end, the one thing she was in short supply of?

"Don't you talk about these things in Spinsters' Club meetings?" Lydia Bennett asked. "Seems to me the spinsters who have married are in a pretty good position to advise the rest of you."

It was a good suggestion. She'd be seeing the ladies day after tomorrow at the box social supper. Maybe during the setting-up time, she'd get a chance to talk to Milly, Sarah, Prissy and Caroline on this subject.

She suddenly remembered she hadn't done anything about decorating the box that would contain her supper or decided what to cook. Tomorrow, she had to get cracking!

Would Gil bid on her contribution, she wondered later as she tried to drift off into sleep, or would he feel he'd betrayed his stance about not courting a non-believer, and deliberately bid on someone—anyone—else's?

"And Lord, please watch over young Runs Like a Deer, and cause his leg to continue to heal," Gil prayed a few mornings later in the church sanctuary. He'd been thinking of the Indian boy this morning, and hoped his leg was on the mend. And that the Comanche band had moved on by now, so they were no longer a threat to the Simpson Creek area. "Thanks for all the blessings You bestow on us, and help us to show others how much You love them—particularly Faith. Lord, help her to believe in You—"

Behind him, he heard the church door creak open, and the sound of bootheels echoing on the plank flooring.

"Pardon me, Reverend…"

Gil opened his eyes and turned, seeing that the speaker was Luis Menendez, Sheriff Bishop's young deputy.

"Deputy Menendez, *buenas dias* to you. What can I do for you today?"

"*Buenas dias* to you, too, sir. Sheriff Bishop was wondering if you could come down to the jail for a few moments. Major McConley is there and wanted to speak to you about your recent experience with the Indians."

Gil sighed inwardly. Just when he had been hoping the cavalry's scrutiny would have shifted to something else…

"Of course, Deputy. Tell the sheriff I'll be right there. I just want to check on my father first." His father had been doing all right in the last few days without the presence of his spinster nurses, but Gil still kept a close eye on him.

He found the cavalry officer ensconced in the chair opposite Sam Bishop's desk, talking to the sheriff. The man straightened as Gil entered.

"Reverend Gil, thanks for coming down," Sam greeted him. "This is Major McConley, commanding officer for the nearby detachment of the U.S. Cavalry.

Major, Reverend Gil is our pastor at the Simpson Creek Church."

The cavalry officer extended his hand. "Reverend, an honor. But, Sheriff, I thought I'd met your preacher—isn't he an older man? I hope he didn't…"

"My father is recovering from the effects of an apoplexy, Major, that's caused him problems with speaking. I'm taking his place."

"I see. He's a fine man, your father. Please give him my best wishes for a return to complete health."

"Thank you, sir, I will."

The major peered at him closely. "Speaking of healing, you appear to be healing up from your scrape with the redskins, Reverend. Sheriff Bishop tells me you were quite the worse for wear."

Gil nodded. "I thank God I was able to escape. Have you…found any sign of the Comanches?"

The major shook his head. "Nary a trace, but there's so much ground to cover…we could have just missed it. Folks still need to be careful."

"But I'm told they're a wandering people," Gil said. "Maybe they moved camp right after they attacked me."

Gil saw the major's eyes narrow and hoped he hadn't come across as a little too eager to believe the Indians were gone. He'd have to wonder why.

"It's true that the hunting and raiding bands range widely," McConley acknowledged. "Sheriff Bishop tells me you started out riding north, but when you ran into the Indians you just let the horse pick his direction and concentrated on escape. Natural enough, I suppose. Can you remember markings on their lances or arrows, or the feathers in their hair, anything like that? That can be distinct to a particular band, and our scouts—often Indians of other tribes or half-breeds—can sometimes identify the band from those markings. Did they wear warpaint? Did their horses? Any particular hairstyle, or I was hoping you'd remembered something else about your experience, something that might help us narrow down the area to search."

Gil thought hard. "It all happened so fast… No, they weren't wearing warpaint nor were their horses painted. Some of them had feathers dangling from their lances, some didn't. Their hair was loose and long, as I recall. I didn't see any of the arrows, but they had quivers of them on their backs."

The major's pale eyes gave nothing away. "That's all you can recall?"

"Yes, I'm afraid so. All my energies were concentrated on escape."

Bishop rubbed his chin and exchanged glances with the major.

"Very well, Reverend," the major said, rising. "I figured it wouldn't hurt to try to see if you'd recollected anything more than what you told Sheriff Bishop before. Appreciate your time, sir."

The three men walked outside together to where the major's mount with its distinctive cavalry saddle was tethered to the hitching post. Gil wondered yet again if he'd done the right thing by being less than truthful with the cavalry officer. He didn't want to save the Indian boy at the expense of the townspeople's safety, but he knew that far too often, the army's version of controlling the Indians had resulted in wholesale slaughter of Indian women and children.

"If you think of anything else, Reverend, Sheriff Bishop knows how to get hold of me," McConley said, extending a hand.

"Go with God, Major," Gil said. He knew that the other man was aware he had made no promise.

"Oh, there you are, Reverend," a man's voice called, and Gil looked up and beheld Yancey Merriwell bearing down on them, pencil at the ready and notebook in hand. "I was wondering if I might get that interview now."

There was plenty Gil wanted to say to Merriwell, but none of it had to do with his Indian encounter, so it was probably best to forestall the encounter until he could control his ire. He noticed that the newspaperman's gaze distracted by the sight of the splendidly uniformed cavalryman preparing to mount his horse, and saw his opportunity for escape.

"Oh, you can interview me anytime, Mr. Merriwell," Gil said with a breezy wave. "Why not talk to Major McConley here while you have the chance? I'll warrant he has some fascinating tales of the frontier to share with your readers."

He saw by the spark of interest in Merriwell's eyes he had been successful in his attempt at distraction.

"True enough, I suppose," Merriwell drawled. "Very well, then, Major, I'm Yancey Merriwell, new associate editor with the *Simpson Creek Chronicle*. Might I have a few moments of your time?"

Gil glanced behind him as he strode away, and felt only a little guilty as he saw the annoyed expression on the major's face.

Chapter Fifteen

Adorning little boxes—or in this case a lidded basket her mother let her borrow for the purpose—was not her forte, Faith thought, surveying the box of fabric scraps in her mother's workroom. There was nothing she could see that would really make the box distinctively hers. And how on earth did one attach the fabric to the basket? She'd seen such boxes before because box socials were a staple of small-town events, but she'd never examined one close-up. Did one have to stitch the fabric to the box somehow?

At least the supper inside the box would be something other than the usual fried chicken. There would be plenty of that popular main dish because it was so easy to prepare ahead, yet still tasted delicious cold. She wanted to make something unexpected, something that would cause the winner to appreciate her originality, yet was still as tasty as fried chicken.

What else tasted good cold? *Ham.* She'd made ham croquettes once under her mother's tutelage and they'd come out well…ham croquettes it would be. Her mother readily agreed to let Faith slice off a portion of the smoked ham hanging in their springhouse. She would prepare it in the morning so she would be available in the afternoon to help the other spinsters set up and decorate the tables in the churchyard for the box social. She'd fill the rest of the basket with slices of fresh-baked bread, coleslaw and angel food cake with peach topping.

She only hoped Gil liked ham as well as the rest of her selections. But would he be the one who bid on her decorated box? Maybe he'd feel that bidding on it would be tantamount to a declaration he was not willing to make, now or maybe ever, as long as she continued in her state of disbelief.

Goodness, what if he didn't bid for her decorated box, and no one else bid, either? How embarrassing that would be!

But she was putting the cart before the horse, she reminded herself. Before a lack of bids could even be a problem, she needed to have a decorated box to offer. But there was nothing in this box of fabric scraps that appealed. Should she go see if Mrs. Patterson had any pretty remnants of calico or gingham to adorn it? She had a few coins saved in a tiny porcelain box in her chest of drawers...

Inspiration struck. She'd already selected a dress to wear to the event, one of willowy green with three rows of a slightly darker green lace starting at each shoulder and ending in a vee at her waist. It had been made for her by Milly Brookfield, who had cut out the pattern at her sister Sarah's house, where she was staying for a few days. Was it possible Sarah kept fabric scraps as Faith's mother did and still had some left?

Folding the dress over her arm and clutching the box, Faith fairly flew up the street to Sarah and Dr.

Walker's house, hoping it wasn't an inconvenient time to be visiting.

She was in luck, for it so happened Sarah had put little Elizabeth down for a nap moments ago and was delighted to see her—even more so when Faith explained the reason for her visit.

Sarah looked at the dress and her face brightened. "Yes, I do have the remnants from that dress. Before little Elizabeth came along, I'd been thinking about making a quilt with the scraps I had. I suppose I thought I'd have all kinds of time while the baby napped." She chuckled. "How silly of me! When I'm not feeding Elizabeth, I'm doing her laundry," she said, nodding toward the window that faced the backyard, where a score of cloths and an assortment of baby clothes flapped in the spring sunshine. "Or cooking meals so my dear Nolan doesn't starve. Then before I know it—" she waved a hand "—it's time to go to bed and I wonder where the day has gone."

Faith clapped a hand over her mouth. "Goodness, I'm sorry. I never stopped to think how busy you must be. If you could just point me toward the scraps, I'll see if you have a big enough piece for the basket and let you get back to whatever you need to be doing."

Now Sarah laughed out loud. "Don't you dare think you're going to just waltz out of here without a good chat! Nolan's been out on a call at one of the ranches, and I'm fairly starved for adult company, especially of the female variety. No, sit right down there," she said, pointing to a chair by the table, "and I'll go get the sack. If I remember right, there's not only plenty to cover your basket, but enough of the matching lace to trim it with, too. Faith Bennett, we are going to make you the prettiest decorated box in the history of box socials."

"But what if Elizabeth wakes?" Faith asked uneasily, with a glance at the slumbering baby in the cradle a few feet away.

"Then I'll nurse her and then you can hold her while I work. This will be fun!" Sarah enthused. "I'll just put the kettle on to boil for tea before I fetch the fabric."

"So, are you hoping Gil will bid on your basket?" Sarah asked some minutes later, while Faith was cutting the fabric remnant to fit the basket under the other woman's direction.

Faith shrugged and kept her eyes on the scissors and the cloth. "I don't know," she said. "Maybe...but we're so different, Sarah. I don't know if it's a good idea..."

"Nonsense, Faith. It's as plain as piecrust Reverend Gil is sweet on you. And opposites attract, don't they? Look at my sister—who'd have thought she'd wed a British aristocrat? And I was so sure I could never love a Yankee, remember? Yet those very differences make for the most interesting marriages, we've both found."

Faith winced inwardly. Sarah couldn't know that the difference between Gil and her ran much deeper than nationality or regionalism. Without commenting, she held out the trimmed piece of cotton cloth.

Sarah took it, then studied Faith. "Or perhaps you're more interested in your papa's new assistant? Polly says he's very handsome." Sarah's tone was teasing and her blue eyes danced with mischief.

Faith raised horrified eyes. "Not if he was the last man in the whole state of Texas!"

"I'm relieved to hear it." Sarah took an egg from a bowl on the sideboard and expertly separating the white from the yolk. Using the tip of her little finger, she dabbed egg white along the edges of the box, then pressed the fabric into the homemade glue. "He doesn't seem your type at all." Her baby began to fuss, and Sarah turned to the cradle.

Certainly Merriwell wasn't her type, but Sarah would be shocked if she knew that both of them were nonbelievers.

Sarah picked up baby Elizabeth, placed her against her chest, patting her back and swaying from side to side. "She often half wakes up like that before she's had a good long sleep, but I can often soothe her back into slumber this way."

Faith marveled at her friend's ease with her baby. Only weeks ago, Sarah had been so unsure of her ability to take care of a baby, but now she seemed to be a natural at motherhood. Would *she* be so competent with a baby? Again, an unbidden image of a child of hers and Gil's, with Gil hovering in the background, rose in her mind.

She dismissed the thought. "I think I can do the trim now that I've seen how you do it," she said, lifting the darker green lace from the box.

"We'll be coming to the box social, too, so I suppose I ought to put some thought into decorating a box myself," Sarah mused. "Though of course Nolan would bid on mine even if I wrapped it in brown paper." She laughed. "I think he's too much the frugal Yankee to understand decorating what is, after all, only a container of food. So tell me, what treats are you fixing for yours?"

Faith described her menu as she cut the lace and glued it to her basket lid to match the V pattern of the lace on her dress's bodice.

"It sounds delicious," Sarah commented, then looked flustered as Elizabeth, contrary to what her mother had said, not only refused to go back to sleep but began to wail in earnest.

Faith had planned to stay long enough to keep Sarah company while her friend worked on her own box, but soon it became apparent that the baby wasn't going to settle down anytime soon.

"I suppose I'd better go," she said regretfully. "Thanks for helping me, Sarah."

"Sorry Elizabeth's so fussy," Sarah said, lowering herself into the rocking chair and preparing to feed her baby. "But I was happy to help. I'll be interested to see what happens tomorrow afternoon at the social. Pray about what you should do, Faith. I promise that will help."

If only Faith could be sure of that, too.

Saturday afternoon, Gil, who'd been going over the church accounts at the kitchen table, heard his father chuckling in the study. He'd thought the old man was still napping in his bedroom, but instead found him standing by the window that gave a view of the church-yard.

"What's so funny, Papa?" he asked, coming to stand behind him. He followed his father's gaze.

Earlier, several of the youths of the town had laid wooden planks on sawhorses to serve as tables, and lugged benches from the social hall to both sides of each one for seating. They'd been paid in cookies and lemonade, courtesy of Sarah Walker. Now, Gil saw, there were several ladies from the Spinsters' Club scurrying around, spreading tablecloths and pinning bows at intervals along the sides of the benches and at the ends of the tables. Others carried out armloads of decorated

boxes and set them out on a table on two sides of a mul-
ticolored china bowl.

Polly Shackleford stood in the midst of it all, pointing here and there and yelling orders through cupped
hands. He spotted Faith working near the end of one
table, looking slender and lovely in a light green dress
that reminded him of spring.

Cautiously, Gil raised the window, not wanting the
ladies to know they were observed—not that they could
have heard the creak of a window over Polly's screech-
ing.

"No, no, Ella!" he heard her snap, when one of the
ladies started to put a last box to the right of the bowl,
"I said, the single ladies' boxes should be on the right,
the married ladies' on the left. We want to make things
easy for the auctioneer, don't we?"

The young woman being corrected protested, "But
I can't tell one box from the other, Polly. The only one
I'm sure of is the one I decorated."

Polly's exasperated sigh was so loud Gil could hear
it from the parsonage window. "The whole purpose of
having the boxes on separate sides is so we can auction off the married ladies' contributions first, because
one can assume only their husbands will be bidding on
them," Polly told the other woman. "Then we can get
on to the more interesting bidding for the spinsters'
dinners. The married ladies have presumably informed
their spouses which box they decorated, but as for us
spinsters, remember, ladies, no one is to give any of the
gentlemen a hint about which decorated box is hers,
do you hear? Not that it takes much guessing when it
comes to *your* contribution, Faith," she accused, pointing at one of the boxes, then at Faith's dress. "How very
obvious of you to decorate your supper box to match

your dress. Don't you know that men like a little mystery, a little surprise?"

He saw Faith bite her lip and could imagine her annoyance at Polly's condescending tone. And from the resentful looks on several other faces, she wasn't alone. Mutiny was brewing among the ranks of the Spinsters' Club.

"*I'd* think men like to know who they're going to sit with, Polly," Maude Harkey retorted. "That's how box socials are always run. You stop picking on Faith and Ella or we'll unelect you president."

Gil closed the window, not wanting to hear any more. He turned to his father. "Sounds like this is going to be an interesting event."

His father nodded, and pointed at Polly, who was pointing a finger at Maude. "B-bossy...g-g-girl."

Gil chuckled. "I can't help but agree. I only hope I don't have to go break up a fight out there." The clock struck the hour of four just then, and Gil glanced up at it. "We'd better spruce ourselves up now if we're going to attend, right? You still want me to bid on Mrs. Detwiler's supper box for you, don't you? There's sure to be chocolate cake in it."

A caterpillar metamorphosing into a butterfly was no more startling of a transformation, Faith thought, than the instant change to Polly's demeanor when the first trio of cowboys showed up at the churchyard. The strident, officious tyrant vanished in an instant, to be replaced with a smiling, sweet-voiced charmer who added "please" to every request.

"Well, hello, gentlemen!" she cooed, as three cowboys tied their horses to the hitching rail. "Have you come for the box social?"

"Yes, ma'am," one of them said shyly. "We got that advertisement the boy brung out to the Lazy O."

"Well, you're certainly welcome!" Polly proclaimed. "You're a bit early, but feel free to take a seat or mingle with our ladies. But you must be thirsty after your ride into town. Faith, won't you please pour them some lemonade?"

As Faith moved to comply, she thought how Polly was almost pretty when she relaxed and stopped ordering folks around. Perhaps she'd catch the eye of one of these ranch hands—although the spinsters had discovered most cowboys weren't really looking to settle down. They just liked a good party with respectable females now and then, because the only other type they usually met were saloon girls. But if one of them flirted with Polly, at least it would keep her from bothering Gil. Faith handed out glasses of lemonade and responded courteously and automatically to the cowboys' thanks, while a part of her longed for Gil to appear. Meanwhile, couples and other cowboys began to arrive, as did Delbert Perry, the former drunkard who had become the town's odd-job man.

As if summoned by her thoughts, Gil crossed the lawn with his father, then helped the old man to sit at one of the benches.

Gil's gaze sought Faith out. "Hello, Miss Faith," he called. "Fine weather for the social, isn't it? There's even a nice breeze."

Before she could even reply, however, Mrs. Detwiler, bearing a box decorated with rickrack in a rainbow of gaudy colors, plopped herself down next to Reverend Chadwick.

"How are you, Reverend? You're lookin' fit as a fiddle!" she crowed, loud enough to be heard halfway down the street. "I'm gonna just give you this box out-right, because I know it's the one you always want."

Polly looked like she'd swallowed a june bug side-wise, Faith thought.

"But Mrs. Detwiler, the decorator of each box is sup-posed to be a secret!" Polly protested.

"Nonsense, girl, I've been making my supper box for the rev'rend at box socials since before you were old enough to put your hair up," Mrs. Detwiler said with a sniff. "And don't try to tell me our preachers have to bid, neither," she added. "It ain't like a man a' the cloth has a lot a' spare pennies lyin' around."

Faith tried to suppress a grin. Polly had certainly met her match, for Mrs. Detwiler had been bossing the town around since the days when her late husband was the preacher, so she wasn't about to be dictated to by the likes of Polly Shackleford.

"Well, of course Reverend Chadwick doesn't have to *actually* pay," Polly assured her, "because of his age and the respect we all have for him…"

"I can afford to pay for one of the supper boxes," Gil murmured, obviously trying to spread oil on troubled waters. "But you'd asked me to judge the decorating, back when Papa was ill—perhaps he could do that in-stead, because he's doing so well now?"

"Of course," Polly said. "What a lovely idea… Now we have that settled, we need an auctioneer. Reverend Gil, would you be willing to do that?"

Faith thought Gil hesitated for a moment before he said, "Certainly, but I'm wishing to bid, too. May I still do that if I'm auctioneering?"

"I suppose there is no reason why not because you must have a supper to eat, too," Polly said, fluttering her lashes at Gil in a way that made Faith want to utter an unladylike snort. "Perhaps I could give you a hint which one I decorated?"

Because Polly's coy question was so patently opposite of the position she'd spouted earlier, it was all Faith could do to smother her indignation.

Gil looked uncomfortable, then relieved as Mayor Gilmore beckoned him over to their table. "Excuse me, ladies," he murmured as he left them.

Polly looked momentarily discomfited at not receiving an answer, but then the direction of her gaze changed. "Why, hello, Mr. Merriwell," she simpered.

Faith looked up to see the dapperly dressed Georgian making his way toward them. He had obviously come with her mother and father, but the couple had stopped at another table to speak with Mrs. Patterson.

Yancey greeted everyone and was introduced to Mrs. Detwiler and Reverend Chadwick. He was his most effusive, charming self, but Faith guessed from the skeptical look in the older woman's eye, Mrs. Detwiler wasn't taken in.

"You look familiar, Mr. Merriwell," she muttered. "Ever been to San Antone? I was just there visitin' my niece…"

Was it Faith's imagination or had the Georgian paled slightly?

Mrs. Detwiler clapped her hands. "I know what it is—you look just like a feller I saw sellin' snake oil to a pack a' gullible fools."

"I've never been to San Antonio, madam," Merriwell said stiffly. "And I'm a newspaperman, not a charlatan."

"Oh, they say everyone has a double," Mrs. Detwiler said, not the least put out by the Georgian's cool tone. "Don't think nothin' of it."

Merriwell's gaze slid back to Polly and then to Faith.

"I've come to cover the first social event since my arrival, ladies," he announced. "But I confess I am also looking forward to bidding on the supper box you put together, Miss Faith." He nodded toward the table, where her box with the others of the Spinsters' Club.

Faith had been irritated when he'd returned to the house on some pretext this morning and found her preparing the ham croquettes. She was sure he'd seen the waiting box on the kitchen table, too. She didn't want him bidding on her entry and then being forced to sit beside him and share it.

Merriwell went on, "I'm very partial to h—"

Faith quickly put up a hand to halt his words. "You must say no more, Mr. Merriwell. Our president," she said, nodding at Polly, "has said we must preserve the mystery and not reveal who decorated which box. I fear you're disqualified to bid on mine in any case by having seen it during the preparation stages." She desperately hoped that because she'd appeared to support Polly's insistence on keeping the makers' identities secret, the other woman wouldn't argue the rule she'd just made up.

"I'm sure there's no such rule," Polly said flatly, dashing Faith's hopes. "Mr. Merriwell, you feel free to bid as you wish. I *had* rather been hoping you'd like to bid on mine, though," she murmured, with an air of graceful defeat.

The nerve of the woman, after just offering to give Gil a hint about which one she'd made, Faith thought, taking a breath before embarrassing Polly in front of Merriwell.

A true lady must remain above the fray, Faith remembered her mother saying, and shut her mouth again.

How inconvenient to have remembered that stricture at this moment.

Merriwell looked uncomfortable again. He could not very well say he much preferred to win Faith's supper box. It would not be chivalrous. "I am beset by two very appealing choices," he said at last. "I shall just have to hope the fates guide me to the right one."

Chapter Sixteen

"It's time for the judging of the decorated supper boxes, everyone," Polly announced a few minutes later. She was in her glory as mistress of ceremonies. "To be followed by the gentlemen bidding on them. Reverend Chadwick, will you come forward and do the honors?"

Assisted by Gil, the old man made his slow way to the front, leaning heavily on his cane, but Faith recalled the day the preacher had been struck down by his stroke and had hung on to life by the merest thread. Perhaps if there *was* a God who cared about people—*some* people, Faith thought, He certainly cared for this man.

"Now, sir, all you need to do is look at all the boxes on this table and indicate which one you think is the most beautifully decorated. There will be a prize for the one you pick—a free dress length of the fabric of your choice at the mercantile. Thank you for that donation, Mrs. Patterson."

As Faith watched, the old preacher bent low over the supper box-laden table, his gaze touching each one of the boxes. There were boxes decorated in all shades of the rainbow, some embellished with ribbons, some with lace, a few with designs made of buttons or beads. Some boxes displayed more decorating skill than others. At last he picked a box decorated to look like the Lone Star flag of Texas.

"Th-this one," he said, pointing to it. "Th' w-winner."

Maude Harkey stood and took a bow. "Thank you, Reverend!"

The old man beamed at her amid the applause.

Gil assisted his father back to his seat, then returned to the front.

"It's time to start the bidding, gentlemen," Polly said. "Please be ready to drop your money into the bowl here, for we will not be able to take your I.O.Us." There was much good-natured groaning from the cowboys and a couple of the husbands. "Remember, this money goes to the Fund for the Deserving Poor of Simpson Creek." She took a deep breath. "Reverend Chadwick will auction off the boxes from this side of the bowl first," Polly declared. "These are the boxes provided by the married ladies. You husbands, I trust you know which one your wife made—if you know what's good for you."

There were snickers from the married ladies.

"Remember, gentlemen, you are to wait until all the boxes have been claimed before you commence to devouring yours—or perhaps I should have said, sharing it with the lady who made it. Reverend, you may begin."

Gil took hold of a pretty box trimmed with gathered ruffles and held it up. "Husbands, who would like to bid for this first supper box? Remember to be generous because the money all goes to charity…"

"Looks like the one I saw my Mary Louise stitchin'," a rawboned rancher called out. "I'll bid two bits."

Beside him, his wife bristled. "Henry Robert Priddy,

you are the stingiest man in San Saba County! You'd better bid more than that or I'll give it away."

Grinning, the man raised his arm again. "All right, I was jes' joshin' with you, Mary Lou. Four bits, then."

Mollified, his wife settled down.

"Are there any other competing bids?" Gil asked.

Of course there were none, so Priddy ambled up to claim his prize.

The bidding proceeded, and soon each of the married ladies' decorated boxes had been auctioned off. Coins spilled from Polly's fingers and clinked against the sides as she dipped her fingers in the bowl.

"Now I'm sure we bachelors can do better than this," Gil said with a wink at the single men, who all sat together in the seats to the left of the auction table. "After all, we don't have the expense of a family with youngsters to support, so let's see some generous bidding!"

It was time for Polly to sit down and let Gil proceed, but instead she dimpled prettily and remained standing by Gil. "We will do things a little differently for the bachelors," she called out, her voice sweetly pitched. "As each supper box is bidden for and won by one lucky bidder, the lady who decorated the box and filled it with delicious goodies will go to sit by the gentleman who won it." She smiled as the cowboys stomped and cheered at the prospect of each having a lady to call his own, at least while the social went on.

"And something else I was thinking, Reverend," she went on, "I had previously suggested that the identities of the box decorators be unknown—"

Suggested? The spinsters exchanged amused glances, and Ella looked like she wanted to shout the truth.

"—so that the bidders would be unbiased, but perhaps we could raise more money for this most worthy charity if each designer was known. Would any of you ladies object?" she asked with wide-eyed and completely false sincerity.

Faith knew exactly what had motivated Polly's changed opinion, and from the knowing glances thrown her way by the other spinsters, they had guessed it, too. Polly hadn't had the chance to hint to Gil or Merriwell which box was her creation, whereas it would be rather obvious that the one decorated like Faith's dress was made by her. Polly was afraid that neither Gil nor Merriwell would know which box was hers when its turn to be auctioned came, and she could end up sitting with one of the grinning cowboys, rather than Gil or Merriwell, as she hoped.

Faith felt sorry for Gil and even for Merriwell, for she could tell neither of them really wanted to share supper with the pushy girl. Now that the identity of each contributor would be known, neither man could take polite refuge in ignorance. Faith knew as sure as she was sitting there that Polly would make both men feel guilty with her entreating, possibly teary, gaze if one of them, at least, did not bid on her supper box. She'd already made sure each man knew she wanted him to win her contribution. What would they do?

Faith was afraid Gil would bid on Polly's supper box just to be kind, and end up the lone bidder. He'd be stuck eating supper with Polly. Then Merriwell would be free to bid on *hers*. Faith was sure she didn't want to have the meal she'd worked so hard on bought by Yancey Merriwell, and be forced to sit with him, enduring his overdone gallantry. Even though he'd been the perfect, respectful gentleman at home since she'd made her feelings clear to her father, she'd much prefer the company of anyone else—the homeliest of the cowboys or a character such as Delbert Perry.

She studied the table carefully as Gil raised the first of the spinsters' supper boxes—the one made by her cousin Louisa. She'd noticed when Gil auctioned the boxes made by the wives, he'd started with the boxes at the front of the table, and progressed by rows until the last boxes in the back had been taken.

Polly's box, a lovely thing adorned with a design of a rose embroidered on cloth and embellished by tiny red beads, sat one row ahead of Faith's. Faith's was the last box.

Oh, dear. That was unfortunate, for if Gil was maneuvered into bidding on Polly's supper box and there was no opposing bid, Merriwell would be free to win hers.

She was certain then that Polly had arranged the boxes thus deliberately.

Polly turned then, and as if reading Faith's mind, flashed a smirk at her.

Oh, well, Faith thought, resigning herself. It was only a box social, and it meant nothing in terms of her future. She had no claim on Gil after all—hadn't they both been of the opinion that they would not suit because she was a nonbeliever? She could make polite conversation with Yancey Merriwell for the time it took to eat the ham croquette supper. After all, her parents were sitting nearby—it wasn't as if the Georgian would dare to behave improperly.

But her heart would have none of her resignation, and suddenly she was aware of Gil's eyes on hers. She could tell he shared her misgivings.

He resumed auctioning off the boxes. Maude Harkey's fetched a nice price and the cowboy who won it had an appealing grin, even if he was bowlegged. The supper boxes made by Kate Patterson and Ella Justiss, two of the newer spinsters, were won by a pair of cowhands from a ranch near Lampasas. Jane Jeffries's box went to a redheaded fellow from the Lazy O. Then Gil picked up Polly's box.

"Who made this pretty rose-decorated box?" Gil said, holding it up. Faith thought his smile flattened somewhat, as if he already knew. He opened it. "Mmm, fried chicken and pecan pie. You fellows who haven't won a supper box ought to be sure and bid on this one."

Faith saw Polly smile brighten. "Why, I did, Reverend Gil, and I promise you, it's the best fried chicken you'll ever eat." She fluttered her lashes at him till Faith wanted to ask her if a speck of dust had blown into her eye.

"Hear that, gentlemen? Who doesn't love fried chicken? What am I to bid?" he asked, but he looked directly at Merriwell. The Georgian grinned as if he knew exactly the fix Gil was in.

Silence reigned. Polly Shackleford began to squirm.

"I'll bid ten cents!" called out Delbert Perry. "It's surely worth more'n that, but that's all I got in my pocket."

Polly went red. Faith knew she wanted to object, but there was no graceful way she could.

"A quarter," Gil said quietly, probably more for Delbert's sake than Polly's.

"Three bits," the Georgian said in a drawl that was more like a purr.

"Oh, come on now, fellows," Gil chided them all. "This box is worth more than that, and it's all for the sake of *charity*."

"I'll bid an eagle," called out a voice from the back,

and everyone turned as one to see who had bid a ten-dollar gold piece.

Faith thought she'd seen the ordinary-looking fellow before, but she couldn't place him. He stood at the back wearing travel-dusty trousers and holding his hat, and his eyes never left Polly.

Polly jumped up. "Bob!" she cried. "What are you doing here?" Her face was suffused with joy.

"I've come back t' claim you, if you'll still have me, Polly Shackleford. Leavin' you was the biggest mistake I ever made."

Then Faith knew who the man was—Bob Henshaw, the druggist who'd answered a Spinsters' Club advertisement sometime back. He'd taken a shine to Polly at Prissy Gilmore's barbecue, and they'd seemed to be destined for the altar. But then he'd claimed he was homesick and fled back to Austin.

"I reckon I got scairt a' what a big step marryin' was," Henshaw confessed. "But Maw died last month, and I reckoned I'd been a pure fool to leave you like I did. Will you let me buy your supper box at least, and we kin sit together and talk about courtin' again?"

"Of course!" Polly called, and went flying into Bob Henshaw's arms. "Oh, how I've missed you!"

"Ain't that sweet?" Mrs. Detwiler opined loudly, and everyone chuckled as the grinning Henshaw, his arm around Polly's waist, walked to the front and plunked his ten-dollar gold piece into the china bowl with a re-sounding *clang*.

In the midst of the celebration, Milly Brookfield arrived in her buckboard. It was driven by one of her cowhands, and after she'd descended, baby Nicholas in her arms, he turned the wagon and headed into town.

Milly slipped into a seat beside Sarah, and Faith heard her whisper she was sorry to be late.

Faith glanced at Gil. He smiled at the happy couple, but there was a worried set to his jaw now.

Faith knew why. With Polly enjoying a reunion with her former suitor, there was nothing to keep Merriwell from bidding on Faith's supper box now. And something about the Georgian's stylish clothes made Faith think he had deeper pockets than a small-town preacher, despite the sad tale of impoverishment back in Atlanta he'd told her father.

There were two other spinsters' boxes to bid on, and those were bought quickly by one remaining cowboy and Delbert Perry.

Everyone sat up straighter, aware that only one supper box was left, but two men. It would be a duel between the Georgian and the preacher.

"Last but not least, a supper box whose ornamentation bears a striking resemblance to Miss Faith Bennett's dress. Might you have decorated this one, Miss Faith?" he asked with a wink.

Faith nodded, not trusting her voice.

Gil lifted the lid. "Ham croquettes," he said. "They look delicious, Miss Faith. I'll start the bidding at fifty cents."

"Ham croquettes—my favorite dish, as it happens," Yancey Merriwell drawled. "A dollar."

"A dollar and twenty-five cents," countered Gil.

"Two dollars."

"Two dollars and fifty cents."

By the time Merriwell bid five dollars, the cowboys were hooting and clapping, but the townsfolk glared at the Georgian and clucked their tongues in disapproval. Murmurs arose about a lack of respect toward a man of the cloth. They wanted their preacher to win supper with the lady of his choice and knew he didn't have endless funds to do so. Faith even noticed her father give his employee a sharp look, but Merriwell seemed oblivious.

Gil's eagerness to win the bidding warmed Faith's heart, but she too knew he couldn't afford it. The salary the town's preacher received was sufficient to cover their food and clothing needs and not much else, and at that they were fortunate. Some preachers had to ride a circuit or take other jobs to supplement their income.

Oh, Gil, just stop bidding, she thought. *This is foolishness. It's all right. It's only a supper.*

There was silence as everyone waited to see if their preacher would top the interloper's bid.

"Excuse me, Reverend Gil," called Milly Brookfield, half rising and holding up a hand.

Folks turned around to stare.

"Mrs. Brookfield, is there something I can help you with?" Gil inquired, the tense planes of his face relaxing slightly at this brief respite from the duel between himself and Merriwell.

Faith saw Milly smile sweetly. "I'm so sorry to be late. Looks like I missed the married ladies' bidding. Because my husband is away on the cattle drive, old Josh was going to bid on my supper box, but I could tell he'd much rather go visit the saloon, because he doesn't get away from the ranch much…"

Merriwell fidgeted at the delay, obviously eager for his victory.

"I've barely met Mr. Merriwell," Milly went on, "just here at church, of course—but I was hoping I could ask him a favor."

Merriwell's expression smoothed. He had to know all

eyes were on him. "Yes, ma'am? I'm at your service,"
he said in his thickest, Deep South drawl, only the most
gentlemanly curiosity present in his gaze.

"Well…I see there's but one box left, and two of
you gentlemen. Because I was late, I have one that's
way too much for me to eat by myself. My main dish
is ham, too, raised and smoked right out on our ranch.
I know our *preacher*—" she gave deliberate emphasis
to the word "—would really like to sit with Miss Faith
for supper, while I'd love to hear all about Atlanta,
and Georgia…" She smiled appealingly at Merriwell.
"Would you do me the kindness of sharing my supper,
and letting Reverend Gil share Faith's?"

Merriwell flushed. He was fairly caught and he knew
it. To refuse and insist on his own preference would not
be the act of a gentleman. Worse, his rudeness would
render him permanently unwelcome in Simpson Creek.

Faith stared at Milly. The former spinster's face was
all innocent entreaty aimed at the Georgian. Faith saw
Gil was as surprised as she was. When she glanced at
Sarah, however, she could tell Milly's sister was trying
to smother a conspiratorial grin.

"Of course, Mrs. Brookfield. I'd be delighted," Merriwell said. He shot a regretful glance at Faith before
striding to the front to claim his prize. When he would
have dropped his eagle in the bowl, however, Gil held
up a hand to stop him.

"Oh, you don't have to pay, Mr. Merriwell. Your gen-
erosity of spirit should be rewarded, I think."

"Lord, we thank You for these supper boxes and the
ladies who prepared them. Bless the food in them to
the nourishment of our bodies. We thank You for the

fellowship we experience with each other and all the blessings You give us. Amen."

After an answering chorus of amens, Gil led Faith to the stone bench under the live oak trees, close to the tables but far enough away that their conversation would not be overheard. He figured the congregation would understand.

He watched as Faith gracefully set out the contents of her supper box between them. She looked happy, though still a little dazed.

He took up one of the ham croquettes, dipped it in small bowl of sweet mustard sauce that she had provided, and took a bite. "Mmm, delicious."

She looked at him, her green eyes shining. "I'm glad you like it, Gil."

He glanced over to where Milly Brookfield was sitting with Merriwell, her sleeping son napping on a quilt at her feet. Gil was relieved to see Merriwell was smiling and talking to Milly—he had been afraid the Georgian would sulk after being maneuvered into sitting with someone other than Faith, but Merriwell had apparently accepted defeat with reasonably good grace.

He nodded toward them. "I think we just experienced a miracle, Faith," he said. "We were rescued out of a disagreeable situation against what seemed like impossible odds."

Her gaze shifted, and he saw she was looking at Milly and Merriwell, as he just had.

"I think it's more like a conspiracy of wonderful friends," she said, skeptical but still smiling. "Sarah Walker just winked at me."

"At the very least, an answer to prayer. I thank God for the deep friendship among you ladies that brought about the blessing."

"I suppose I would say amen to that, if I was a believer," she said lightly. "But you said you prayed about it?"

He nodded. "Before the auction, and again when it seemed I would have to watch Merrifield eating supper with you."

Her eyes widened at what he had implied.

Yes, that means I would have been jealous. I don't know what is going to happen between us, given the impasse we face, but I would have been jealous, watching you with him.

When she spoke again, she made no reference to his implication. "Do you think God wants to hear about such little things?" she asked, as if she hadn't even considered such a possibility.

"I do, Faith. The Bible says He cares if a single sparrow falls. I knew you didn't want to sit and eat with that fellow, and I asked Him to make it possible for me to do so instead."

He watched delightedly as a pink blush rose into her cheeks.

"I can't imagine how they managed the timing," she marveled.

"Timing?"

She chuckled. "You don't think Milly's lateness was an accident, do you? I wouldn't be surprised if old Josh was hiding in the bushes somewhere in the trees by the creek, so Sarah could signal him when to bring the wagon around to the church to cause Milly to arrive just *after* the bidding for the married ladies' suppers."

"And the unexpected appearance of Polly's former fiancé, just at the right time?" He nodded toward the end of one of the other tables, where Polly sat with Bob Henshaw. Neither one of the reunited couple was eating—they were both too busy staring into each other's eyes. "If that wasn't a miracle, I don't know what is."

"Whether it is or not, I'm happy for her," Faith remarked. "She's been so miserable since he left. It's why she's been so bossy, I think."

And flirtatious. Gil was relieved to think he wouldn't be fending off Polly's coquettish behavior toward him anymore, because he hadn't been able to return her feelings.

Because he was in love with the woman across the table from him. *Help me, Lord. Help me win Faith for Your kingdom.*

"Yes, I think I'll be performing another wedding soon," he said.

Faith chuckled. "I only wonder if Polly will move to Austin or she will talk him into opening a druggist's shop here."

Later, when the planks-and-sawhorse tables had been taken down and put away, and the last of the cowboys, spinsters and married couples had departed for their respective ranches or houses in town, Gil walked Faith home.

"Your supper was delicious, Faith," he said, as they walked down the quiet street. "I'm so glad your friend did what she did to make that possible."

"Me, too," she murmured. "I'll have to thank Milly when I see her in church tomorrow. I think she was just going to stay the night with Sarah because tomorrow's Sunday."

"I'll make it a point to do the same."

Once again, Gil wished Faith lived farther than she did from the church. He wanted to spend more time with her, discover what on her mind. *In her soul.* But they had only to walk past the parsonage and the doctor's office, and there was the Bennett home. And from the light he saw through the curtains, it looked as if her parents might still be in the parlor. He didn't want to talk with her on the porch, aware that their conversation might be overheard through the open windows.

"Perhaps we could go for a buggy ride tomorrow afternoon?" he asked, keeping his voice low.

He could feel her hesitance. She stared up at him in the dim light.

"Gil—"

"Are you worried about running into Comanches? I happened to speak to Major McConley and Sheriff Bishop the other day, and from what they were saying, there haven't been any other Indian sightings since my encounter with them. I think they probably left the area after that, fearing I'd report the incident. In any case, we wouldn't go far."

"No, it's not that," Faith said. "Like you, I think they've gone. But I thought we agreed we weren't going to do anything that looked like courting."

"It's not—not unless…well, you know. I'm thinking of it as spending time with a friend."

She looked skeptical at his argument. "Gil, I can't help thinking that spending time with me is keeping you from courting the right woman."

You are the right woman! he wanted to exclaim. *If only—*

If only. He could not wish her into something she was not.

"Faith," he said instead, "I want you to rest easy on one thing. As nice and pretty as the other ladies in the Spinsters' Club are, I do not feel led toward any of them. If you weren't here, I don't believe that would change."

She didn't look convinced, but she agreed to go.

Chapter Seventeen

"Did you have a nice supper with the preacher? You certainly seemed to be enjoying yourself," Merriwell said from the parlor, as she stepped into the house.

Faith whirled from the hat rack, where she had hung her light muslin shawl.

"Oh! I thought Mama and Papa were sitting there," she said, looking around the room as if they still might be lurking in the corner somewhere.

"They went on to bed," he murmured in his smooth drawl, and waited.

She realized he had asked her a question, and she had not answered. Something about the man put her so off balance.

"Yes, we had an enjoyable time," she said. "Reverend Gil is my friend. I always enjoy his company." She was aware she sounded a little defensive.

"Careful, Miss Faith," he said, keeping his voice low. "For all your protestations of being a freethinker like myself, I believe he's trying to transform you into one of his sheep."

Better a sheep than a sly goat like yourself, she thought but didn't say it.

He sighed. "But it's none of my business, I suppose."

"That's right. What I do and think is my own affair."

"Pity. We could have made quite a team, you and I. Your father doesn't appreciate what a keen mind you have, you know. I've seen it, though. Working on the newspaper together, we could have been quite a force for freedom of thought in this town."

She stared at him. *How had he known how much she longed to be a part of the newspaper business? To be important to her father?* Merriwell tempted her with the very thing she longed so much for.

She remembered Gil's father once doing a sermon on Christ's temptation in the wilderness, how the Devil had led him up to a summit and tempted him with worldly power. Had Jesus felt the pull of what could be, like she did?

"And what would Simpson Creek look like, with more people like you here, I wonder?" she murmured out loud. "No, Mr. Merriwell," she said, deliberately using his last name instead of Yancey, as he'd asked her to before. "I think I like Simpson Creek just as it is." *Before you came, that is.*

It was a pointed reply, and she knew he got her point by his swift intake of breath.

"Very well," he said after a moment. "If your mind is quite made up, do not fear that I will press you further. But you *do* have to make up your mind as to what you are, you know. Sooner or later you will trip up, and reveal yourself for what you are. Already, I'll wager, you've come close, haven't you? How will they treat you when they find out you're different?" He chuckled. "They won't act so *Christian* to you then, I believe."

She couldn't quite stifle a shiver, remembering the times she'd left her eyes open and her head unbowed during prayer—either out of rebellion or absentmindedness, only to have someone in the congregation look up too soon and see her. Or the time when she'd daydreamed during one of Papa's table blessings over the meal, and kept her eyes shut, only to hear her mother laugh and tell her he'd said amen a minute ago?

"Don't worry, your secret is safe with me, Miss Faith. I wonder, though, does the Bible thumper suspect?"

"Gil's never thumped a Bible in his life," she said indignantly, though she was careful to keep her voice down, too, lest her parents hear her. "But yes, he knows. I would not keep such a thing from him. And he does not condemn me."

Merriwell arched a brow. "I give you credit for your honesty, then—with him at least. How very noble of him. But he can never marry you, can he, as things are? What do they call it, those Christians, an 'unequal yoke'? Yes, that's it, as if you were both dumb oxen."

She felt as if he'd struck her. "*No,* he can't," she breathed, her throat so thick and tight with that truth it threatened to choke her. It was all she could manage to utter, with the wild sorrow and anger swirling inside her. "And as it doesn't concern you, you have no right to talk about such a thing," she seethed.

"I suppose not. My humblest apologies, Miss Faith," he said, his regret patently false. He moved toward the door. "I believe I will take a walk before I turn in. Good night."

Going out to smoke one of those smelly cheroots, Faith guessed, or perhaps to have a drink at the saloon. She'd smelled both tobacco and whiskey on him before, and had heard the door open late at night, after the household had gone to bed. She supposed her father didn't care as long as his employee did these things away from the house.

Now she stared at the door long after it had closed behind him, knowing the anger he had aroused and her uncertainty about what she should do about Gil would keep her sleepless for hours.

Gil lay awake for a long time, too, pondering his course just as Faith was doing. Yet when the insistent knocking at the door came, it woke him from a deep sleep.

"Rev'rend, we need you! Wake up!" shouted a voice outside.

His brain still fogged with sleep and the remnants of a dream, Gil stumbled out of bed. Coming out into the hallway that divided the two bedrooms, he saw his father struggling to get up.

"Papa, I'll see who it is," he said. "You can stay in bed."

George Detwiler stood on the doorstep, his collarless shirt splashed with crimson.

"Reverend, y' got t'come to the saloon! She's cut bad…I think she's d-dying!" George cried, his eyes wild, his hands raised in entreaty. They were bloodstained, too.

Faith! But no, the saloon owner hadn't said her name, Gil realized. He'd been dreaming about her just before the knocking. There was no reason to think Faith would be at the saloon.

"*Who's* been cut, George?" he asked. "Did you tell Doc Walker?"

"Yessir, I notified him first, and he ran on down, but she said she was gonna die and she wanted th' preacher," Detwiler said. "It's Dovie, one of the two

girls workin' in my saloon, Rev'rend. She went upstairs with one a' the customers—that's strictly between
them and the men, y'understand, I don't tell them they
can or they can't, and I sure don't take no part of any
money—"

Gil raised his hand from the shirt he'd been trying
to button. "I don't need to know that right now, George.
Just tell me what happened as we go," he said, joining
the man on the step. "Papa, I'll be back soon as I can,"
he called back into the house.

"Rev'rend, there was a handful a' cowboys drinkin'
in the saloon, and that fella from Georgia, too," Detwiler said as they walked. "I wasn't payin' no special
attention, but then I saw Lupe was the only one servin'
drinks, an' she said Dovie'd gone upstairs with that
Georgia feller. An' then we heard this unearthly scream,
and we ran upstairs, and there was blood everywhere…
He cut her *everywhere,* Rev'rend…"

The Georgia feller. Yancey Merriwell.

"Where's Merriwell now?" Gil asked as they passed
Gilmore House. They were nearly to the saloon. "Sheriff Bishop have him in a jail cell?"

The saloonkeeper shook his head. "Nope, we heard
a clatterin' on the roof as we ran up the stairs—that
was Merriwell slidin' off the roof to escape. Then we
heard a horse gallopin' away, and one of the cowboys
yellin' that he'd stolen his horse. Bishop and th' deputy
are ridin' out after him, but I reckon that scoundrel got
a good start," he said.

They reached the saloon then, and pushed the bat-
wing doors open. A handful of cowboys milled around
the bottom of the steps, staring upward, but they opened
a path for Gil and Detwiler as they approached.

Gil's first thought on seeing the young woman

stretched out on the narrow bed with its cheap white-painted iron headboard was that she was several shades whiter than the threadbare, dingy sheet she lay on.

Instantly the bare-board walls of the little room faded and Gil was standing in another saloon, in another city, at another time, standing over another bloody saloon girl. Only that girl was dead—and her baby inside her, too. *His baby.*

Nolan Walker raised his head from the bloodstained bandage he was pressing to her chest, his face grim, his eyes devoid of hope. He shook his head at Gil.

Gil thought he meant she was already dead, too, and his heart sank. *Lord, how could this be happening again?* But then the doctor smoothed her hair away from a sweat-pearled forehead and said, "Dovie, the preacher's here."

The saloon girl's eyes fluttered open and she stared at Gil as he knelt beside the bed. "Preacher, I'm…not gonna make it," she said in a voice so devoid of strength he couldn't be sure he'd actually heard it. "Wan' you to pray for me. I ain't been…a good woman."

Gil had never met the woman, but now he called her by her name as if she'd sat in a pew every Sunday. "Dovie, Doctor Nolan's here, and he's doing everything he can for you. You've got to hang on. I'm going to pray that you get better."

The injured woman shook her head with a vigor borne of desperation. "No…stabbed me in th' lung, I think," she said, gulping for air like a landed perch. "I ain't got…much time. Wanna repent my s-sins…"

Gil met Nolan's eyes, and the look in them confirmed his fears and Dovie's own words. He closed his eyes, asking for the right words.

"Dovie, Jesus told the thief on the cross that he was

forgiven for his sins, and you must believe He forgives you, too, for whatever you've done. Are you asking Him for forgiveness, Dovie?"

She nodded, gulping again for air. There was a bluish-gray cast to the skin around her mouth now, and the irises of her staring eyes widened. "Wanna go to Heaven," she murmured. "Don' d-deserve to..." Her eyelids sagged halfway over her eyes as if she no longer had the power to hold them open.

"None of us do, Dovie, but He forgives us and takes us home to be with Him," Gil murmured, holding her cold, clammy hand.

She made an attempt at a smile, exhaled shakily and went still.

Her father returned to the house just as Faith and her mother were finishing breakfast the next morning. His face was drawn, his eyes stricken.

"Robert, what's the matter?" her mother asked, rising.

"I went out to see if anyone had seen Merriwell," he said, sinking into a chair. "His bed hadn't been slept in, so I thought maybe he'd overindulged at the saloon last night. Thought he mighta got into trouble, so I checked at the jail. No one was there, but I ran into George Detwiler, and he told me Yancey'd killed a woman in his saloon last night. One of the—" he darted a glance at Faith "—one of the women who works there."

Faith covered her mouth in horror. She heard her mother ask, "Is he in jail?"

Her father shook his head. "Apparently he stole one of the horses at the hitching rail and lit out. Sheriff Bishop and his deputy rode after him, and they haven't come back yet." He laid his head on his arms and his shoulders shook. "Lydia, how could I have been so wrong about a man?"

Her mother went to him and put her arms around him, laying her head on his. "Robert, you couldn't have known…"

Faith stared at them without really seeing her parents, remembering last night when the Georgian had said he was going out for a walk. There'd been a darkness in Yancey Merriwell's eyes, and she could almost see the anger radiating from him in waves. He'd taken her rejection of him out on another woman, and the woman had paid with her life.

"Detwiler said there's no church service this morning, just the mayor leading folks in prayer if they want to participate," her father went on, his voice muffled and thick with unshed tears. "He said young Gil came and comforted the woman until she…passed. He's apparently taking it real hard. No one knows where he went."

"G—Reverend Gil left?" Faith cried. "Where would he have gone?" Surely he wouldn't have tried to apprehend the murderer himself. Not in a buggy.

Her father lifted his head. "Detwiler said his mama is sitting with Reverend Chadwick now," he said.

She had to find him. She ran upstairs, got enough coins from her small savings to rent a horse and headed for the door.

"Are you going to church, Faith?" her mother asked, half rising. "Wait a moment, and I'll go with you—"

"I have to find Gil!" she called over her shoulder.

Her father shouted something after her, but she was out the door before he could complete his sentence.

Faith wished she believed enough to pray, at least enough of a prayer so she would go the correct way.

But she figured it wasn't right to pray just for a selfish wish like that, if you weren't first on speaking terms with the One you prayed to.

Hoping she was picking the direction Gil had gone, Faith headed the rented gelding eastward at a lope. She was nearly all the way to San Saba when she spotted the buggy sitting under the shady bows of an enormous live oak.

She nudged the horse forward, but only at a walk. The back of the buggy faced the road, so she couldn't tell if Gil was in the buggy or had left it.

She found him sitting in the buggy, his head bowed in prayer. He was so intent he hadn't even heard her approach.

"Gil?" Faith called softly, not wanting to startle him.

He raised his head slowly, as if coming out of a trance, and she saw that his eyes were full of torment.

He blinked, his eyes struggling to focus. "Faith." His voice was dull.

"Are you all right? I was worried about you, Gil," she said, peering into the buggy from the back of her mount. She was still worried about him, she thought, seeing his red-rimmed eyes.

"Have they found Merriwell?" he asked.

Faith shook her head. "I passed Sheriff Bishop and his deputy riding back into town as I was leaving it," she said. "They tried to track him as soon as it was light, but they lost his trail after he forded a creek in a rocky area. They're putting the word out to other towns nearby."

"Is Papa all right? I shouldn't have left him like that, but he said it was all right. That I needed to go pray."

"Mrs. Detwiler is with him, so I'm sure he's fine," she said. "Gil, it's horrible what Merriwell did. That poor girl…but…" Her voice trailed off. As awful as the murder of the saloon girl was, Gil seemed to be grieving over more than that. Unless—*had he had some sort of liaison with her?*

She tried again when he said nothing else. "Gil, did you…know her?"

"Dovie Maxwell? No," he said, "I'd never met her before last night."

She was startled by the extent of the suffering in his eyes. "Doctor Nolan says you…you comforted her," Faith said.

Gil nodded. "She died a believer," he said. "She went to Heaven, I'm sure of it. Thank God."

"Then why…" She couldn't ask him why he was so upset. Surely he viewed that as some sort of victory in the midst of tragedy. "Can we— Would you like to get out of the buggy and sit with me underneath the tree?"

Something flickered in his eyes, and his gaze became shuttered, distant. "Perhaps we should stay as we are," he said. "You should ride back to town, Faith. Your parents will worry about you. You shouldn't be out here alone." He turned away.

I'm not alone, I'm with you, she wanted to say. *What had happened to the smiling man who had spoken of miracles last night?*

"You have to tell me what's wrong," she insisted, when he said nothing else. "As awful as it is, there's something more bothering you than that poor woman's death."

He moved to descend from the buggy. "All right, I'll tell you, but then you must ride back."

She dismounted and tied the gelding's reins to the back of the buggy, then stood in front of him. Gil made no move to sit down, but he faced her at least.

"I should have told you about it long before this," Gil said, his eyes on his shoes, "so you wouldn't think so highly of me. But I haven't told anyone, not even Papa. If the congregation knew…well, I'm sure they would appoint another preacher," he said, and lifted his eyes to hers.

"Knew what, Gil? What could you possibly have done?" Faith realized this conversation was similar to the one when she had confessed her lack of belief to him. But surely nothing Gil Chadwick could have done was as bad as what she had told him.

"What happened to Dovie—the girl at the saloon," he began, his voice thick and hoarse with emotion, "happened to my wife. She died in a saloon, too."

His wife? But how could that be? Gil had fought in the war, then went to a seminary before coming to Simpson Creek. He'd never made mention of a wife, let alone a wife with such a scandalous background. A preacher would never ally himself with such a woman.

Any more than he would marry a nonbeliever, a voice inside her whispered.

"I fell in love with a girl while I was at seminary at Independence," Gil finally continued. "Suellen wasn't at her…place of business when I met her, so I didn't suspect what she was. I was already head over heels in love when I found out she worked at a saloon. I'd already done more with her than a man should do unless he's married to a woman," he admitted. A tear trickled down his cheek.

"Then she told me she was…with child. Naturally, I wanted to do the right thing, not only because it was right but because I loved her. I married her. I was only months away from graduating, and I told her we'd go far from there and no one would ever know about her past. I knew she didn't believe in God…in anything but herself really. I told myself my example would rub off on her, and she'd learn to be a good preacher's wife."

Faith just stood there, unable to think of anything to say.

"I rented some rooms—a humble place, but it was decent and safe, and I promised her we'd be leaving town soon. I gave her as much money as I had for food and clothing. But I guess she missed the excitement, the baubles men would buy her, the attention they paid her. Guess she figured she'd better get what she could before…before the baby started showing. She'd sneak off to the saloon to work in the afternoons, then sneak back to our lodgings before I got home."

In one of the tree limbs overhead, a catbird called.

"Go on," Faith said.

"One day she wasn't there when I got there. I sat down and waited, thinking maybe she'd gone out to buy something for our meal and was late getting back. I waited for hours… Then one of the girls from the saloon came and told me there'd been a gun battle at the saloon, and Suellen had been caught in the crossfire. She was wounded and not expected to live.

"I didn't believe what the girl said," he said. "Not till I saw Suellen. She breathed her last breath an hour after I arrived, despite all the desperate praying I did, all the promises I made to God… And our unborn child died with her." He was weeping again, silent sobs that shook his shoulders.

Faith gathered him in her arms, and he did not resist.

Chapter Eighteen

He had to let go of Faith, he had to, he told himself, but he felt like a drowning man holding on to the only thing that kept him from being swept under.

But at last he had no more tears left, and he pulled away from her, knowing she'd been sobbing, too.

Her eyes were like wet emeralds.

"I'm sorry," he said. "What a weak man I must seem, weeping on your shoulder like that."

She shook her head. "I don't know who made it a rule that men should not cry, but it's a foolish rule. I think those tears have been held inside you a long time. They needed to be released."

He tore his eyes away from her. Faith was right. Other than a few tears once he'd regained the privacy of his lodgings after arranging for Suellen's funeral, he'd not allowed himself to fully mourn her. He couldn't very well tell the dean of students what had happened.

"Thank you, Faith," he murmured. She hadn't condemned him for becoming involved with such a woman, or even expressed disapproval that he'd had a secret marriage.

She took hold of his hand, forcing him to look at her. "I'm sorry for what happened back then, Gil. But you did the right, honorable thing by Suellen. You loved her, you married her and you planned to provide a good home for her and the baby. It wasn't your fault that she was killed."

He shook his head. "Maybe not. But I involved myself with her, a woman who was not a believer, knowing it was wrong. Even if she hadn't been killed, it wouldn't have worked in the end. Sooner or later she would have grown tired of my profession and the responsibilities that go with it, the high standards expected of a preacher's wife, and she would have grown to resent me."

She waited as if she knew worse was coming.

"Don't you see? I can't do it again."

She stared wordlessly at him, her eyes enormous in her pale face.

"When I watched Dovie die last night, it took me back to that time…when I sat at Suellen's bedside," he said. "And I realized I'd let myself fall in love with you—despite what I said, despite knowing you weren't a believer. Despite what had happened before when I… loved someone who had no faith."

He saw a tear slide down her cheek then, and sadness rose in him, that he should be the cause of that tear, and the others, and perhaps more to come. He only wanted to bring her happiness.

He looked deeply into her eyes. "Faith, I love you. I want to court you and marry you. But I can't keep fooling myself that it would be right for us to continue as we have been when you're not a believer. You tried to tell me as much before."

She took a step toward him, holding out a hand. "Gil, I—I *want* to believe… I want to…to share that with you. But…what if I let myself trust God…and He lets me down again?"

She was thinking about her brother, he knew. He wished he had some easy answer to give her, some answer that his theological training had given him. But he didn't.

"Believing is a leap of faith," he told her.

"That's what Mama said about love, too," she murmured.

"Very true, because God created love. But don't believe in Him just because of me. You have to believe for your own sake."

Faith whirled away, fists clenched, as if she couldn't listen anymore. "I have to think…"

When she thought, she would probably come to the conclusion that after what he'd done, he had no right to tell anyone what to believe. That he was a fraud, a hypocrite.

Please, Lord, teach her about the grace You offer. The forgiveness. I'll do whatever I must to become a completely honest man, not one who keeps secrets, but let Faith see Your love.

"Yes, think. Maybe you should confide in another believer you can trust. And pray, Faith. Even if you don't know if He's there. He is and he'll listen, I promise you."

"I—I'll do that," she said.

"You should go back now," he said gently, when she didn't move.

"Are you coming?"

"In a few minutes. I expect they'll be wanting me to say a few words over Dovie."

There would be no grand laying to rest for the saloon girl, no more than there had been for Suellen. The little amount of cash Gil could lay hands on then had made sure his wife at least had a coffin, rather than merely a shroud. The Fund for the Deserving Poor that the Spinsters' Club sponsored would probably provide a coffin for Dovie. But there would be no one to properly mourn her. He wondered if George Detwiler knew of any next of kin who should be notified.

Meanwhile Dovie's killer ran loose, probably heading for new territory where he could assume a new identity, his violent tendencies unknown. Thinking of this, Gil clucked to the horse and turned him in a circle, heading back for town, always keeping Faith in sight on her rented gelding. It was highly unlikely that Merriwell was hiding out anywhere close by, but he wouldn't take any chances with Faith's safety. And there were always Comanches to watch out for, too.

Makes Healing waited until he was invited to sit next to Panther Claw Scars in front of his fire. The two men were born in the same summer, but Panther Claw Scars was the chief, and so worthy of respect even from the medicine man, for had he not been marked on the face by a panther and lived to tell about it?

"Your son's leg heals well?" the chief inquired, passing his pipe to the medicine man. He nodded toward Runs Like a Deer, who sat among a group of other boys nearby. They played the Comanche game called Button in which one boy held a button made from a knot of rawhide, then strove to confuse the watching boys as to which hand the button was held in by shifting it from hand to hand and making distracting gestures while the watching boys beat time on little drums or leather parfleches.

Makes Healing nodded. The boy's crutch lay close

to his hand, but Runs Like a Deer relied on it less and less. "His bones knit fast."

"It will not be many summers before he makes his vision quest," Panther Claw Scars remarked, after taking a puff from his pipe and passing it to the medicine man.

"Yes, and then he will leave the games of boys and join the young braves," Makes Healing said. He pointed with the pipe where the young warriors sat at their fire, laughing, talking and smoking tobacco in rolled-up corn shucks.

"Will he choose to follow the peaceful path your moccasins have made, or will he lead the young braves? Already he rides his pony with more skill than any of the other boys."

It was true. On horseback he wasn't slowed by the healing leg, and he rode with verve and daring. "Who can know these things at this time?" Makes Healing said. "His vision quest will reveal this when it is time."

The chief nodded agreement, then narrowed his eyes as one of the louder young braves stood up and began boasting in front of his friends. They could not hear what his boast concerned from where they sat, but they could guess—he bragged of his prowess on raids, which would earn him much respect and his choice of wives from among the people.

"Has Black Coyote Heart said anything more of a disrespectful nature to you?" the chief asked, keeping his gaze fixed on the young warrior and not on his medicine man.

Makes Healing's jaw set as he remembered the scornful remarks Black Coyote Heart had made after Makes Healing had persuaded the chief to release the white holy man without so much as a disfiguring scar, much less torture. Black Coyote Heart felt he'd been robbed of sport by having to escort the holy man back to the white man's road, but Makes Healing had threatened him with a curse if so much as a hair on the head of the white man was harmed. While the young man feared the curse enough to let the white man go relatively unscathed, he'd made scornful remarks within Makes Healing's hearing whenever possible—until he was reprimanded by the chief.

The worst of the remarks was the younger man's assertion that his insistence on releasing the white holy man proved that Makes Healing had lost the life force that made a Comanche warrior a man to be feared on the plains, and was fit only for the old men's smoking lodge. Makes Healing had always preferred the path of peace, hunting buffalo and practicing the healing skills, over making war on the whites or other Indians such as the Kiowa, but surely this was an undeserved insult. He had pointed out that the young holy man deserved to be released for his bravery in trying to bring Makes Healing's son back to the camp when he had been injured, but the arrogant young brave didn't care.

"No, he has made no more scornful remarks," Makes Healing told his chief. "But he is restless, and he makes the other young men restless, too. It is not enough for him to hunt game and steal cattle. He wants to go on raids among the white men, to steal horses and take scalps and capture white women to keep or sell to the Comancheros. He wants to be made war chief." There had been no new war chief named since Makes Healing's older brother had been killed in a battle with the bluecoats.

"What do you think should be done?" Panther Claw Scars asked.

Makes Healing hesitated. He realized that the chief was according him respect by asking him his advice— he could have made a decision on his own. He did not want Black Coyote Heart's actions to bring the blue-coats down on them, yet a Comanche who did not raid and count coups was a pitiful creature, worthy of derision.

"I will go on and seek a vision from the Great Spirit," he said at last. "It will make our path clear. I will leave at dawn tomorrow."

Dovie's burial service was held at dusk Sunday evening. Faith attended, and was the only other one beside George Detwiler, Sheriff Bishop and his wife, and both Chadwick men.

"*'I am the Resurrection and the Life,'*" Gil read aloud from his open Bible. *"'He that believeth in Me, though he were dead, yet shall he live. And whosever liveth and believeth in me, shall never die.'* Dovie had only moments to live for Jesus, but I'm as sure as I'm standing here that she's in Heaven today because she believed His promise, just as Lazarus did."

The service didn't last long. Soon the unvarnished pine coffin was lowered into the ground and Sheriff Bishop and George began shoveling the dirt over it.

"Thank you for coming, Miss Faith," Gil said. It was all he said aloud to her, but his eyes were eloquent before he turned away. Old Reverend Chadwick patted her shoulder, then said his thanks in the slurred, hesitant voice he'd had since the stroke.

She walked out of the churchyard for home after that, not wanting to torture herself being near Gil. It was up to her not to tempt him to abandon his resolve, she told herself. Yet she could not resist a final look back at him.

As if he felt the weight of her gaze, he looked up and their eyes met. She could not be sure, but she thought the corners of his mouth turned upward ever so slightly.

Her parents were sitting in the parlor when she returned. Her father looked up from the Lampasas newspaper. He and the editors of neighboring newspapers exchanged publications, and each was free to borrow from the other, as long as each gave proper attribution to the writer.

"Busy day tomorrow, Faith," her father said.

"Yes, Papa." In all the turmoil, she'd forgotten tomorrow was printing day. "I'll be ready to distribute the newspapers as usual."

"Good. Then come back and see if you can write out an account of the events at the saloon Saturday night."

Her mother looked up, startled. "Robert, is that wise? Surely the death of a saloon girl is not a subject a young lady should even know about, much less write about," she said.

"Horsefeathers, Lydia. Thanks to my apparent misjudgment, a poor woman is dead and I'm without the assistant I thought would be so perfect. Faith's expressed her eagerness before to try to help. I'll put my byline on it this time, if you think it best because of the subject matter, but I'm going to give our daughter a chance to prove herself. I know I can trust her not to sensationalize the account. I suppose I should check to see if Sheriff Bishop's going to need wanted posters for that scoundrel Merriwell, too."

Faith's heart lifted. "Thanks, Papa! I'll be happy to help you. I'm sure I'll need you to edit and proofread it, but I promise you, I'll get better with practice."

"Good. Now, mind you, this is just till you marry

your young preacher, Faith. I'm sure he'll be able to keep you plenty busy after that," he said with a chuckle.

Faith hoped her parents did not see her wince. In time they would notice that she and Reverend Gil were no longer keeping company, and she hoped she wouldn't be asked about it. She didn't want to add lying to her other shortcomings.

She was thrilled and encouraged that her father was willing to try making her a more important part of his newspaper business at least. Maybe in time she would convince him of her capability, so when time went on and she did not marry, he would eventually turn the newspaper over to her with confidence.

Yet when she lay in her bed that night, it wasn't excitement over her enlarging role with the *Simpson Creek Chronicle* that kept her awake. It was the words Gil had read from the Bible, and his firm assertion that the saloon girl had gone to Heaven.

Gil had told her to pray, and that believing in God was a leap of faith.

"Lord, are You out there?" she whispered into the darkness. "I wish I could see some sign of You to prove You're there. How can I be sure You hear me?"

No sound reached her ears but the hoot of an owl wafting through her open window, and the gentle rasp of her father's snores from down the hall.

Gil had also urged her to confide in someone. She wasn't sure if he'd said it because he thought someone else could help her because he hadn't been able to, or because he just didn't want the temptation of being near her when she asked question, but she found herself eager to do as he'd suggested. But whom should she talk to?

She wasn't willing to take the chance with her

mother. If she was upset and disillusioned to hear her daughter had been living a lie ever since Eddie's death, Faith could irreparably damage her relationship with her. It was too much to risk.

Then who? Reverend Chadwick would be willing to listen, but he couldn't speak well enough to answer any question she might have. And going to see him would entail seeing Gil. He might think it was just a ploy to be around him.

Then it would have to be one of the spinsters. There were several of them whom she could trust to be discreet—probably all of them now that Polly was blissfully reunited with her beau from Austin—but who would be best?

Sarah or Milly. She had known them the longest. Sarah would listen sympathetically, but their conversation was too apt to be interrupted by the cries of her baby, or by her husband, who ran his doctor's office on the other side of their dwelling. Dr. Walker had always seemed like a nice man, but perhaps he'd be so shocked by learning that his wife's friend had been a secret heathen all this time that he'd refuse to allow Sarah to associate with Faith.

Whereas Milly's husband was somewhere on the trail to Kansas with hundreds of longhorns, and would never know. And Milly had shown herself sympathetic to Faith and Gil by diverting Merriwell into having supper with her so Faith could sit with Gil.

Perfect. She would rent the gelding again and ride out to see Milly. It couldn't be tomorrow because she'd be far too busy working at the newspaper office, but the next day for sure. She could hardly wait. As Faith lay there in the dark, she rehearsed ways to reveal her secret before asking Milly about returning to the Lord.

* * *

"This will do very well, Faith," her father said, looking up from the sheet of paper he'd been peering at through his spectacles. "It shows compassion without being maudlin—although you still suffer from an injudicious use of commas." His eyes twinkled as he said that, though, and Faith began to believe her father was finally coming to see her value. "Well, I'm off to the office to work on those wanted posters. If I had a little more money to spare, I'd put up reward money for that Georgian's apprehension myself."

Faith watched him go, relieved that he apparently hadn't noticed she wore a split skirt for riding. If he had, he might have asked her destination and admonished her not to go alone. When her mother had left for the mercantile, Faith had told her she was going out to see Milly. Lydia Bennett had made some remark about Faith riding in the buggy with Gil, and Faith hadn't corrected her assumption. *Was that lying?*

Black Coyote Heart watched a departure, too. The stupid old medicine man blessed his son before mounting his spotted horse. He carried nothing with him but a knife—no food, no bow and arrow, for he was going to seek the will of the Great Spirit.

Black Coyote Heart had no use for such foolishness. The only will he cared about was his own, and it longed for blood to be spilled. He itched to take white men's scalps and hear the cries of their women as he carried them away. He longed to possess some of their fine horses—he could use them to buy a wife. Perhaps Eyes of an Antelope would suit him, he thought, spotting that girl eyeing him over a hide she was tanning. He'd bring her a captive woman as a slave, and then

Black Coyote Heart would effectively have two women to meet his every need.

He gestured to the other young warriors who looked to him as leader. "We ride," he told them. "But let us say it is only to hunt," he added, keeping his voice low. "The chief would have us wait on the advice of that stupid medicine man before raiding. We will take paint for our faces and our horses and apply it once we are away from camp. The people will thank us when we return with plunder, and then that old man Panther Claw Scars won't dare to object."

He became aware then of a boy standing nearby, leaning on a crutch, watching the braves gather with their horses. It was the medicine man's son, Black Coyote Heart realized. It had been he who had caused the white man to ride close to their camp.

Seeing the wistful expression on the boy's face, Black Coyote Heart called to him.

"You want to go with us, Runs Like a Deer?" Wouldn't that put a frown on his father's face when the old man heard his son had ridden on a raid, perhaps taken his first scalp?

"Where do you ride?" the boy asked.

"We will take horses and cattle, and spill the white eyes' blood," Black Coyote Heart told him. "There will be captives to torment afterward, and scalps. Are you ready to become a man, boy?"

Runs Like a Deer looked uneasy. "I have not gone on my vision quest yet."

One of the other braves snorted, and mimicked what the boy had said, but in a high voice like a woman's.

Runs Like a Deer's face darkened and his black eyes flashed sparks.

"So? Maybe you'll have a vision while you kill your

first white eyes," Black Coyote Heart said. "A vision of taking back our land for the people. Are you up for it, boy? Or do you want to stay with the women?"

The others hooted with laughter.

Runs Like a Deer turned, leaning on his crutch, and walked away.

Chapter Nineteen

Whoever had said "The road to a friend's house is never long" had never ridden under a hot Texas sun on a cranky, swaybacked mare that seemed reluctant to go any faster than a jarring trot. The amiable smooth-paced gelding she'd ridden out to find Gil two days ago had been taken out by an earlier customer at the livery. It was just as well she met no one on the road who would have witnessed her battle of wills with the obdurate beast.

She soon forgot her discomfort once she arrived at the Brookfield ranch, however, for Milly was delighted to have an unexpected guest. Her thirst soon quenched by some of Milly's delicious lemonade, Faith spent the first half hour of her visit admiring baby Nicholas's progress in walking and improvements inside the ranch house and out of it. Then she helped her friend take a pot of soup and sandwiches out to the bunkhouse for the ranch hands before they sat down for their own meal— a peach pie which Milly had just taken from the oven.

They ate with relish, feeling like schoolgirls who'd

stolen a treat because they were making a meal out of dessert.

"Mmm, this is wonderful," Faith murmured. "I can't believe Sarah used to do all the cooking here. It's the flakiest crust I've ever eaten."

Milly grinned. "Thanks. Be glad you never tasted my earlier attempts. It took a lot of patient teaching from my sister and even more practice before I deserved any praise. I'm afraid, though, that I've gotten into some lazy cooking habits I'll have to break myself of before my husband gets back from the trail drive," she said, with a rueful nod toward the toddler, who was smearing mashed peach all over his face. "It's just gotten too hot to eat a heavy meal at noon, though of course the cowhands still need one, because they work up an appetite."

Faith pretended to concentrate on cutting a second piece of pie, wondering how to broach the main purpose of her visit. She'd just finished telling told Milly about the dreadful murder of the saloon girl and Merriwell's subsequent disappearance, and her father's plan to use her assistance more.

"So what's on your mind, Faith?" Milly asked suddenly. "I can tell something is, and I've been waiting for you to spill it. Is it about Reverend Gil?"

Faith nodded, grateful for her friend's perceptiveness. "I don't know how to begin," she said at last. "I have something to tell you about myself, and afterward you may never see me the same way again. You may not want me as a friend anymore."

Milly's eyes widened. "I can't imagine anything you could tell me that would make me feel that way—"

"Milly, I've been keeping a secret. An awful secret."

"I hope you know you can rely on my discretion,

Faith," Milly said. "Don't worry about how you're going to say it. Just blurt it out."

So that's what Faith did, although she had to wait a moment while Milly wiped her protesting son's face with a damp cloth and set him down to play. She told Milly everything, how she had stopped believing in God when her little brother had died and had faked her conformity with the faithful of Simpson Creek to the point that Gil had believed she would make a perfect preacher's wife. She told her about confessing her disbelief to Gil, and how Gil had told her he loved her and wanted to court her, but he could not marry a nonbeliever.

Milly nodded as Faith spoke, occasionally encouraging her to go on.

"Then Dovie, the girl at the saloon, was killed and…" Faith stopped, remembering she could not break Gil's confidence about his late wife. "Well, somehow that tragedy reminded him that he must not court me, not as long as I'm not a Christian. And I know the most awful thing I could do would be to *pretend* to believe just so I could marry Gil."

Milly nodded, her face thoughtful. "And how did you respond?"

"I told him I *wanted* to believe…believe again, that is…I *did* believe before Eddie died, Milly. I was baptized in Simpson Creek by Pastor Detwiler before he passed on, remember?" She hadn't thought of that day in so long.

"You wanted to believe, but?"

"But I don't have enough faith," Faith said, her voice almost a whisper. "My name is ironic, isn't it?"

Milly smiled. "How much faith do you think you need to have, dear friend?"

Faith shrugged her shoulders. "More than I have anyway. I'm so afraid of trusting in the Lord again, only to have some awful thing happen." Milly hadn't sent her from the house in outrage, she thought in amazement. Instead, she'd called her "dear friend."

"Faith, tragedies happen in life. People we love die of old age or illness or accident. Danger threatens—from animals, natural disasters, outlaws, Indian attacks—but we know that through it all, God loves us and we will be with Him in Heaven someday. If you were a Christian, you would see your brother again one day."

Milly got to her feet then, went to a cabinet and rummaged among some small bottles that appeared to be spices. She brought one of them to the table.

"Wild mustard seeds," she said, holding out the bottle for Faith to see. "Look at how small they are."

Faith waited.

"In the Bible, Jesus tells us that our faith need only be as big as a mustard seed. You can manage that much faith, can't you?"

Slowly, tentatively, Faith nodded, then more emphatically, as tears of joy trickled down her cheeks. She was laughing and crying at once.

Milly embraced her, laughing and crying, too. "Just believe that little bit, Faith, and ask for more faith, and I promise you He'll give it to you," Milly said. "You'll still have questions, there will be things we can't understand in this life, but Gil will answer what he can—and I will, too, as best I am able."

"Yes, he will," Faith said, beaming through her tears. "Oh, Milly, I can't wait to tell him! You…you wouldn't mind if I went on home now, would you? I want to see him as quickly as I can!"

"Of course I wouldn't mind for a reason like that,"

Milly said, smiling. "Why don't I ask one of the hands to ride back with you? There hasn't been any more trouble with the Indians, but—"

"Oh, I don't think that's necessary," Faith said. "I didn't see a soul on the way here after all. You see, I'd really like to do some praying aloud, maybe even some hymn singing on the way back," she added, when she saw that her friend was about to argue. "I can't very well do that if one of your men rides along."

"I don't know, Faith…I don't feel right about letting you go off alone," Milly said, her eyes troubled.

"But I'll be talking to the Lord," Faith reminded her. "When could a person be safer than that? Besides, like you said, there hasn't been any more Indian trouble. I'd feel silly taking one of your men away from his work to escort me."

Milly sighed. "I can see you're determined. All right, then. I can't wait to hear what Gil says."

He heard her before he saw her, singing in that peculiar out-loud way of the white eyes. It was not a low religious chant such as the shaman would sing, but somehow Black Coyote Heart thought it had something to do with the white eyes' religion. Perhaps it was one of the songs he'd heard escaping from the open windows of white men's worship houses when he'd crept up to them in times past to see how close he could come to them without being discovered.

And then he saw the woman, riding around the bend below him on the road, singing as if she didn't have a care in the world—or any need to be wary. No woman of the People would have worn such a ridiculous hat which blocked the sides of her vision. She did not even compensate by looking around her, or she would have easily seen him sitting on his horse at the edge of a clump of juniper on the rock- and cactus-strewn hillside. The whites were so foolish. What man would let one of his women ride out alone without protection, whether she was a wife, a daughter or a sister?

She had dark red hair, he saw, as a breeze blew her bonnet off her head and sent it bouncing from its strings on her shoulders. Not as prized as yellow hair, he thought, but even from here he saw that it shone as if fire danced with the sun on it.

Perhaps she was mad, he thought, as she switched from singing to talking out loud. He was even surer of his theory when he heard her laugh out loud. Yes, mad, but he could discipline that out of her.

He'd stayed behind to guard the rear after he and the other braves raided a ranch of its horses and cattle, but so far there had been no pursuit. The fire arrows that had set the ranch house ablaze, and the knives that had shed the blood of the white men who had swarmed out like ants to protest the destruction of their anthill had apparently terrorized anyone left alive there. Black Coyote Heart had been just about to ride after his fellow warriors, who were herding the stolen livestock toward the camp. He'd been hoping he could catch up so he could bask in the admiration of the people when they admired the booty. He thought perhaps Eyes of an Antelope would appreciate the silver-backed hand mirror he'd taken from the ranch house before they'd burned it.

He was glad he'd remained behind. Now none of the other braves could dispute his claim to the woman. He could take her red hair, but he decided he'd rather make her his captive. He'd beat her into terrified submission before presenting her to Eyes of an Antelope as a slave.

The white woman could serve his sister, Crow Echo, until Eyes of an Antelope became his wife.

The horse the white woman rode was hardly fit for even a pack horse. That was another mystery to Black Coyote Heart—why would a white man allow one of his females to ride such a beast? Surely it weakened his medicine. He'd take the horse along with the white woman. They could load possessions on it when it came time to winter on the staked plains, and then slaughter it when the People grew hungry.

Black Coyote Heart grinned at what he was about to do, then uttered a blood-curdling scream and charged his pony down the slope toward the white woman.

Gil and his father had just sat down to a late supper—he'd been making wedding arrangements with Polly Shackleford and Bob Henshaw and had lost track of the time—when the knocking sounded at the door.

Gil smiled ruefully at his father. "I guess getting interrupted at meals is part and parcel of being a preacher, isn't it?"

His father smiled back and nodded as Gil went to the door.

Robert Bennett stood on his doorstep, his face anxious, his fist poised to pound at the door again.

"Is my daughter with you?" he demanded before Gil could even open his mouth to greet the man.

"No," Gil said. "I haven't seen her all day. Have you checked with—"

"Didn't you go out to the Brookfields' with her today? My wife said she was going out there with you to visit Milly."

Gil stared at the frantic-eyed man. "No, we had no plans to do that." This certainly wasn't the time to explain to Faith's father why he and Faith wouldn't be going anywhere together as things stood now. "She didn't ask me to go anywhere with her, Mr. Bennett. Perhaps she went with one of her spinster friends, and they decided to stay the night?"

"She wouldn't do that," Bennett argued. "Not without telling us first, and I sure wouldn't have given her permission to go out there with just another female or two. Not with Yancey Merriwell on the loose. Anyway, we've checked with her friends in town, and they're all here…" His wide eyes begged Gil to give him reassurance.

Gil's blood ran cold at the thought of Faith in peril, but he kept his voice calm for Bennett's sake. "Why don't we ride out to the Brookfield ranch? She'll be there, you'll see. Surely there was some reason she had to stay, for I know she wouldn't make you worry without a good reason." He didn't really believe what he was saying, but his words seemed to reassure Faith's father.

"I'm sure you're right, Reverend. I'm going to give her such a talking-to when we find her there for scaring us so! Yes, let's do that."

"I'll go get the buggy," Gil said, knowing Bennett wasn't much of a horseman. "Do you think your wife could stay with Papa till we get back?"

When she came to, Faith found herself lying on her side on some sort of fur rug with her arms tied together at the wrists behind her, and attached to her bound feet so she was arched like a bow. Her mouth was full of a foul-tasting gag and her head ached as if it was trapped inside her father's Washington press while it printed.

Where was she? Faith looked around as much as her bindings would allow, which wasn't much, and saw that

the side of the dwelling appeared to be of some sort
of hide stretched over poles. A faint light filtered in
from the open top of the dwelling where all the wooden
poles met.

She lay in a tepee. Now it all came back to Faith
in a rush of terror—the sudden, out-of-nowhere spotted horse charging down the hillside, its demoni-
cally painted rider shrieking like a banshee before he
wrenched her off her mount. She'd struggled frantically,
and then there had been a sickening blow to her head
and everything went black.

She'd awakened in a head-down position, felt a rocking motion and seeing the ground blur by her as the
horse's legs gathered, then extended, below her gaze.
The knowledge that she was being carried away to an
unknown fate by the Indian who had seized her was
enough to convulse her with such unreasoning panic
that she struggled to throw herself off the galloping
horse.

It was then that she discovered her wrists were bound
to her ankles beneath the horse's belly, and that she
couldn't fling herself off if she tried. The Comanche
leaned down and shouted something at her, then struck
her head with the heel of his hand so hard that she sur-
rendered to the blackness once more.

And now she had awakened in a Comanche tepee,
alone—as far as Faith could tell. She could hear voices
outside, speaking in their incomprehensible tongue,
and the crackling of a nearby fire. The hide wall was
thin enough to faintly see the light cast by the dancing flames.

She could smell meat cooking over the fire, but the
savory smell evoked no answering growling in her

stomach. Hunger was impossible, because of her over-powering fear.

The day of the Comanche attack on Simpson Creek a couple of years ago flooded her brain in vivid detail—the sudden appearance of the first bloodied, arrow-studded victim tied atop his horse appearing in the midst of their Founder's Day celebration, the townspeoples' panicked run to the recently built fort as mounted Comanches poured across the creek, the savages' blood-curdling war cries as they galloped their ponies around the fort, shooting fire arrows and stolen rifles at the defenders shooting back from inside, the desperate prayers of the women and the men too old or injured to fight. And then, the sound of hooves pounding away from the town, the sudden quiet. And the discovery of mangled bodies in the street.

Faith moaned in fear. *Oh, God, I put my trust in You again, and this is the result? One minute I'm singing and praying to You, full of joy, the next I'm trussed up like a slain deer? Is that what You meant to happen?*

Faith heard a sound in back of her, and then fresh air swirled around her, tinged with the smell of wood smoke and some sort of gamey-smelling grease. *Someone had come in!* Quickly she shut her eyes again, seeking safety in feigning unconsciousness. She heard footsteps nearing her on the hard-packed earth, and then someone knelt beside her, bringing the smell of smoke and grease nearer.

She felt a nudge on her shoulder, then another and another. A voice shouted in her ear, a female voice, guttural and insistent. Faith fought the urge to flinch, maintaining her stillness by sheer effort of will. Maybe if she continued to pretend to be unconscious, they would leave her alone—at least until later. She was merely postponing her fate, she knew, but every moment she could buy was a moment she was not being tortured.

Without warning the nudge became sharp, and aimed at her ribs, and was followed by a slap so hard she could not help but recoil.

Faith's eyes flew open, and she beheld an Indian woman's coppery face, framed by short-cropped raven-black hair, just inches from hers, the obsidian eyes full of curiosity—and malice, too. She called something over her shoulder, and another pair of moccasined feet neared Faith. As they came to a stop by her, she noted the beaded design on the moccasins resembled some sort of dog or wolflike gray creature with an irregular black-beaded shape midway between his shoulders and forelegs.

The wearer of the moccasins—a huge, powerfully built brave—bent over and stared at her, his gleaming long black hair, warpaint and hideous grin sending Faith into another paroxysm of terror.

Lord, if You love me—if You ever loved me, please help me!

Chapter Twenty

Her kidnapper spoke to her in Comanche, then leaned over and untied the leather thongs that bound her wrists and ankles.

Faith rubbed her wrists to bring back the circulation in her numb arms, never taking her eyes off the brave. She longed to rub her ankles, too, but dared not expose them to the big Indian, who watched her every move with avid eyes.

He said something to the woman behind him—his wife? Yet there was a similarity to their features, so perhaps she was his sister. The Indian woman stepped forward then, and Faith saw that she carried a leather pouch and a crude wooden bowl. She dropped the bowl in front of Faith, then upended the leather pouch over it. What fell onto the bowl looked like dried meat mixed with grease. She pointed at it, uttered another unintelligible word, then pantomimed picking up the stuff, putting it in her mouth and chewing it.

Faith's stomach rebelled. It certainly wasn't the savory-smelling meat she'd been smelling from the campfire outside. And even if she wanted to, she couldn't eat with that grinning, evil-looking Indian man squatting inches from her and watching.

He barked what sounded like a command at Faith; then, when she just stared at him, he clenched a fist and boxed her left ear.

Faith straightened, feeling tears stinging her eyes, blurring her vision. The brave held a hunk of the meat mixture under her nose. He shouted the same word he had said before he'd hit her.

He was ordering her to eat, but was the meat poisoned? Would she feel it burning her throat as she tried to swallow, then double over in agony as the evil substance did its work?

He pulled a wicked-looking knife from a sheath hanging from the belt that held up his breechclout then, and waved it at her face. The message was clear—*eat or die.*

Perhaps it would be a quicker death than the fire...

The meat mixture was chewy and greasy, but intensely sweet and surprisingly palatable. Faith suddenly realized she was hungry, and so she chewed the substance and reached for more. This must be pemmican, the meat and honey mixture that frontiersmen had learned to make from exposure to Indian ways, and indeed she realized now that *pemmican* was the word the man and woman had been saying to her.

The brave relaxed somewhat then, sitting on his haunches and watching Faith eat. The woman brought Faith a gourd full of water, and Faith washed down her food, then watched the brave warily.

He turned on his heel, said something to the woman whom Faith had decided was his sister and left the tepee.

Sister muttered something, then took hold of one of

Faith's hands, yanking her to her feet. She brandished a knife from her own belt, then indicated Faith was to follow her from the tepee.

Would she be tied to a stake and burned now? The woman's obsidian gaze was impenetrable and gave Faith no clue, but when she left the tepee, there was no gathered throng waiting for her. Comanche men sat eating, while half-naked children ran and played and women stirred pots. They looked up at Faith with mild interest, then went back to whatever they were doing.

Sister marched her out of camp into a clump of scrub, then barked something, pointing first to Faith's riding skirt, then at the ground.

Faith finally understood she was to take care of her personal needs. Face burning with humiliation, she did so, and then Sister marched her back to the tepee and retied her, shoving her down on the buffalo hide she'd awoken on. She pantomimed closing her eyes, and left the tepee.

Sleep? How was she to sleep not knowing what her fate was to be? Gil, I'm sorry I didn't listen to you sooner—then I wouldn't have needed to go talk to Milly, wouldn't have foolishly ridden out and back alone...

But maybe she'd been right all along about God, that familiar voice hissed inside her. Hadn't that been proven by her present circumstances? If God existed at all, how could He care about His people when He allowed this to happen to her right when she'd begun to come back to Him?

No one would likely ever know for sure what had happened to her. They'd speculate certainly. Perhaps they'd think she'd been caught by Yancey Merriwell, and redouble their efforts to find the Georgian scoundrel. She wondered if he was even in Texas anymore.

She wasn't sure if the savage who had brought her here had been out by himself, or if he'd been part of a raiding party. When Sister had taken her out of the tepee, Faith had spotted a makeshift pen full of milling, restless cattle, so perhaps there had been a raid. She hoped it wasn't they hadn't struck Milly's ranch after she had left or Caroline's. Perhaps one or both of them had been killed defending their homes.

She heard the tepee flap lift again, and she stiffened, but this time it was only a boy who stood there peering at her. He leaned on a crutch, though both feet were planted on the hard-packed dirt floor at the entrance of the tepee. There was no threat in his gaze, only inquisitiveness.

"Hello," Faith whispered. "Who are you?"

He murmured something in Comanche.

"I'm sorry. I don't understand your language, any more than you do mine," she said. Was he her captor's son? But somehow she didn't think so. He had probably only come to satisfy his curiosity about the white captive. He'd probably never seen a white woman before—or perhaps he had, and he knew what would happen to her. If only she could talk to him!

Was this the same band whose braves Gil had encountered? Had the same savage who had seized her from the road and struck her when she tried to resist been one of those who'd chased Gil?

Now she'd never get to tell Gil of her regained faith, never get to kiss him, never hold his child… She felt a tear trickle down her face despite her resolve to remain stoic in front of this boy.

"Oh, Gil…" She was not aware of speaking aloud until she saw the spark of interest in the boy's black-as-midnight eyes.

"Geel," he repeated. *"Geel."*

Then the boy uttered a spate of Comanche words. He reached some distance above him, then leveled his hand, as if indicating height. He put his hands together, as if praying.

Faith's jaw dropped. "Did you meet Gil?" she breathed. "Was he here?"

As if he could understand her. He was merely parroting her word. *You'll have to learn English from someone else, child,* Faith thought. *I may not live long enough to teach you.*

"Gil," she said again.

The boy stared at her, then made two circles with his thumbs and forefingers, and placed them over his eyes—like spectacles. He smiled at her.

"You've met Gil," she said. *Had this boy ridden with the braves who had attacked Gil? Dear God...* Could she somehow get the boy to try to find Gil and bring him here? But how was she to convey that idea?

"I am Faith," she said, pointing to herself. *"Faith."*

"Fait," the boy repeated. Perhaps they had no "th" sound in Comanche.

Before they could say anything more, however, the tepee flap was opened again and her captor reentered. As soon as he straightened, he saw the boy and snapped something at him, his voice both angry and scornful.

Without a backward glance, the Comanche boy scampered from the tepee.

It was dusk by the time Gil and Mr. Bennett reached the Brookfield ranch, only to be told that Faith had left the place hours ago and should have been home by midafternoon. The blood drained from Mr. Bennett's

and Milly Brookfield's faces. Gil's blood turned to ice
in his veins.

Bennett groaned, "Merriwell's caught her, then.
What are we going to do now?"

"We don't know it was Merriwell," Gil reminded
him, not wanting to panic the man or Milly Brookfield.
"Perhaps her horse went lame and she had to stop in at
one of the ranches along the way."

But Faith's father wasn't willing to be reassured.
"Dear God, no…"

"You think Yancey Merriwell took her?" Milly demanded. "While she was here, Faith told me what he'd
done to that poor saloon girl."

Milly took a fortifying breath, then continued. "I *told*
Faith to let one of the men ride back with her, but she
wouldn't listen, said she wanted to be alone…we'd been
talking, you see, and…" Her voice trailed off, and she
darted an uneasy glance at Faith's father, who looked
as if he might pass out, too.

"Mr. Bennett, let's go inside. Let me get you some
water," she said, firmly taking the older man by the
arm. With Gil's help, she shepherded Faith's father inside the ranch house.

"Can I borrow a fresh horse?" Gil asked in a low
voice, once they had Mr. Bennett sitting in an armchair
with a glass of water.

"Of course," she said.

"Where are you going?" demanded Bennett, still
looking too pale for Gil's comfort. "I'm coming, too.
It's my daughter—" He winced then and placed his
open palm over his chest.

"No, you're not, Mr. Bennett, you're obviously exhausted. I can go faster without you," Gil said kindly

but firmly. "You can ride back in the buggy in the morning."

"But it's pitch-black out there," Milly said. "At least wait until first light."

"There's a moon. I can follow the road well enough if you'll lend me a lantern, too, Miss Milly," he told her. "By the time I get home, check on Papa and let Mrs. Bennett know her husband is resting here, it'll be dawn. I'll leave word at the jail that we didn't find Faith here, but that you're all right. Better bring your men in close because we really don't know what happened." Gil knew from the look in Milly's eyes that she'd already intended to do just that.

"And then what? You'll join a search party?" Bennett asked.

Gil nodded. There was strength in numbers. He'd kill Merriwell himself if he'd harmed a hair on Faith's head.

Runs Like a Deer stood outside the tepee, wondering what to do. He'd heard enough of Black Coyote Heart's boasting to know that he considered the white eyes woman his to either keep as a captive or kill, as his whim dictated. Being a captive, one who might eventually marry a warrior and became one of the people herself, would not be a bad fate for a woman, he mused. There was no finer life than that of the People—free as the wind, moving from place to place as they wished, at one with nature and the Great Spirit... He'd seen male captives in this band and others on the staked plains become Comanches, too, some of them fiercer than their adopted tribe.

But he also knew Black Coyote Heart's spirit—it was as dark as his name. He would not treat the white woman fairly, rewarding obedience with increasing trust. He would abuse her, and on a whim, kill her if it suited him. He'd heard the other braves egging Black Coyote Heart on to tie the woman to a pole and do the scalp dance.

Panther Claw Scars would not intervene, even though the boy knew the chief preferred that his band not take captives from the whites. Mexican captives were safer—their people would not ride over the Big Long River to save them for fear of the Texans. But the taking of captives was a long, honorable tradition among the people, and in any case, the boy suspected the old chief was a little bit intimidated by Black Coyote Heart in the absence of his medicine man, Makes Healing. He would not forbid Black Coyote Heart to do as he wished with the white woman.

This woman knew Gil, the white holy man. Perhaps she was even his woman. And Gil had been kind to him, speaking in a fatherly tone and courageously helping him return to his tribe—at his own expense, as it turned out. Gil would not want this woman to be tortured and killed. He would want her back.

But Runs Like a Deer did not know where to locate Gil, the white holy man. He wouldn't be able to find him even if he was brave enough to ride his pony into the closest white eyes' town, and they might take him captive and torture *him*.

He had to go get his father to intervene. Makes Healing was on a spiritual retreat, and he had not disclosed where he would be meditating. In all likelihood he hadn't even known himself when he'd left. But it didn't matter. Runs Like a Deer would have to find him.

He would mount his pony and leave at dawn, telling no one where he was going.

* * *

His father was already sitting in the kitchen with his Bible in front of him when Gil arrived back. Quickly Gil explained that Faith wasn't at Milly's, so he was going to find the sheriff and form a search party to look for her.

The old man seized Gil's hand and stared up with that keen, penetrating gaze of his, and for a moment father and son just stared deeply into one another's eyes. Then his father pulled downward on Gil's hand, and Gil knew his father wanted him to kneel.

He felt his father's hand on his head. The old man's prayer was silent, but Gil knew the old man was praying for his son's protection and success in finding Faith.

"Thank you, Papa," he said, when the hand was lifted from his head. "Try not to worry about me."

The old man shook his head and smiled faintly. "No...I pr-pray."

Gil straightened. "Where's Mrs. Bennett?"

His father pointed toward the parlor. "Sleep."

Gil strode into the parlor and found her asleep on the horsehair sofa, covered with her shawl. Gently he woke the woman, wishing he had better news to tell her.

The woman sprang awake at his light touch. "I can't believe I dozed off, Reverend. You didn't find Faith with Milly?" she said, her eyes desperate and wild.

He shook his head and explained he was going to form a search party. "Your husband is spending the night at Mrs. Brookfield's ranch," he added. "He was done in, so I suggested he wait till morning to drive the buggy back."

"But—"

"I'll look till I find her, Mrs. Bennett," Gil promised. "We'll ride out as soon as it's light." A glance outside the window revealed the first faint graying of the dark. That wouldn't be long, and he had to get a fresh horse.

"Please, Reverend," Mrs. Bennett begged, fresh tears streaming down her face. "I can't bear to think of what that monster Merriwell might do to my little girl!"

"With God's help, we'll find them," he promised again. "Please keep praying."

"Oh, I will, of course. Go with God, Reverend," Mrs. Bennett said. "Take some of my biscuits with you on the trail. You…you have a gun?"

He nodded. "Miss Milly wouldn't let me leave without one," he said, then left to go wake Sheriff Bishop.

In an hour, they rode out—Gil, Sheriff Bishop, Dr. Walker, Jack Collier, who'd been told of Faith's being missing by Milly and had brought a couple of his ranch hands, and Andy Calhoun from the livery. Bishop left his deputy at the jail in case some sort of ransom demand was brought there.

Gil prayed they weren't too late to save her. And that he'd be able to conquer his urge to kill the Georgian when they caught up to him.

Chapter Twenty-One

Faith woke with a cramp in her left calf, but still bound hand and foot, she could do nothing but endure the stabbing pain. She gritted her teeth so she would not cry out and awaken the snoring Comanche woman sleeping a few feet away from her. Finally the spasm passed, leaving her with nothing to do but imagine what would happen today.

It might be her last day on earth. A tear slid down her cheek at the thought.

She had wandered far from the Lord, and had only made the first few steps back toward Him. She hadn't had a chance to do anything that would make her worthy of forgiveness.

Gil had said that if she believed in God, she would see her brother in Heaven. But had the prayer she prayed been enough that He would forgive her for her past faithlessness? She still had so many questions—questions she'd planned to ask Gil the next time she could speak with him alone, and now she would never have the chance. She would never get the chance to show him how much she loved him, or what a worthy wife she could be for a preacher.

By now, she figured, it would have been discovered that she was missing. Someone would have ridden out to the Brookfield ranch to see if she'd merely stayed the night with Milly, and a search would have begun. Was Gil part of the search party? Was her father?

Her parents would be worried sick. She remembered what her father had told her about his heart, and her anxiety kicked up several notches. Would the stress of fearing for his daughter cause a fatal heart seizure? Her father did love her—she knew that now. True, he'd been clumsy at showing it for some time after Eddie had died, and he'd taken her for granted many times, but she'd begun to realize her father's quiet pride in her when she'd begun helping him more at the newspaper office after Merriwell fled.

Her poor mother—losing daughter and husband at the same time.

Or this might be her first day of a long and miserable captivity. Gil and her family would never find her, for the Comanche camp was well hidden. How long had they existed here, with no one in Simpson Creek the wiser? And they wouldn't stay here forever, wherever here was. The Comanches were a roaming people and would move on whenever they felt like it.

Then she became aware that the Comanche woman's eyes were open, and staring at her across the floor of the tepee.

Once again, she was taken out to see to her needs, then given pemmican and water. Faith hoped this meant they did not intend to kill her today, for surely they wouldn't waste food on her if she was to die within hours.

Then she was tied back up, and spent an endless day where she could do nothing but stare at the tepee wall or at a rotating group of women guards, who alternated staring back at her with scraping the flesh from hides, sewing pieces of tanned leather together into clothing, or stitching beading onto new moccasins.

Twice, the big brave who had captured her came in and stared at her, his eyes greedy and threatening, and she closed her eyes until she heard him leave. Once, she heard what she thought was his voice, raised in angry discussion outside her tent.

She spent the hours praying, napping and wondering what Gil and her parents were doing and what would happen to her.

Gil and the other men of the search party camped on the banks of the Colorado River that night, tired, saddle-sore and discouraged. They'd ridden miles in every direction around Simpson Creek and the rest of San Saba County and had found no trace of Faith or Yancey Merriwell, nor had anyone they encountered seen them.

"We'll split up in the morning and go farther," Bishop said, as they ate whatever food they'd been able to pack and bring along. "Half of us will go north, half south—"

He stopped as the braying of a mule and the creaking of wagon wheels announced the arrival of a newcomer, a bearded mule skinner hauling freight.

"Mind if I share yore fire, gents?" the mule skinner asked. "Got my own grub, but I wouldn't mind some company, after what happened t'day a coupla miles southeast a' here."

"And what would that be?" Bishop inquired, gesturing that the mule skinner could come in and join them.

"Comanches burned a ranch, killin' every soul there and drivin' off their stock. So ya see why I ain't hankerin' t'camp alone. What're you fellows out fer?"

Gil barely listened as the sheriff explained their purpose, for the mule skinner's mention of an Indian raid had sent a chill skittering down Gil's spine.

What if Faith had been taken not by Merriwell, but by Comanches? The possibility that Merriwell's recent flight had nothing to do with Faith's disappearance on the way back from the Brookfield ranch had occurred to him before he joined the search party, but the rest of them had concluded Merriwell was the most likely culprit.

The longer Gil sat there, eating what Mrs. Bennett had packed for him while he listened to the mule skinner talk about the carnage he'd seen at the burned ranch, the surer he became that Faith had been taken by Comanches, not Merriwell. And he knew what he had to do.

Bishop looked thoughtful as the search party considered how the mule skinner's report might affect their plan.

"Those redskins can travel like the wind," Andy Calhoun said. "They could be fifty miles or more away by now."

"Not if they're driving cattle," Jack Collier said.

"But they might have split up," one of his ranch hands suggested. Faces around the campfire were somber as they all realized the very real possibility that Faith Bennett might be an Indian captive and never found.

"I'll need a man to ride back to town at sunup and

have my deputy contact the cavalry—they need to know what we just found out. We'll keep searching, but if Miss Faith is a Comanche captive, they have a far better chance of rescuing her than we do."

"I'll go," Gil said.

Bishop nodded, probably figuring a preacher not used to hard riding was the man they could most easily spare. "Let's all get some shut-eye, then."

Gil would have liked to leave right then, but he had no lantern to light his way as he had had the night he rode to town from the Brookfield ranch. And every bone and muscle he possessed screamed with exhaustion. He needed to sleep if he could, so when tomorrow came, he could do as he'd told Bishop he would, then get a fresh horse and ride off to where his heart told him Faith would be.

The next morning began as the previous one had, but as soon as she had broken her fast with the inevitable pemmican, she was yanked out of the tepee and lashed to the post in the middle of the camp.

Hours later, Faith winced as yet another round-faced Comanche woman poked at her with a sharpened stick in passing, then ducked as much as the leather thongs binding her to the pole would allow when the woman's bright-eyed child chucked a handful of pebbles at her. One caught Faith on the cheek in spite of her efforts, and she bit her lip against the stinging pain.

Most of the tribe went about their business, however, merely giving her sidelong, opaque glances from time to time. There was no brush piled up around her feet as if they meant to burn her, at least yet. Perhaps the purpose of leaving her tied to the pole was to provide humiliation and distress for the captive and a source of amusement for the women and children—before escalating the torment.

Faith faced another post stuck in the ground. It was sharpened to a point at the top, and just below the point several scalps were impaled. She did everything she could not to look at that hideous sight, and hoped none of the victims had been people she knew. *Please, Lord, protect the people of Simpson Creek, especially Gil, Mama, Papa and all the Spinsters' Club.*

She'd been tied to the pole since early morning and not been given food or water since shortly after sunrise. The inside of her mouth felt dry as the middle of a haystack. Her head pounded dully as the summer sun beat down on her. At first, she'd been clammy with perspiration beneath her long-sleeved shirt and heavy skirt, but her sweating had ceased, and she could feel her skin of her scalp and cheeks being scorched with sunburn.

Once, she dozed, only to jerk awake when a stolid-faced squaw pelted her with rotten meat. Some of the stinking mess clung to her ripped, stained riding skirt.

Her captor passed by once, flanked by a trio of his friends. When he saw that she had seen him, he pulled out a knife and fondled it while watching her. He chuckled when she turned her head away.

Faith hadn't seen the inquisitive Indian boy who had come into the tepee her first night again, although a half-dozen boys of similar ages had passed by carrying bows and arrows. At first she thought they might be preparing to use her for target practice, but they kept walking until they passed by out of sight of the camp. Where had the boy with the crutch gone? Something about him—the apparent fact that he had met Gil? The kindness in his eyes?—had been comforting. Maybe her captor had punished the boy for entering his tepee and looking at her, and he had been forbidden to come near her.

As the afternoon wore on, the tantalizing smells coming from the cooking pots began to taunt her, but no one showed any interest in feeding her or relieving her thirst. Laughter erupted from several sides when a boy walked past her, throwing a gourdful of red ants at her which he had apparently scooped up from an anthill.

Most of the ants bounced harmlessly off her clothing and fell to the ground. A few, however, found their way inside the neck of her blouse, and Faith couldn't help flinching and whimpering as she felt their tiny, vicious biting. Her audience seemed to find her flinches and outcries the height of amusement.

Soon everyone took their cooked food and went inside their tepees, and she was left alone with her thoughts.

Lord, I don't understand why this is happening. Please, let Gil find me...

As soon as he reached Simpson Creek, Gil lost no time in delivering his message to the deputy and checking on his father. He didn't tell Faith's mother that they now thought Faith might have been taken by the Indians. It would have given her added anguish for no good reason, and he would have had to stay longer to try to console her. Instead, he let her believe he was rendezvousing with one of the search parties, and went to retrieve Milly Brookfield's now-rested horse from the livery.

What if he never found the camp? Gil wondered as he rode north out of town. He couldn't be one-hundred-percent certain it wasn't Merriwell who had taken her after all, and if Comanches had been the culprits, he had no reason to be certain it was even the same band he had encountered when he'd found the Indian boy. A raiding party from another band might be miles away with her by now.

Or it might not even have been Comanches at all, Gil thought. Kiowas, enemies of the Comanches, raided in Texas from time to time, too.

Lord, only You can help me find her, and only You can save her. Please lead me to the right place, even if it means I must die.

He figured there was very little chance he would come out of this alive if he found Faith, even if he did somehow persuade the Comanches to release her.

But if by some miracle I do survive—whether I'm able to find Faith, Lord, I know there is something I need to do—something I should have done a long time ago.

He needed to tell his father about his long-ago sin with Suellen, and then confess it to the congregation. The Lord had long ago forgiven him, but because he had kept his sin secret, perhaps there would be some in Simpson Creek Church who would feel he wasn't worthy to be their preacher after they learned what he'd done.

But all that would take place in the future, he thought. He left the road and began to climb into the hills.

As the sun began its descent into the hills to the west, Black Coyote Heart took yet another look at himself in the mirror he had taken from the dead white eyes, and which he had yet to give Eyes of an Antelope. He was the best-looking male of his tribe, that was certain. No one had such a wealth of long, raven-black hair as he possessed. No one had such a fierce, eagle eye. He was taller than most and powerfully built. The many coups he had counted showed in his proud bearing.

Grinning at his image, he dabbed on another slash of crimson war paint. When the white woman saw him, she would surely faint from terror.

He heard the murmuring of the people outside the tepee, and the beginning throbs of the drum beating in a slow rhythm.

Crow Echo, his sister, lifted the flap of the tent. She had painted her face in slashes of black, as was traditional among the tribe's women when the scalp dance was to take place.

"It is time," she said.

He lifted the flap of the tent, and saw that Panther Claw Scars sat in the place of honor, as befitting a chief. Black Coyote Heart's fellow warriors and the young women were already dancing and chanting around the pole to which the red-haired woman was bound. She hadn't seen him yet, but she already looked terrified.

None of the warriors had died during the raid, so there was no clamoring for the captive to be killed. The purpose of the dance was to subjugate the woman with terror. After that she would be compliant and meek, always afraid that she could be tied to the pole again and killed the next time.

The drum beat sped up. All eyes were on Black Coyote Heart as he stepped into the circle of dancers, pulling his knife from its sheath with a ceremonial flourish. The woman saw him now and the knife he held, and shrank back against the pole, her green eyes impossibly wide in a face leached of all color.

Eyes of an Antelope saw him, too, he noted with satisfaction. She was staring at him as if she could not

get enough of his magnificence, and her father also
looked suitably impressed. Perhaps it would take only
three horses instead of four—plus the captive woman,
of course, to purchase his bride.

He began to dance, weaving closer and closer to the
white woman each time he passed in front of her, feint-
ing at her with the knife as if he meant to cut her throat,
pantomiming the act of scalping. Once he lifted a lock
of her dark red hair with the blade of his knife, then
cut it off. She'd had her teeth clenched before that, but
now she whimpered with fear.

*Yes, the red-haired white woman would give him no
trouble after this.*

Gil thought he knew a little of what it was like for
the Lord to wander forty days in the wilderness. He felt
as discouraged as Jesus must have felt just *before* the
devil showed up to tempt him power and worldly riches.
Gil wasn't being tempted with anything like that, of
course, just to the possibility of giving in to despair.

*Lord, can it be Your will that I don't find Faith, even
though I'm willing to give my life for her?* He couldn't
believe it could be so. Yet the sun was sinking and he
had found no trace of horse tracks, no scrap of clothing clinging to a shrub, nothing.

With God, all things are possible.

And then the wind carried a snatch of sound to his
ears—a sound so faint and so low that he couldn't be
sure that his mind wasn't playing tricks on him, for it
seemed to be coming from beneath the ground. A ca-
denced, low reverberation like the beat of a drum. He
paused, listening, then inched the horse forward, his
eyes scanning his surroundings for anything familiar.

Seek and ye shall find.

All at once he spotted a mesquite some fifty yards ahead of him and stared hard at it. *Yes*—he'd seen that scrubby tree, split down the middle by lightning, ahead of him before. While tied to the post in the middle of the camp, he'd spotted it perched right above the lip of the overhanging ledge that hung over the Comanche camp.

Now Gil could hear the drumbeat clearly, a beat echoing in the thudding of many feet and chanting voices keeping time to the drum's throbbing. Wanting to see what was happening without being seen as yet, Gil dismounted his horse, hoping it wouldn't stray far. He crawled the rest of the way on his belly to the lip of the canyon and peered over it.

At first he could make out nothing, for his eyes were blinded by the campfire, and then he spotted Faith, tied to the same post he had been not so long ago. Painted savages danced around her, the firelight reflecting off their skin.

He felt sick at the confirmation that she was exactly where he feared she would be. He was outnumbered perhaps forty to one. And that was just counting the young braves. There were as many or more women of various ages, and half as many older men, including one he guessed was the chief by his ceremonial headdress. Nowhere did he see Makes Healing or Runs Like a Deer. Had they been banished—or something worse— because the medicine man had aided him?

As Gil continued to watch, unable to decide what to do, he was horrified and enraged to see a Comanche woman lean in as she capered past, jabbing Faith with a stick. He saw her flinch back, clamping her teeth over her lip to keep from crying out.

He had to rescue her! How long before they would progress from torment to real torture? He had the will

to do it, to ride in there and hope they would be willing
to free her in exchange for him, but he had no reason
to believe they would do anything more than laugh at
him, then kill them both. Lord, why couldn't he have
been born to be a rough-and-ready cowboy or a soldier skilled in firearms? He'd left the pistol back in his
saddlebag—he could get it, but what were six bullets
against such a murderous horde below?

*All David the shepherd boy had were five smooth
stones. And he felled the mighty Philistine giant. I will
go with you.*

All right, then. There was nothing else to do but to
attempt the impossible.

He turned, intending to crawl back to his horse, remount, then ride boldly into the camp. He knew now
where the land dipped, several yards to the east of the
lip of the canyon, forming a narrow trail into the camp
itself.

He froze, for there were four Comanches standing
just a couple of yards behind him, and a fifth holding
the muzzle of his horse so the beast couldn't nicker
and warn him.

Faith had been so sure the only thing worse than
the taunting and hideous pantomiming of her weaving, swooping captor and his dancing friends could
be the time he would actually inflict a fatal wound or
set her on fire with a burning brand. But the sight of
Gil, his arms tied behind him, being pushed down the
trail into the camp and into the circle of firelight was
much, much worse.

"Gil!"

He heard her over the crackling flames nearby and

the monotonous drumbeats, thumping feet and chanting, and raised his head. "Faith!"

She could see that they had beaten him. Even in the flickering light she could see one eyelid was reddened and would probably swell shut soon. They had broken his nose. A thin trickle of blood ran down over his lips and onto his chin.

Her captor had circled back around the pole and saw him now, too. He stopped in midstep, pointing at Gil and shouting a question at the Indians who had brought him into the camp.

One of them pointed at the overhanging ledge above the camp, indicating, Faith thought, it was where they had found him.

Rage suffused the hideous face of her captor at the interruption. Then, in a lightning change of mood, he laughed and pointed his wicked-looking knife right at Gil, calling out something to the others.

Loud whoops lifted from a score of throats at whatever he had said, and they seized Gil, dragging him past her to the post in front of her and binding her so they faced one another about ten feet apart. She guessed he hadn't seen the scalps that so hideously decorated the top of the post, but he had only to look up and he would.

She had thought that she had lost every bit of moisture in her body, but impossibly, she felt a hot tear slide down one cheek, then the other. Was she going to be forced to watch him die before they killed her, too?

"What are you doing here, Gil?" she cried, when the whooping died down enough that he could hear her. "You can't help me—they'll kill you, too!"

Her captor apparently didn't like her speaking to her fellow captive, for he ran at her with his huge palm open. His slap stung like a hundred red ant bites at once. He screamed something at her, his eyes bulging in his fury.

She looked beyond those fiery obsidian eyes to Gil's face, and saw him shaking his head at her, warning her not to anger the Comanche further. Resolutely, she looked away—away from the face of the man she loved, away from her captor whose evil face was only inches from hers.

The drumbeat began again. Her captor whirled away from her and lunged at Gil, slashing with his knife. In a motion almost too quick for Faith to see, he jabbed at Gil, opening a diagonal slash in Gil's right cheek. Pointing his knife, he screamed something to the men and women who had been dancing with him. He seemed to be trying to incite the others to do as he had just done.

No! Faith wasn't sure if she had shrieked aloud or silently inside, but the Indian in the headdress stood then and raised his ceremonial lance. The others paused, and the drumbeats halted.

He said something in that impenetrable tongue of theirs and pointed.

Riding down the narrow defile was yet another Indian, an older man like the chief, and following him on a smaller pony was the boy who had come into the tepee.

Chapter Twenty-Two

Now Faith saw frustration join the anger on her captor's face, its focus shifting from her to the mounted older man riding toward them. The older Indian pointed toward them and shouted something that sounded like a command.

The younger Comanche's face darkened still further and he clenched the hand not holding the knife into a fist at his side.

Now the chief barked something at him, and her captor went rigid. Jaw clenched, he sheathed his knife. He shouted something at the Indian on the horse, who by now had ridden down to the chief; then, raising a fist, shouting and gesticulating, he stomped over to the two older Indians. The other young warriors swarmed behind him, doing likewise, obviously enraged by whatever the mounted Indian had said.

Was the newcomer disputing her captor's right to do with her as he willed? She watched, but could glean no hint of what was being discussed, so she turned to Gil. Who knew how long the Comanches' attention would be diverted?

He felt her gaze and looked at her. "My darling Faith, are you all right? Have they— *Has he*—" he jerked his head toward her captor "—hurt you?"

"Not really," she said. None of her cuts and bruises hurt now that he was with her, even though there was nothing he could probably do but die with her. "But you—your nose…"

"It doesn't matter," he said. "I had to find you. I didn't know if I could locate this camp again, or if they'd even still be here, but I had to try…"

"'Locate the camp again'?" she echoed. "So you *have* been here. That boy knows you, doesn't he?" She nodded toward the boy on his pony, who had followed the older man to the chief. He was looking over his shoulder at Gil now, worry etching his young features.

"Yes…his name is Runs Like a Deer. I'm sorry, Faith, I didn't tell you the whole truth about my encounter with the Indians," he admitted, shamefaced. "I found him in the hills. He'd fallen from his pony and his leg was broken. I had to find his people—I couldn't just leave him out there alone and in pain… Then those braves found us, and attacked me. I was taken back here."

She said nothing, just watched him steadily. *Who knew how long they would have to speak together before the Comanches turned on the again?*

"Those young braves wanted to kill me that day. I was bound to the same post you're tied to now. They would have, too, except that Makes Healing, there—" he indicated the older man who was now dismounting his horse "—stopped him. He's the medicine man of this band, and Runs Like a Deer is his son. He was grateful that I had helped his son and interceded for me apparently, so they were forced to release me."

"But why…"

"I didn't feel I could tell anyone about this place," he said, "because the cavalry would come down on them, and the medicine man and his son might well be killed. It seemed a poor thanks for the mercy he showed me."

How like Gil to return gratitude and mercy—even to an Indian—for the gratitude and mercy he'd been shown.

"But it seems I was wrong," Gil went on sadly, "because if the cavalry had eradicated this camp, they couldn't have taken *you*. Or attacked a ranch out near Lampasas. Faith, I'm so sorry."

"You couldn't have known this would happen, Gil." The cattle she had seen penned up at the edge of the camp must have been from that attack. And so were the scalps hanging above him.

Both fell silent, for one of the warriors was returning to them now.

His face unreadable, the brave untied Faith, then retied the leather thongs behind her back. Keeping a hand on the binding between her wrists, he pushed her toward one of the tepees. Once inside, he pointed to a tanned hide on the ground, and when she had lain down, bound her legs, too, so she was once more tied and helpless as she had endured the night before.

A moment later he returned, pushing Gil ahead of him. He was followed by an older squaw who seated herself across the floor of the tepee. In moments Gil was bound just as she was and lying a couple of feet from her, facing her.

It suddenly seemed to occur to the brave that they might be thirsty. He offered water from a drinking gourd to first Faith, then Gil. They drank thirstily, as much as he would give them, even though it was awkward to drink in that position and much of it spilled.

As soon as the brave had left, Faith darted a cautious glance at the older squaw, but she seemed much more interested in the bowl of stew she had brought with her than in the captives she'd been set to guard.

"Gil, what will happen to us now?"

He hated to quench the flicker of hope he saw in her eyes.

He looked away. "When I was here before, Makes Healing told me if I ever returned he wouldn't be able to save me."

Her eyes widened. "He…he'd *let them kill you?*"

He was done with lies and half-truths. "He said if I ever returned I would die."

Tears trickled down her pale cheeks once again.

"It's all right, Faith, if that's what must happen. But I'm hopeful I can persuade him, somehow, to let you go." He had to find a way to do that, he thought, desperation squeezing his heart. He'd seen the way that brave with the red war paint had been threatening Faith. Gil would let them kill him a thousand times if it meant removing Faith from that monster's clutches.

"We must pray that both of us are released," she said then.

Something about the way her eyes shone with an extra brightness alerted him then.

"'We'?" he repeated, his eyes searching hers.

"When I went out to Milly's I asked her things about faith and—" She shut her mouth then, for someone was entering the tepee again.

What had she been about to say? Had she regained her belief in God?

It was Makes Healing, Gil saw as the older Comanche straightened.

"Gil Chadwick," the man said. He assisted Gil to sit up, then lowered himself to his haunches next to Gil. His eyes gave nothing away.

"Hello, Makes Healing," Gil responded.

"He speaks English!" Faith murmured in surprise.

"You should not have come," the medicine man said, allowing Gil to see the sadness in his black eyes. "Did I not warn you?"

"Yes, but I had to try to rescue the woman I love," Gil said. He nodded toward Faith, lying on the other side of him. "Makes Healing, this is Miss Faith Bennett, the lady I want to marry." How surreal it seemed to be making an introduction as if they were sitting in a parlor, instead of in a Comanche tepee.

The Comanche nodded solemnly at her, and she at him.

"My son rode through the night to find the place where I sought a vision," Makes Healing said. "He told me that she is your woman, but Black Coyote Heart took her for his slave."

"What a fitting name," Faith said tartly. Then she focused on what else the medicine man had said. "Then they weren't going to kill me? But I'd rather die than be a slave!" she declared.

Gil saw Makes Healing transfer his gaze to Faith. "If a slave does not obey, she *will* die," he told her. "A slave who obeys is given more trust and kindness, and in time may join the tribe. A woman slave can become the wife of her captor, or if another man gives horses for her, the wife of that man."

"Never," she said.

"Makes Healing, please, can't you make them let

her go as you did with me?" Gil asked. "I'm willing to pay the price for returning here, but she's done nothing wrong. I kept faith with you—I told no one this camp is here."

Makes Healing looked down at his hands for a long time. "You are a brave man, Gil Chadwick, for coming here to rescue her when you knew it meant death. Black Coyote Heart considers your woman his property, and the other young braves lust for blood. Panther Claw Scars, our chief, does not wish to always refuse them. I do not know if I can change their minds."

"Please," Faith said. "I'll stay here, if you can get them to release Gil."

"Faith, no!" Gil exclaimed. "You must not make such an offer!"

Makes Healing gave Faith an approving look. "Your woman loves you and is a woman of spirit. But it would never work. Your people would do anything to save a captive white woman. We would be hunted."

"That's true," Gil said. "So it would be best for the tribe if she was released. The cavalry would ride in and rain destruction down upon your people. Perhaps they would kill Runs Like a Deer," he added, hoping he was not going too far.

Makes Healing's eyes narrowed dangerously. But Gil knew he was bargaining for Faith's life, and he was willing to risk it. After all, he was going to die anyway.

The medicine man rose to his feet. "I will speak to the chief. He will decide what is to be done. I will not return tonight. You will be told at sunrise of the chief's decision. He must seek the will of the Great Spirit."

"The Great Spirit is your name for the Lord," Gil said boldly. "His Son, Jesus, wrote in the Good Book which our people read, 'Blessed are the merciful.'"

Makes Healing looked at him for a long minute. "Do not try to escape," he said. "There are braves outside the tepee standing guard. If you try, they will not be merciful or wait for the chief to decide what to do with you." He left the tepee.

"As if we could," Faith said, jerking her head to indicate the leather thongs that bound both of them hand and foot, and the squaw who now watched their every move with beady black eyes that missed nothing.

Gil nodded ruefully, although he couldn't help but remember how both Peter and Paul had been loosed from jails in the book of Acts.

He wanted to distract Faith from her worry, so he asked her what she had been about to say when the medicine man came to the tent.

Her eyes brightened again in the fading light. "It was all so clear after I spoke to Milly. She said I only had to have faith the size of a mustard seed, and it would be enough. I still have questions of course, but I am a believer once again, Gil!"

"Thank God," he breathed. "I'm so glad, Faith." At least if he wasn't able to buy her freedom with his blood, Faith was a child of God.

"Your coming here to save me, offering your life for mine, is like Jesus coming to the world to save us," she said solemnly.

"No sacrifice I could make could equal what Jesus did for all of mankind," he said. "But yes, he died to ransom us."

"But we're going to pray for a miracle," she told him. "God is a God of miracles, isn't he? If He wills it, He can save both of us."

Gil nodded. *If God only chose to save Faith, that would be miracle enough for him.*

They prayed for their miracle then, first Faith and then Gil, both of them ignoring the suspicious eyes of the Comanche woman across from them. Faith also prayed for her parents and for Gil's father.

Lord, wouldn't she make a wonderful preacher's wife now? Gil thought. *Maybe You could find some other young preacher for her to marry if I don't make it through this.*

Faith fell asleep after that, but Gil lay awake for a long time, listening to the crackling of the campfire and the occasional murmur of the braves outside the tepee.

Simpson Creek Church would go on without him, as it should. He prayed that Faith and his father also would be able to. Gil hoped she would be able to report he died bravely, and prayed God would give him the courage he would need so that it would be the truth.

Thy will be done, Lord.

At dawn the squaw left the tent, returning minutes later with food. One of the braves—not Black Coyote Heart, she was relieved to see—removed their wrist bindings so they could eat.

Faith was given only water and more pemmican, but Gil was given a hunk of roast venison and a bowl of boiled mashed corn with his water. He tried to share with Faith, but that seemed to upset the Comanche woman, so Faith insisted that he eat all he'd been given. Her stomach felt as if it was too full of grasshoppers for her to be hungry anyway.

Makes Healing returned to the tepee in the morning shortly after they finished their breakfast.

"You have eaten well, Gil Chadwick, and that is good, for you will need every bit of strength you have."

Gil raised an inquiring eyebrow, but waited in silence for the medicine man's explanation.

"I have persuaded Panther Claw Scars to give you a chance to win your freedom and that of your woman, Faith. It is not much of a chance, for you are a holy man, not a warrior as Black Coyote Heart is. But being a holy man gives you strong medicine, Gil Chadwick. You are to fight Black Coyote Heart to the death."

Gil was pale, but Faith saw him nod resolutely. "If I win, Faith goes free and we leave here together," he said.

"It is so," Makes Healing said. "But if you do not win, your woman will die. It is clear to the people that she would never be content to live among us. If you die, she will die, too, to honor your death."

Chapter Twenty-Three

Gil swallowed hard. He had known he would be fighting for Faith's freedom—now he was fighting for her very life.

He shifted his gaze from Makes Healing to Faith, and saw that even though she was very pale, her eyes met his steadily. "It's all right, Gil. If the worst happens and you die, I wouldn't want to live anyhow."

He winced. *Lord, I'm a preacher, not a fighter. Couldn't the odds be more in our favor?*

Gil turned back to Makes Healing. "When?"

"The fight is to take place when the sun is at its highest point," Makes Healing said.

"Will we be using weapons or is this a bare-knuckle fight?" Gil asked, then wondered why he bothered. It wasn't as if he was good with any weapon.

Makes Healing pulled a long-bladed knife from the sheath at his waist and proffered it. "I would be honored if you would use mine. I have said a blessing over it, for I hope for your victory. Black Coyote Heart does not follow the way of peace that the chief and I would prefer. His spirit is evil and full of hate."

"The honor is mine, Makes Healing," Gil said. "Thank you." If only he'd done more with a knife than just some whittling as a boy. He'd known men in the army, during the war, who could throw a knife with deadly accuracy and were lethal in a hand-to-hand knife fight, but he hadn't been one of them.

"You will have until the sun is high to prepare your spirit," Makes Healing said. "But you must not leave the tepee."

It would have to be a time to pray *and* say all the things to Faith he'd been holding back for so long, all the endearments he could think of until they met again in Heaven.

The moment the medicine man left the tepee, Faith flew to his arms. He'd never dreamed their first kiss would take place inside a tepee, with red men eager to kill them surrounding it. But the moment Faith's lips touched his he forgot all that and concentrated on the sweetness of them, on the warmth of her, the steadfast beat of her heart.

"I love you, Gil," she said, when they finally drew apart. "I always have, even when I thought I had no right to. When this is over, I want to be your wife just as soon as we can possibly get married."

He could see her faith in him shining from her eyes and wished he deserved such faith and trust in his ability.

"I love you, too, Faith,' he said. "With all my heart. And if God gives us the victory, that's a request I'll gladly fulfill."

They spent the rest of the time on their knees, holding hands and praying for that victory.

At noon, they were led out to the middle of the camp. The entire tribe lined the open space, whooping and cat-calling at them. From somewhere near the chief's tent, a drummer kept a steady beat on a tom-tom. Everyone seemed to be wearing their best, Faith observed as they tied her to the post once again—beaded buckskins and moccasins, their hair black and flowing, feathers in the scalp locks of the young men. The young braves who had ridden with Black Coyote Heart jeered as Gil took his place in the center of the open space. The women, especially the younger ones, looked at Faith with implacable hard eyes.

She spotted Runs Like a Deer standing at his father's side next to the chief. He looked worried, but when he noticed her looking at him, he gave her a hopeful smile.

Her heart was touched despite the danger she and Gil faced. No wonder the man she loved had wanted to protect this boy.

Gil waited in the open space, his face resolute. He had told her he would not look at her once the fight began, and asked her to do her best not to cry out. He would need every bit of concentration he possessed.

Black Coyote Heart came out of a nearby tepee and strode toward the circle then. The young braves cheered and lifted tomahawks and lances into the air.

He had painted his face with a combination of red, black and white paint so he looked even more hideous than he had the day she had been seized on the road from Milly's ranch. He darted a scornful glance at Gil, then sidled up to the pole Faith was bound to and favored her with a leer that turned her blood instantly to ice. He leaned closer, so close she could smell his sweat, mixed with the pungent tang of the buffalo grease in his hair. With a fiendish laugh, he drew his knife with painstaking slowness from its sheath and slid it along her throat from one ear to the other, not so hard that it would draw blood, but leaving her with no doubt as to how eager he was to actually cut her throat.

He turned and pointed at Gil, then took his knife and rolled the flat of the blade along his own scalp. The message was clear.

She tried her best to suppress a shudder. *Ignore him, Gil. He's trying to rattle you.* The Indian's gesture had tightened Gil's jaw, she noted, but he merely shifted his gaze to the chief, who stood and appeared to be giving instructions to the combatants. The medicine man translated for Gil, but Faith couldn't hear what he said.

Black Coyote Heart made a ceremony of removing his buckskin shirt, tossing it to one of his warrior friends among the onlookers. Gil merely rolled up the sleeves of what remained of his dusty, stained shirt.

Lord, I believe You can give Gil the victory if it is Your will. Please, Lord, save us!

The chief held up his hand. Both men tensed and the drumbeat sped up. Then suddenly the chief let his arm fall and the battle was on.

Quick as a striking snake, Black Coyote Heart lunged at Gil, jabbing at his left forearm, his knife leaving a long gash. He shouted and raised a triumphant fist at achieving the first "coup," and his warriors cheered.

The sight of the crimson rivulet running down Gil's skin sent waves of nausea churning Faith's stomach, but he merely wiped his arm on his pants and kept his eye on the Comanche, dancing out of reach when the Comanche lunged again.

Jeers erupted from the crowd as they saw Gil retreat, but Faith saw his strategy. He was less powerfully built than the Comanche, but that made him more agile.

The Indian shouted something at Gil. Makes Healing called a translation—"He says if you give up now, he will kill you both quickly and not make you suffer. Do not believe him, Gil Chadwick!"

The next time Black Coyote Heart sprang at him, he waited till the last possible moment before jumping aside, then raked his knife down the Indian's right arm.

The Comanche bellowed in rage, his eyes blazing with hatred. Gil had cut deeper than he had, and now the blood flowed over the hand that held his knife, no doubt making the rawhide-thong-wrapped haft slippery. The throng murmured uneasily, but Faith thought she detected a measure of admiration for Gil, too.

Black Coyote Heart bared his teeth and threw himself at Gil, but Gil feinted just in time. The Indian's knife, however, managed to tear a red stripe down Gil's ribs—not deep, but long.

Faith closed her eyes as lightheadedness threatened her consciousness. *Give him strength, Lord, don't let him get dizzy from loss of blood!*

When she opened her eyes, Gil was once more crouched, readying himself for the savage's next move, seemingly oblivious to the blood that dripped into the dust. The air was full of the sound of the men's harsh breathing now and the smell of sweat and blood.

The Indian snarled, apparently ready to stop playing with Gil, and sprang at him. This time Gil wasn't able to dance out of his grasp, and the two went down in a tangle of red and white skin.

She heard a thud as Gil got in a punch, and used the moment that his opponent was stunned to roll out of his grasp. He jumped to the balls of his feet and waited.

Black Coyote Heart spat out a tooth, leaving a trickle of red dripping down his jaw, then charged Gil like a maddened bull. Gil let him come, then danced aside again, but reached out and grabbed hold of the brave's flying black hair, yanking him back.

The Comanche nearly lost his balance on ground that was now slippery with both men's blood, but recovered and threw himself at Gil. Once again Gil wasn't able to dodge and the two grappled with each other. Then Black Coyote Heart managed to hook a leg around Gil's and both men went down, the Comanche falling heavily on Gil.

Faith saw a knife skid away from the two men—*but whose?* It didn't matter, for now the two men struggled for sole possession of the one knife between them.

Now Gil was on top, but was he losing his grip on the knife? The arm that Black Coyote Heart had lacerated fell away from the hilt.

Faith's heart quailed within her. She shut her eyes, afraid to see him lose the fight and die at the hand of the murderous Indian.

But no, he'd only pretended to falter to distract his enemy and land a haymaker to his opponent's jaw. Then he slammed a fist down on each of the Indian's wrists in turn, and Faith heard bones crack. She saw the big Comanche's arms and limbs flail and then grow limp and his eyes rolled back in his head.

Gil rolled out off Black Coyote Heart, gasping for breath, but keeping a wary eye on the fallen Indian.

"Kill him, Gil Chadwick," Makes Healing said. "You are the victor. It is your right."

"It is not right for me as a man of God," he panted, "for our holy book says 'Thou shall not kill.'"

Black Coyote Heart was stirring now, but with two broken wrists, he could only stare dully at Gil. He muttered something, then let his head fall back limply in the dust.

Makes Healing said, "He begs you to kill him. He is disgraced by losing to a white man and will have to be fed like a small child until his bones heal."

"I won't kill him," Gil said. "My God gave me the strength to achieve the victory, but all I want is to take my woman—" he darted a glance at Faith, and winked "—back to our people."

The chief raised his feather-trimmed lance and said something.

"He says you would make a good Comanche if you ever wanted to join the tribe," Makes Healing said. "And he will grant you your wish to leave with your woman in peace."

"Thank you," Gil said as the medicine man and his son strode over and began to untie Faith. As soon as Faith was free, Gil took her in his arms and kissed her. The Comanches seemed to find this as much a cause for war whoops as they had the combat of a few minutes ago.

After Gil had bathed and his wounds had been dressed, they were fed a victor's dinner of roasted antelope, boiled corn and pemmican. Then their horses were brought around. Makes Healing offered her a spotted Indian pony in trade for Faith's swaybacked mare, saying the bony creature was not a worthy mount for her. The pony was a pretty horse, but Faith explained she had to return the rented mare to the liveryman who owned her. She was rather afraid that the Comanches would have made a meal of the mare.

"May your wife-to-be give you many sons," the medicine man said, and Runs Like a Deer grinned up at them.

Faith felt herself blushing, but she managed to smile back at the boy.

"Thank you. Go with God," Gil said then, his voice sober. He added, "Makes Healing, you understand we will not be able to keep it secret among our people what has happened to us as I did before. We have been gone too long, and Faith's people have been worried about her. They will demand to know where we have been."

"Do not worry about us," Makes Healing said with a half smile. "Even if they could find this place, we will be gone from here by the next dawn. The white eyes will not be able to find us. Many Coups will guide you to the road," he added as one of the young braves rode forward on a gray horse. "You can trust him, for he will obey the chief. Black Coyote Heart's leadership of the young braves has been broken."

Once they'd reached the road and their Comanche escort had ridden back into the hills, Faith and Gil talked about all that had happened.

"I was so afraid when you were fighting," Faith said. "But I just kept on praying."

"I'm sure it made all the difference, because I'm no fighter," Gil said. "I don't mind saying I had more than a few anxious moments myself. Every time I thought Black Coyote Heart was about to gain the upper hand and end my life, though, I got this sudden surge of strength from out of nowhere."

"From Heaven," Faith smilingly corrected him.

Then Gil told her about the vow he'd made to confess, first to his father, then in front of the church what had happened when he was away at seminary, how he'd gone astray and gotten involved with the ungodly Suellen, only to lose her and their baby.

"We'll talk to them together," Faith said. "I think I have some confessing to do, too, about living a false

Christian life—and some testifying about how the Lord brought my faith back and saved both of us from death."

Gil smiled at her. "Faith Bennett, you're going to make a perfect preacher's wife. I love you."

"And I love you."

Then, they stopped their horses for a long, heart-felt kiss.

There was a round of applause in Simpson Creek Church as Gil and Faith finished their confessions the next Sunday morning. They began to step back toward their places next to her parents and Reverend Chadwick in the front pew so that the song leader could lead the final hymn, but then her father stood and made a motion for the couple to stay by the pulpit.

"Reckon we've all had some big sins at one time or another to own up to. I think I speak for everyone when I say, Reverend Gil, that we think your shortcomings have made you a wiser man today. I have a sin to come clean about, too. There was a time when I was swamped by my grief at losing our boy," he said, looking at his wife, "and I let our daughter get the mistaken notion that she wasn't important to me. Maybe that's why she lost her faith for a time, because her earthly father was so weak he couldn't help her see how her Heavenly Father never stopped caring about her. I regret that, Faith, and I hope I've begun to show you just how proud of you I truly am. I'd like to have you continue to help with the newspaper after you marry, just as long as you want to. You've picked a good man to wed, Faith, and I'll be proud to call him son," he added, grinning at Gil.

"Oh, Papa," Faith managed to say before giving way to happy tears. Her father closed the distance between the front pew and pulpit in a few quick strides, and embraced both his daughter and his future son-in-law.

Reverend Chadwick and Faith's mother both beamed, and started the applause that built to a thunderous pitch.

"Thank you, Mr. Bennett," Gil said as the older man stepped to his daughter's side. "And now I'd like to announce there'll be a wedding taking place here next Saturday, with Reverend Barnes coming in from San Saba to conduct the ceremony."

"I hope you can all be here to help us celebrate," Faith added with a broad smile.

There are some that hold that cheering and hollering aren't proper in church, but none of them were present in Simpson Creek Church that summer morning. And when the cheering died down, Gil said, "We plan to live in the parsonage with Papa, of course, but if the Lord sees fit to bless us with children, we're hoping y'all would help us build onto it a bit?"

"You got it, Reverend Gil!" someone called, and there was a chorus of agreement. Soon the air was full of suggestions about how many extra bedrooms they'd need, names for about a dozen children and how many should be boys, how many girls.

Faith blushed so deeply that Gil decided it was time for the final hymn. He gave a signal to the song leader, who began singing in a rich baritone, "Praise God from whom all blessings flow," which seemed to fit the situation perfectly.

* * * * *

*Look for Laurie Kingery's next story
in her* BRIDES OF SIMPSON CREEK *series,
coming in 2013 from Love Inspired Historical.*

Dear Reader,

Thank you for choosing *The Preacher's Bride,* whether it's your fist Brides of Simpson Creek book or you've read each book in the series as it came out.

When I was deciding which of the Spinsters' Club members to gift with a spouse next, my eyes fell upon the name of Faith Bennett. What unique story could I craft for her? Hmm…what if Faith *had no faith?* Her name would be so ironic, if that was true. And who would be the most unlikely choice for her true love? *The new preacher,* Gil Chadwick, of course.

Many of us who are believers have had friends and loved ones who have lost faith or never had faith, so I hoped the story of how Faith regained her faith, with the help of the man who loved her and her loving friends, would be an important story for Christians dealing with this issue today.

I suffered a loss during the writing of this book—the unexpected death of my beloved dog Tango, a Belgian Tervuren and the most beautiful, neatest dog ever. While of course it doesn't compare with the loss of a human loved one, I know those who love pets will understand. I'm blessed with a husband and family who understand, and two other dogs who seek to fill the gap—and most of all a Lord whose "eye is on the sparrow."

Blessings,
Laurie Kingery

Questions for Discussion

1. In the story, Faith has lost her faith. Have you ever lost your faith? Why? How did you recover it, if you did?

2. How does Gil's father's stroke affect the course of the romance between Gil and Faith? How might it have developed had that not happened?

3. Gil thinks he dare not share the mistake he made while in seminary. What difficulties does this make for him? What would have been a better way to handle it?

4. Why didn't Faith have a bigger role in her father's business? How did the way her father treated Faith after her brother died have an impact on Faith?

5. If you are a believer, have you ever dated a person of a different religion, or who was an atheist or agnostic? What was that like for you?

6. What qualities do you think the ideal preacher's wife (or husband) should have?

7. Do you think it's easier or harder to lose or regain faith today, as compared to the small-town world Faith knows?

8. Have you ever been around someone like Polly Shackleford? How did you deal with her?

9. How did the Texans of 1868 view the Native Americans, especially the Comanches, compared to how we look at them today? What are the differences? The similarities?

10. We all suffer losses or tragedies in our lives. Why do you think God allows these things to happen? Have you ever seen good things come out of tragedies? Please describe.

11. Have you ever met someone like Yancey Merriwell who initially seemed too good to be true? Was that person all that he or she seemed to be, or were flaws later revealed?

12. How did the dangers the people of the post–Civil War Texas faced, such as Indians, outlaws and natural disasters, affect the way they lived? How does that mirror how we deal with similar dangers today?

13. If you've read any of the other Brides of Simpson Creek books, who is your favorite character? Which spinster would you like to see meet her true love next?

REQUEST YOUR FREE BOOKS!

2 FREE INSPIRATIONAL NOVELS
PLUS 2
FREE
MYSTERY GIFTS

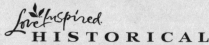

Love Inspired.
HISTORICAL
INSPIRATIONAL HISTORICAL ROMANCE

Love Inspired HISTORICAL

celebrating 15 YEARS

Author

LYN COTE

brings you kindred hearts in a wild new land.

No one is more surprised than Sunny Licht when Noah Whitmore proposes. She's a scarlet woman and an unwed mother—an outcast in her small Quaker community. But she can't resist Noah's offer of a fresh start. Noah, a former Union soldier, sees Sunny as a woman whose loneliness matches his own. He'll see that she and her baby daughter want for nothing...except the love that war burned out of him. Yet Sunny makes him hope once more—for the home they're building, and the family he never hoped to find.

Their Frontier Family

Wilderness Brides

Available November wherever books are sold.

www.LoveInspiredBooks.com

LIH82939

Ellie St. James is a bodyguard on a mission to protect her newest client from dangerous threats…without letting her client's handsome grandson distract her.

Read on for a sneak peek of the exciting new Love Inspired® Suspense title,

CHRISTMAS STALKING
by Margaret Daley

Lights off, Ellie St. James scanned the mountainous terrain out her bedroom window at her new client's home in Colorado, checking the shadows for any sign of trouble. The large two-story house of redwood and glass blended in well with the rugged landscape seven thousand feet above sea level. Any other time she would appreciate the beauty, but she was here to protect Mrs. Rachel Winfield.

A faint sound punched through her musing. She whirled away from the window and snatched up her gun on the bedside table a few feet from her. Fitting the weapon into her right palm, she crept toward her door and eased it open to listen. None of the guard dogs were barking. Maybe she'd imagined the noise.

A creak, like a floorboard being stepped on, drifted up the stairs. Someone was ascending to the second floor. She and her employer were the only ones in the main house. She glanced at Mrs. Winfield's door, two down from hers, and noticed it was closed. Her client kept it that way only when she was in her bedroom.

She slipped out of her room and into the shadows in the long hallway that led to the staircase. Another sound echoed through the hall. Whoever was on the steps was at the top. She increased her speed, probing every dark recess around her for any other persons. She found the light switch, planted her bare feet a foot apart, preparing herself to confront the intruder, and flipped on the hall light.

Even though she expected the bright illumination, it took her a few seconds to adjust to it while the large man before her lifted his hand to shield the glare from his eyes. Which gave Ellie the advantage.

"Don't move," she said in her toughest voice.

The stranger dropped his hand to his side, his gray-blue eyes drilling into her, then fixing on her Wilson Combat aimed at his chest. Anger washed all surprise from his expression. "Who are you?" The question came out in a deep booming voice, all the fury in his features reflected in it.

Can Colt and Ellie work together to fight the danger that lurks in the darkness? Don't miss CHRISTMAS STALKING *by Margaret Daley, on sale November 2012 wherever* Love Inspired® Suspense *books are sold.*